MW01259083

Other books by Marian Coe:

- *On Waking Up, Welcome to the Ultimate Personal Trip*
- *Women in Transition*
- *Legacy*
- *Eve's Mountain, A Novel of Passion & Mystery in the Blue Ridge*
- *Marvelous Secrets*

KEY TO A COTTAGE

KEY TO A COTTAGE

Enjoy!
Marian Coe

BY

MARIAN COE

ISBN: 0-9633341-9-0
Library of Congress Control Number: 2002093455

Cover by Mayapriya Long
Interior design and typography by Publishing Professionals

SL
SouthLore Press
730 Grouse Moor Road
Banner Elk, NC 28604
(828) 898-3490

In Appreciation of

This author wishes to thank the many writer friends who encouraged me to complete this story—which took courage—also editors along the way including Betsy White.

Thanks and appreciation go to publishing consultant Sylvia Hemmerly and staff of Publishing Professionals for their expertise and personal interest.

Also: For Hawaiian information, Shaka. Workshop feedback from members of Pinawor Writers in Pinellas County, Florida; High Country Writers in Boone, North Carolina. Writer friends whose interest in this story helped include: Niela Dakota Eliason, Bethia Caffery, Kay Yount, Lisa Raphael, Jack R. Pyle, Taylor Reese. And always, husband Paul Zipperlin and daughter Carol Coe Verbit of Cambridge, England and Normandy, France.

Table of Contents

"There is only one journey.
Going inside yourself."

Rainer Maria Rilke

Fort Lauderdale

May 1998

From wherever you are, Vyola, can you see me tonight, standing here on a South Florida balcony? I need to talk, to feel you listening.

As aunt to the kid I was, friend to the woman I became, you helped me through many a quandary by your patient listening. Never told me what to do, did you, but reminded me that choices were the way to move past stone walls.

Six floors below this balcony, a jeweled snake of traffic races along on Galt Ocean Mile. That's Fort Lauderdale, out on the town for the evening. I could be there if I cared to tonight. You've called me a survivor who doesn't give herself credit. I wish you knew—perhaps you do—this survivor has made her way here in this money-driven palmy paradise. Behind me, inside glass doors, those designer-perfect rooms are my earned comforts.

There's a man in my life here. Other women murmur he's one to die for—meaning he's straight, looks good, smells of money and can be charming in the way a powerful man can afford to be. When he retires months from now we're supposed to marry. Being a man accustomed to agreement, he assumes I want this. He intends to play hard and "wants me along." Not a romantic offer, but I know women in this town who would drop lovers or husbands to "go along." They murmur, "That self-contained Rae Kendall has it made."

No one knows, he doesn't know, that something holds back in me. Why don't I want this after earning my own way all these years? Vyola, I wake from convoluted dreams, left with a sense of something unfinished, or missing, or not yet found. Can't give it a name. I ask myself, *What else did you intend to do with your life?* Get no answer, only a beat of urgency in the pulse.

Behind my public face, I hide a crazy desire to stop the world and get off—long enough to deal with this. Go somewhere alone to hear myself think and dare to listen. What happened to me on the way here? I've slammed a mental door on the past.

To claim private time, put my life here on hold, would risk everything I've worked for. Status quo waits for no one, especially in this place where momentum is fast-forward.

There I've said it, Vyola.

In the bright sun of tomorrow morning, behind the wheel of my Mercedes, caught at a red light, I shall berate myself for this. Shame myself for the inner tumult I hide, knowing how many women have no choices.

Once the traffic light says go, the non-stop day started, I'll deny all this and go with the momentum as usual.

But tonight, I had to hear myself say it, the way I used to confess to you, Vyola, at other crossroads in my life.

If I dared to get away, you know where I'd go, don't you, Vyola.

The Cottage

Montgomery, July 1967

"It's downright embarrassing." I admit with a sigh. "Being seventeen and engaged and never been anywhere out of Alabama except to Daytona Beach."

"So now you will," Aunt Vyola says in her calm, husky way. "You'll see San Francisco and so much open country in between."

We've spent the afternoon talking and drinking lemonade. I can ask and confess things here I wouldn't dare mention at home. Mostly I do the talking. She murmurs back.

She's stretched out in the wicker lounge, smoking a Pall Mall, wearing one of her pink striped housecoats that makes her look taller yet. This is the nicest shady spot on the hottest afternoon with old wisteria vines reaching from the porch to cover the arbor.

"Daddy would never drive far as California only he sold enough insurance this year and got invited to the convention out there. My family thinks Alabama is the center of the world."

"Home is usually one's center," Vyola says.

"But you left yours to marry Uncle Vance. And then stayed here when he died." I'm always hoping for more of that story.

"Sometimes you find a new home," she says, calm as usual. "I found a work that nourishes me and a Southern niece for the daughter I would never have. One who asks a lot of questions."

We're quiet again, just listening to wisteria and honeysuckle vines rustle overhead. Summer can be as awful hot in Montgomery as Birmingham, yet it's nice here. Used to talk to Vyola about being angry at God for letting little sister Molly die back there when I'd prayed so hard she'd live. Wouldn't dare say that at home. The last two summers I've asked about love and sex.

Vyola says learning about sex has nothing to do with love.

This time I've confessed the problem I have with Charley when he gets back to Birmingham for a few days. We park after a movie. I don't let him go as far as girls I know do with their boyfriends, because I'm so afraid Mother would guess. She looks at me hard—so worried, when I come in. I'd die, simply die, if she knew.

"If you can't handle him, Rae, be glad he's back at the Air Force Academy." My school teacher aunt sits up and douses her cigarette into a saucer on the ground. "This trip is your opportunity to give thought to whether you want to marry so soon."

"It's sort of decided for next spring."

"Too soon."

I finger his high school ring on the chain, resting between my breasts just under my peasant blouse. Charley Kendall is the cutest thing in the world, and he's going to be this Air Force officer. Christmas I'll have the real engagement diamond. The idea is thrilling yet it pushes on me somehow.

Vyola gets up, looking down at me. "Rae, right now you're standing on the edge of everything that's yet to happen to you. Choices—we've talked about choices—lead in so many different directions. Give some honest thought to marrying by spring. If your folks feel pressed now, you could come down and stay with me next September and go to Huntington. I could help." She ducks out under the vines. "Wait here. I have a gift for you, to take on the trip."

She goes into the screen porch and into the house. I wait in my wicker chair, fingering Charley's ring again, trying to imagine him in his Air Force uniform, sitting in some class maybe, or in a fighter jet. No, it's the San Francisco trip I keep thinking about.

Late sun is turning the back of the house bronze, sky and garden Technicolor, like magic. I call this house the cottage because that sounds romantic. Vyola doesn't mind. The peaked roof for the attic does make it look like a storybook place. Love coming here. Last summer from the window up there I watched a tall red-haired boy hop around with his basketball over in the Shaw's backyard next door. Once I went over there to watch. He told me he intended to go to the moon. I didn't laugh. Boys get to do great things out there in the world. Not girls. He must be out of college now. It's true, I wish I could go, even if it's East Lake College at home.

Nobody says so at home, but Mother and my other aunts don't like Vyola. I figure it's because she's from Quebec and not a Baptist and because she married Uncle Vance and made him happy before he died, without his ever breaking down and going to church and getting saved.

Have to thank Daddy for telling Mother, "Cripes, Martha, let Amy Rae take the bus and go visit the woman if she wants."

The screen door whines. She comes out and puts a book in my lap. It's the tooled leather folder she brought back from Italy, a soft brown thing. Inside, a special three-ring notebook of clean pale green pages, little metal rings at the holes.

"Rae, this is not a diary but a journal. I've written on the first page. You have all the other pages to fill."

The edge has a neat hidden zipper. In the Technicolor light, I read her message in fresh purple ink.

My Dear Rae,

You are a searcher after answers that ring true to your own heart. For this you will be forever challenged, but also blessed. Seekers do find, though it may take a lifetime of searching.

A journal can be one's private confession booth, one's Delphic oracle. Write your life as you live it. Put down the questions that seem to have too many answers or none.

Write the high moments and the hurtful. Record as honestly as your heart knows at the moment, without protective ego. In time you will discover what your heart seeks, and the path that takes you there, even if you have to turn back pages to recognize what you missed before.

Always, Vyola
July 1967

Summer Of Love

August 1967

Dear new Journal:

I'm writing this down, heart-honest, the way Aunt Vyola says to do, though I'll never, ever forget what I'm seeing. We're rolling up the California Coast Highway, a scary road hugging the mountains above the Pacific Ocean. Waves way down there are rolling in, beating and foaming against the actual edge of the USA—imagine!

The radio keeps playing the sweetest song about when you go to San Francisco, wear flowers in your hair. And here I am, Amy Rae Calhoun of Birmingham, Alabama, heading there, like it's some kind of fate, even if it is for Daddy's insurance convention. Greatest deep-down thrill I've ever had in my life.

I'm supposed to write down my thoughts as well as the scenery, so here goes. This feels like the first time I climbed to the high dive at Cascade Plunge, to bounce up there, scared and tingling, about to dive into the deep part, where everything would look different.

In the front seat, Mother's scrunched over to the right since we went over that scary bridge. Keeps staring out her side, afraid to look past Daddy where the road drops down to the ocean. Bet she's stopped worrying about how her new perm will look when we get to the convention.

Daddy keeps his eyes straight ahead, grumbling under his breath. I tell them I'm doing poetry back here so they won't ask what I'm writing. Mother keeps looking back at me with her frown so I'd better close this up for now. . . .

"Yessum," I say. "It is scary, but I want to look."

Daddy is grumbling out loud now. "Why in the name of heaven did I take this roller-coaster highway? Where did these gypsies come from?" He means the dusty vans painted with swirling colors passing us and coming too close to our bumper.

Mother stares out at one whipping past. "Why, it must be those love hippies I saw in Look Magazine."

A purple van honks behind us. I get on my knees like a kid to look back at them. Fellow driving looks like Jesus giving me a devilish wink. I drop down to watch them pass. The girl at his side leans way out, waving, her blond hair blowing in the wind just like the song says. I crank down the window quick and wave back.

Wonder why she's on her way to San Francisco with a boy who looks like Jesus in a van with curlicue words—"I am a hope freak."

There's that song again on the radio. Like a magic message.

Mother has to use the bathroom and sit down with coffee to get over being dizzy, so we're stopping at this place just ahead, even with hippies and painted vans parked along the road. It's called Nepenthe. Everybody rolling through Big Sur for San Francisco must be stopping here. Oh, exciting.

I peer into a woody shop of crazy posters that smells of sandalwood and downstairs to a room of costumey dresses. Come back up to see people on the wide open patio that spreads to the edge of the bluff. A low wall that must be the only thing stopping you from falling off, down to the ocean if you weren't careful.

Who do I see sitting on the wall, not being careful at all, but the blonde girl from the purple van.

She looks like Rapunzel, pale yellow hair down her shoulders, shiny in the sun, and wearing a long cotton dress, the kind pioneer women wore in covered wagons going west, at least in movies. She waves her arm like a dancer in a ballet. Wants me to come over.

Her sea-green eyes sparkle. "Isn't this place alive and real?" Her voice is bell clear and sounds like someone who grew up in a Yankee private school. "Doesn't the air make you want to open your arms and soar?" She pats the wall for me to join her.

I sit down and here we are talking. She wants to know where I'm going, what am I looking for? I'm looking at her perfect ivory skin and a thin straight nose people call patrician.

What to say? I ask right back where is she going in a purple van and why.

She finger combs the long golden hair and starts telling me everything. Her name is Chloe now. Changed it from Christine when she left Barnard College for Columbia where she'd met Garth McCullough. Saw what power he had, turning on a crowd. When he was ready to cut out of there she went with him. They took off for California three weeks ago.

I listen, wanting to know more.

She nods, looking dreamy-faced. "I'm looking for a different life totally open to love. I've left behind the other, and the kind of education that Kafka says kills the creative spirit and initiates students into the lie."

Never heard of Kafka but I nod. "What about your family, aren't they angry or worried?"

She shakes her head, looking far out to the ocean before turning back. "Your eyes are full of questions. That's the soul showing, you know. What are you looking for?"

What can I say except that I had wanted college, but everyone expects me to get married soon as Charley finishes flight training out in Colorado. Told her my mother is the worrying type, and she'll be relieved when I marry.

Chloe looks right into me, as if she's heard a sad thing. "You can't live by others' expectations. My own mother did, and now—" She looks away again, shrugging her thin shoulders. "Now, she's sleek and cold as a mannequin in a Saks' window."

I stand up, worried my folks would be looking for me. Here comes her friend Garth striding up. Wow. Six foot tall, or more. Tight jeans, leather vest over an Indian looking shirt, sandals on lean brown feet. Up close he looks more like a shaggy-haired Gregory Peck or some Indian scout than Jesus.

"Who's the lost child? This fresh-hatched chick?" he asks, and without warning cups my face in his hand so I'm staring right into brown eyes glinting under heavy lashes and smelling his funny breath. Oh wow. I blink and breathe hard and back up like some silly lost child for sure. He pulls Chloe to him and starts telling me how she'd left her "Daddy Warbucks and society mater" for a more ecstatic trip and to be his old lady and why didn't I come along, too? Just like that—inviting me into the purple van.

I answer as sassy as I can, that I have my own ride to the Fairmont Hotel and a big convention. Well, this Garth gives a disgusted groan and starts lecturing about the "hypocritical world," and how the establishment is a "vast technological apparatus where human qualities are lost." Talks fast as an angry teacher, but I gather the hypocritical world includes his father and his professors back at Columbia.

Chloe puts a hand on his arm, very loving, or to shut him up. He grins, gives her a rough hug, while she tells me in this clear soft voice that Garth is talking about the whole society, how it needs a new vision of love and freedom.

I say good-bye and streak across that open place through hippies, to get back to the car. My folks are waiting, Mother frowning, Daddy patient. I drop in the back seat, hoping I didn't look dumb back there.

All the way into San Francisco, I keep wondering about them. How could a girl like Chloe walk out on a paid-for college tuition and I bet an apartment full of clothes out of Glamour Magazine? Exchange all that for granny dresses and letting some man call her "my old lady." Her folks back in Boston must be having a fit, even if her mother is "a cold mannequin," not a sweet pudgy lady like mine who watches my every breath.

Even if what they're saying is true about society and all, how do they think they're going to change anything by walking out of college and going to California in an old bus?

I feel like a dumb kid standing on the outside of something important that's happening. I'd sure like to know what's going to happen to them.

❧

Fairmont Hotel

Journal:

Here I sit in the room. Mother and I were going to Cost Plus down near the wharf where they have all sorts of imported dishes and stuff. But after the stage business this morning, she's lying in there with one of her sick headaches. Don't blame her. I watched some of it. The men and their wives have to wait backstage during a lot of speeches. Then they come out, one couple at a time, to stand up there next to some important fellow from the Prudential home office who gives the husband's sales records and introduces "his lovely wife Jane" or "his lovely wife Mary" or whatever.

I watched Mother up there, clutching her purse, blinking in the spotlight, getting called "his lovely wife Martha." Bet anything she wasn't worrying about her too-tight perm, but about what they expect of a "lovely wife." I know what that is. It's dinner on the table every night at five-thirty so the husband can get back to selling more insurance.

Heck, I'm going out and ride one of those trolleys. I just might find a way to get over to Golden Gate Park.

Nobody back home will believe what I'm seeing, this grassy park seething with "flower children" or "love hippies," whatever they're called. Regular tourists standing around the edges, staring. Not me. Walk right though a bunch stretched out on the grass, passing around fancy pipes, hugging and waving banners. The cold crisp air smells like those pipes. Dope, right out in the open, with all the singing and talk and clinking tambourines.

A funny looking girl, young as a kid sister, gives me a wilted flower and in a squeaky voice, says, "Let's make love not war," like it's something she's supposed to say, before she weaves away. Barefoot, in some skimpy thing, she has to be freezing because I'm shivering in my brown sweater.

There's a bunch of boys with shaved heads, in yellowish robes, jumping up and down with their tambourines. A circle of girls in granny dresses rocking together singing *Let It Be*. I know that one. I keep on walking past the weirdest conversations and then I see the purple van. Chloe is sitting in the open back end, bare legs tucked under her big skirt, arms crossed, rocking herself like one shivering Rapunzel. Sees me and waves, then reaches down to hug me. I have to get up there and sit with her.

We start right off talking like old friends. My questions, her answers. That private school voice of hers is soft and excited, too, saying how our generation has to teach the people in power that love is the true energy and war and greed are killing the planet.

She doesn't sound angry like Garth saying these things. She says it with all this feeling like someone who has discovered a terrible, wonderful secret and has to do something about it.

Behind us in the van—a mess of blankets and scattered books where they sleep. I pick up one about a guru and scrawl my address on the back because she's promising to write me. Not that I expect her to remember.

"Look at him," Chloe says, warm and dreamy, nodding to Garth out there, squatting down like an Indian, sun lighting his curly dark head. He's smoking and talking to a ragtag bunch huddled around him. One girl sits close, rubbing her face against his leg.

Chloe keeps finger-combing her long hair and watching. Says right out, "Garth has a power that draws people to him. He's a highly sexed man, they sense the energy but he's a genius, too. A leader." Then she goes right on telling some really embarrassing details about how often they do it.

My face is hot. I must be more dumb about what other girls do than I'd thought. At home, even the brides don't come out and tell that much for goodness sakes.

Garth waves off his grass sitters and ambles over to us. Hands the skinny cigarette to Chloe. She sucks on it, eyes closed. I figure it's time to get away because he's looking me over, saying, "Damn, if it isn't our fresh-hatched baby."

I pull back, tell Chloe good-bye and walk away fast as I can, breathing hard, angry at my goose bumps.

Fairmont Hotel

Journal:

Sitting here writing of this beautiful lobby with its chandeliers and thick carpets. Told Mother I wanted to come back down here to write a poem about this place.

Watching people stroll past. Women who look like fashion pictures in Vogue *magazine and holding on to the arms, and purring up to the men who look rich and sure of themselves. Guess this is the Establishment they're talking about, not anybody I know at home.*

Wow, do these people know what the hippies in the park are saying? I won't forget Chloe and the rest of it. All I know for sure is, what they're running away from is what I'm going back to. Birmingham and East Lake College for a semester and getting married in the Baptist Church.

Maybe our conversation felt so special because of the way the sun hit the waves below, the green smell of eucalyptus trees and sound of ocean. Then meeting again at Golden Gate Park, talking like honest friends about things girlfriends back home don't mention.

There's one thing I intend to change for myself. The name I wrote down for Chloe with my address was not plain old Amy Rae Calhoun, but what Aunt Vyola always calls me.

Rae.

Charley

Birmingham, May 1968

"You've got a lot of loot here for the housewifey job," Josey says, picking up and putting down Pyrex bowls and cookie jars and cutesy potholders. The whole dining room table is covered with presents and curly ribbons. I go on making a list for thank-you notes now that everybody's gone. Thank goodness, the last shower.

"Not to mention the other duty." Josey lifts a shiny blue gown we agree won't look the same after the first wash.

Depend on Josey to say things like that. I don't mind. She's my favorite cousin and more honest than girlfriends here today who giggled and pretended to swoon over everything I unwrapped. Especially Charley's sisters, Bertie and Louella. Thank goodness they're all gone now except Josey. Mother and Aunt Sarah are fussing around in the kitchen, washing the plates. Mother's actually cheerful.

Josey keeps on picking up stuff looking under for prices. "I know you wanted to go to college. You could have come up to Auburn with me and roomed with some smart ass from Long Island who could have really wised you up. You're getting married for the same reason girls around here do, to get away from mama at home."

I keep on writing names while Josey fusses about foolish girls who marry at eighteen. "They're stuck. Marriage and kids are a roadblock to a girl's intellectual curiosity."

I fire back, “I don’t know how intellectual you’d call it, but I have a lot of curiosity.”

“Once you sat through a psychology class, you’d question every notion you ever found in the kind of stuff you read, or what you’ve heard at church.”

“I shouldn’t have told you about the Cosmic Consciousness book. But it’s happened to some people and doesn’t that prove it’s possible? To actually be in tune with the whole universe for an utterly magic minute? Maybe more people have had that happen, or little glimpses, but don’t talk about it.”

She shrugs. Poor Josey, with her earnest sallow face and limp black hair. When she says boys are afraid of her brain, I don’t mention she’s never had a date, just say well, maybe someday you’ll find one who likes your brain.

She’s peering under a casserole dish. “Those two who’ll be your sisters-in-law are going to be on your neck all the time.”

“Oh, groan, I know. Bertie and Louella think Charley is handsome as Prince Valiant and more wonderful than Elvis. That’s okay only they act as if I don’t deserve him. It’s because I don’t gush the way they do.”

“You’d better hope any daughters you have will get your cheek bones and curly brown hair and not their stringy white blonde and Bertie’s pink moon face.”

“You aren’t very encouraging.” Right now I’m worried about how they’ll look in the wedding. I’m glad Josey turned down being a bridesmaid. She’d look like a beanpole in the fancy pink dress, standing by Charley’s sisters who will look like short, white muffins in pink icing.

“Did I tell you? I won Mother over about my dress. No white satin, but a long pretty white cotton thing with ruffles on bottom.” Not telling Josey or anybody it reminds me of one I saw on a hippie girl in Golden Gate Park last summer. “I’ll be glad when this is all over next week.”

“Hey, it’ll be just starting, Cuz.”

⁂

MacDill Air Force Base, Tampa
May, 1968,
Dear Journal:

Been writing nothing but thank you notes and getting used to living here. The base is flat and drab but Tampa Bay can be romantic in moonlight. All the teapots and towels and stuff help to make this "quarters" look like the place is ours, but I keep thinking of all the other couples who must have lived here. I feel like I'm playing a part being Rae Kendall.

I don't have to worry about Charley reading any of this. He thinks this leather folder is poetry which he says is not his bag. His interests are flying, what's for dinner, and let's hit the sack. Besides he's not always here. They're testing some fighter plane out in the desert. So lonely in bed without him.

Another lieutenant's wife—Marty, about thirty, sun-browned from golf, no children, a chain smoker—comes over a lot. She checks out all the new brides. About sex. Well, it's none of her business. I do a lot of shrugging and nodding but she must have guessed what I wasn't saying.

I didn't want to tell her Charley makes me think of a big blond bear going after his prize and this leaves me sort of floating around in a new space, stirred up, but looking on from the outside. Maybe this is because I'm new at this? Matter of fact, I think Charley is new, too, only for sure I didn't tell her that.

Or men must be in too big of a hurry to be romantic. When it's over, I lie there brushing the crinkley hairs on his arm and chest, like yellow gold, feeling mellow inside but he's already sleeping like a log. I haven't told Marty that.

That Marty. "You're a dumb kid, Rae Kendall, still believing in being romanced," she's told me, puffing away on her cigarette. "You have to tell the man a thing or two or he might never catch on to how to move the way it counts for a woman. The bastards never want to be told anything, in the bed or out."

I did tell her I hadn't counted on the mechanics being a problem in making love.

"Love is one thing, honey. Sex is another."

Marty is so sarcastic. Bet her lieutenant husband thinks the same. She's always looking at other husbands. Sally, who comes over, too, says it's awful. I think it's sad.

June / MacDill

Happy day. A letter from my hippie friend Chloe. She found my address I scribbled on her book. Mother forwarded her letter from Birmingham with a note, "Who on earth is writing you from California?" Chloe has a PO box now in Berkeley—her father made her get one. She wants me to write about what I'm doing.

How can she be honestly interested in me out here in the ordinary world? "Stuck in establishment expectations," as her boyfriend would say. All I have to write about is being married here on the MacDill Air Force Base, counting Pyrex dishes and teapot sets, talking with other wives and waiting for Charley, who's gone days at a time, testing the fighter jet out in the desert somewhere.

July

Dear Rae:

Thought of you last week when five of us bused down the coast to Esalen, a marvelous mountainside place along Big Sur. You would have loved being there. We did Gestalt sessions, but the best was two days sitting in silence meditating to experience the God within, as personal contact, not some remote being from some man-made doctrine.

Back now in Santa Cruz. Garth has been arrested after leading a protest against the war. They can't keep him. He's teaching alternative politics at a small college. What power he has.

Write to me, tell me what it's like for you, married on a military base, Do your friends there know what's happening, the ills in our country, the hated, senseless war? Does your Charley understand?

Rae, read the Greening of America *about the revolution of the new generation. We must be open to new ways of being. Write me again. You know I feel we were friends in a former life. By the way, since you asked if I have let my family know where I am. I did try to call my mother. They wouldn't take my collect call. I say to you what I tell myself. Stay open to love, wonder and joy.*

Your friend, Chloe.

❧

I read and save her letters but don't talk about her to Charley. He would never understand.

August / MacDill

Here comes Sally expecting coffee and ready to deliver more lessons in how to be a military wife. I put away my new

Chloe letter, not something to share here. Well, friends are friends no matter how different they are. You can't always mix them.

Sally loves to talk about being a real army brat, living in Germany and France, when her father was a general. She skips over the fact her parents are divorced and she hasn't seen him in ages. I listen, and want to say I think you're angry at him and not at your husband for not being like him.

Here she comes, bursting in, a cute little thing with tiny waist and big round hips and gushy way of talking. She gets going on "isn't it awful" subjects. Today it's about the convention in Chicago, the riots in the street, police using tear gas and having to bust heads.

I pour her a cup, sit down across the table to agree it's awful that police have to bust heads as if the demonstrators were foreign enemies or space invaders.

Sally glares. "Are you taking up for the counterculture hoodlums?"

"Well, I met a war protester once in California who looked like Gregory Peck and was this good student at Columbia before he got angry with his professors and the government. It's that kind of people out there." Oh, big mistake. I might as well have said I know a nice Commie.

Sally sits straight up, brown eyes wide. "You realize, these are the long haired draft-dodging creeps who burn the flag. While our husbands have to go to Vietnam for this country and maybe get killed."

"And for what good?"

"Rae! You are so . . . so gullible to believe those creeps deserve anything but being dragged to jail."

She walks out. I feel bad. She comes right back in with a magazine, flipping it open, reading Walter Cronkite saying, "The young are deeply disillusioned." And a man named Burroughs says the "youth rebellion is a worldwide phenomenon, a new hedonism with ominous overtones." She leaves it and flounces out.

I sit here thinking, Chloe, I'm worried about you and what to believe myself.

ॐ

September

Journal:

This Tampa Library is my favorite place to read the news and write some in my journal. Coming here, the car radio was playing a Bob Dylan's song, You Don't Know What is Happening Do You, Mr. Jones. *Who does, for sure?* Look Magazine *has pages about "flower power" and "counter culture" with pictures of those gypsies I saw last summer. They're all smoking pot and "doing LSD and mescaline and hash" out there in California. Maybe that's happening other places too.*

I could never do what they're doing. Because I'm too stuck-in-the-mud cautious? So far I have had the nerve to turn down bridge lessons. That got me some frowns. Instead, I spend time here in the library. I do try to be looking nice and smelling good when Charley gets home. He is away again this week. Makes me shiver to imagine him up there above the clouds. Yet he has such a happy look on his face when he talks about it.

November/ MacDill

Dear Vyola:

Tried to call you this afternoon just to hear your husky voice. Won't try later because Charley is due in.

Thanks for the books. They help. I can sit under the fan and forget the awful heat here. Not complaining. Charley is so sweet, really, swaggering around like a man who has everything he wants going for him. That's flying and me. He wouldn't mind if I got pregnant but I'd just as soon wait a while, until I'm twenty-one, though the wives here with babies have something to do besides play bridge.

I am reading the Carl Jung book about dreams and Anne Lindbergh's Gift from the Sea. *It isn't only for older women. I went to the beach all by myself to read it. I love* The Prophet *so much I read the part to Charley about marriage being like two trees, only I don't think he got it. He grinned, "I'm supposed to be a tree, standing next to yours? No way, Honeybabe, I want your sweet limbs wrapped around me." Some things you can't explain to some people.*

There's one wife here who's on my wave length. Belle is what Mother would call "black as the ace of spades." Mother doesn't know first thing about bridge cards, just knows that old saying. Belle is the first Negro friend I've ever had. She's read Edgar Cayce. Says what he could do really blew her mind. We've talked about the powers he had—real psychic powers in his trance sleep though he was a good Christian, reading the Bible all the time during the day. The people at home, not just my Baptist and Methodist aunts, would call what Cayce brings back from his dreams "mental delusion."

Vyola, you've called it "a gift of rare and finely tuned intuition." Belle and I both believe it's more than that.

I look at the wives here, talking bridge and babies and recipes and husbands and promotions and Air Force moves. Do they ever wonder about fate and free will and all that? I feel like an outsider to other people's lives—both the hippies and these women.

Till later,
Lonesome Rae

November / MacDill

Waiting. Was about to go walking at sunset when Sally called, voice a squeak as if she's crying. Told me to stay home, she's coming right over.

Waiting and frightened. pacing this place that seems strange. In the kitchen the cherry pie is waiting. Made it today for Charley. His favorite. "Love to see him eat. Can't wait until he walks in tomorrow," I say aloud. It comes out a whisper.

When he drives up I'll put it in the oven to have it hot when he comes in looking grimly proud, and wanting to peel out of his uniform and pull me into the shower with him.

I hear a car. Sally always walks over. Have to open the door. An officer and a chaplain stand there with Sally.

I have to let them in, my throat closed up, chills creeping over me. I watch their mouths moving like a bad scene I'd already rehearsed in a dream. I hear myself giving them permission or something, addresses for my parents and his in Birmingham, and Vyola's, too. Sally sits on the couch with me, her shoulders shaking. I'm too numb to feel, think. The chaplain's mouth is moving. In my head, I'm seeing Charley's plane crashing in that desert, burning in that wide open place, happening this morning while I was making a damn fool cherry pie.

The officer and the chaplain leave. I'm still watching fire behind my eyes, knowing every vague idea I had of a future is going up in that smoke.

Dark outside now. I made Sally go. She trailed around watching me dump out the pie, afraid I've gone crazy because I can't talk and I'm not crying and I've taken the phone off the hook so I won't have to talk to anyone.

I promised to take the sleeping pills they left me. Let her watch me swallow two before she left. They must be powerful. They pull a curtain down over my mind where the plane is still burning.

The phone beeps. No. They all know I'll be flying to Birmingham tomorrow. Don't make me have to say it.

Birmingham / November 18, 1968

I have to get away. Too many faces keep waiting for the poor girl to cry.

Charley's sisters the worst, puffy-eyed, wondering if I'm pregnant, as if they're at least entitled to that.

Or would they hate me for owning what's left of him?

Had to walk out of the house, run all the way to the park. Same old park where I played as a kid, dreamed as a teen and walked with Charley when he was my high school steady.

What did we talk about then?

Kissing and hugging seems enough when you're living a movie love song in your head, imaging he's singing it to you. Why am I seeing high school years with MacDill already fading? Yet, I can remember Charley's weight moving on top of me, burying himself in me.

Today I can't sit on this empty bench. Have to stretch flat on the grass and look up. Endless blue up there. Wish I could fall into that space Charley loved so much. Maybe more than he loved me. I didn't mind.

A plane up there now, a small one drifting over, moving along easy as if there were no such thing as crashes and closed coffins and people having to pretend a hard blond body is inside. I hate believing in something and finding it's not true.

Where are you, Charley? Already I don't know you.

They played taps for you, really for all of us standing there, throats tight. Such a sad sweet sound I used to think in movies. Now I know what it really is. An awful wail from a million battlefields. A forlorn blast of bravado, echoing heartaches of all the people standing silent by the open grave, trying to make noble what seems senseless while somebody folds the flag and puts it in your arms.

Taking that thing, I felt like somebody I don't know, having to play a role.

A folded flag is a burden you can't bring back to your old room at home, to hang with high school pictures.

November 20, 1968

I can't stay here. Have to go somewhere, breathe different air before I can imagine what to do next. I need to go stand in Charley's desert and scream out everything caught inside me. Can't talk to anyone or listen to their pity. Not even Aunt Vyola. There's only one person I want to talk to because it's away from here. Do I dare? I'll tell Mother I'm going back to the base to pack. Won't tell her I've already told Sally to take all that stuff.

Lies are justified when they save explaining what can't be explained. Chloe, I want to come see you. You'd understand. You would know how I can live past this.

Birmingham / November 29, 1968

I've done it. Bought a round trip ticket, packed one small bag for two nights, three days. Need to breathe different air, get away from faces waiting to see what I'll do. Going in the morning without knowing if Chloe has my letter. Sent it to her address, a real address, the apartment her father is paying for so she'd get back into school even if it is Berkeley. Thanks goodness Garth is going on to Santa Cruz without her. He's scary as beautiful lightning or crackling electricity.

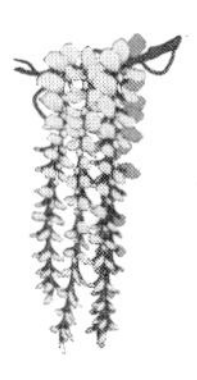

Berkeley

November 1968

Finally we're landing, my ears roaring, chest tight with all the tears I haven't let out caught in there, turned to hard ice.

The terminal now. Strange cold place crowded with hippies, but not like the summer before, not like Golden Gate Park. Here they look rag-tag and angry waving that sign, LBJ how many babies did you kill today? More freaky kids sitting on the floor, smirking at me. I must look the freak here, in a blue going-away suit, shiny shoes and clutching my carry-on bag.

Outside, colder yet. A slow moving traffic jam. How to get to Berkeley? An oily-faced driver leaning against his cab looks me over, mumbles something like, "Little sister, turn around and go home right now if you're here looking for somebody in the Haight."

I shake my head, dig in my bag for Chloe's address.

He's still glowering. "You have to step over them, stoned out of their minds. Worse rats in those buildings are the hippies living there. What's your choice, kid?" Looks at the address, shrugs, tells me to get in.

Crazy ride, huddled in the rumbling back seat, shivering, sick at the pit of the stomach, still breathing around what's frozen inside.

Roller coaster streets and crowded sidewalks rush by. Then the high Bay Bridge, meter ticking away, ugly housing down there along the water. Finally, Berkeley. Street noise. What's happening? Driver growls back it's the afternoon revolution at the People's Park. The Hippies built it. Police put up a chain link fence to keep them out.

I ask what's wrong with a park, knowing it's an innocent, Alabama question.

"University property. I don't give a shit about that, but these freaks. . ." He growls out a tirade about the Hippies and the Yippies.

Mister, you talk pretty crude to a lady passenger. I just think it, don't say it. We're rolling along a street of tall houses turned into sad old apartment buildings.

Driver says, "This is it, Sister.

I'm left standing in front, in sharp wind and gray cold afternoon. Inside, a tiny vestibule with ancient mailboxes, no names. Dim-lit stairs rise up. I sit on the bottom step, holding on to the little satchel like a lost urchin in a dumb blue suit and shiny shoes.

From above, footsteps. A tall girl in a long black sweater and Chinese kind of pants, pads down in clunky leather sandals. Long blonde hair to her shoulders, not gold as in the sunshine at Big Sur. But it's Chloe, the sea-green eyes alive in the pale oval face, arms open in greeting, voice clear as sparkling crystal.

She hugs me and steps back holding on my arms smiling, saying, "It's my friend, Rae," as if it's the most natural thing in the world for this Alabama person to be found on her doorstep. I see how thin she is under the black sweater.

Does she know about Charley? Yes, she got my letter. She doesn't ask more. I'm thankful.

We climb the stairs together, Chloe's perfect profile nodding, listening. I'm holding on to my little bag, explaining how I'm here for only three days, have to go back and start East Lake College that's right up the street from my parents' house.

Talking in gasps. How awful if all the locked up tears burst loose now. When would they ever stop?

Here's her door, the apartment her rich father made possible. We go in. Gray light from two tall, ancient windows show a gloomy, almost empty place. Books and blankets spill from two boxes. On the floor, against one wall, an Indian print and piles of pillows cover a big mattress on the floor.

Chloe lights fat white candles in dishes, explaining how she's sent the furniture back. She's going to Santa Cruz with Garth after all. Looks up to say that, her face glowing in the first flicker of candlelight. "We're going to a house there with some others. But not yet, Rae, not until after your visit."

I'm so weary I have to sink down on the floor mattress. It sloshes. A water bed. I'm thankful there's a tiny kitchen behind a folding Chinese screen and a bathroom with an old yellowed tub. I pull out her gift from the bag, the long white cotton that was once a wedding dress. She holds it up against her black sweater, thanks me in that clear flute voice for a wonderful gift.

I want to fall back, bury my face in the pillows, cover up and sleep but she comes back with a glass of red wine. It tastes strong and warm on my throat but it doesn't touch what's frozen in my chest. "I'm so tired it's unreal," I confess.

"Of course. Emotions sap the psychic energy, Rae. We'll talk later, but first I'd like us to go out tonight. For just awhile."

She's digging for something in one of the boxes. "You need to see and feel a different kind of energy," she says, coming up with a wool shawl.

It would be awful if I did fall back, wine dizzy and too tired to go. So I get up, let her put the shawl around the shoulders of my blue suit. Downstairs, outside in early dark, the cold wakes me up.

"Want you to see the co-op," Chloe says, striding along.

I keep pace, holding on to the shawl.

The co-op—food bins and whirling lights and speakers thumping out a beat, loud and angry sounding, but exciting even to my weary body.

"Rolling Stones," Chloe says, as if that explains everything. She leaves and comes back saying "Jefferson Airplane." Brings me a huge ripe peach like a gift. I bite into the sweetness, cold juice running down my wrist.

People stop at our little table. They seem to be paying court to this thin blonde girl in the long black sweater. She sits listening, serene, I think, as a water lily in a swirling current. The hyper talk is about rallies and teach-ins and tripping on speed and smack and who got busted. It's about the SDS and the city pulling the buses off "the Haight" and what happened at Altamont when the Hells Angels started whacking heads.

Looking on, eating the peach, I wonder if Chloe does all these things. A skinny girl weaves up. Her tee-shirt has a picture of Bobby Kennedy dead on the floor. Says, "This is all a shuck." Wanders off to sit on the sidewalk, looking at nothing.

Another one in a long dirty skirt, bells on her ankles, gauzy blouse showing her flat breasts, sidles toward us. "Get ready for Medea," Chloe murmurs with a set smile.

Medea's tangled mess of dark hair would be called a rat's nest by mothers back home. She gives me a quick smirky glance before leaning close into Chloe's face, asking where Garth is hanging out tonight. She goes on to talk about balling—words I've never heard out of the mouth of a boy, much less a girl. I keep eating my peach. Have to swallow past my tight throat and aching chest.

Chloe inhales deeply and lets it out with a sigh. "Good-bye, Medea."

Medea gives me her final surly glance. "What kind of cat are you . . . hanging out with this goddamned princess?" She shouts up to the night, "I'm a cat in heat," and wheels away.

Under the dark blonde lashes, Chloe's eyes stay half-closed a moment before she stands. "You're shivering. Let's go."

We start back, quiet for minute. I have to take a deep breath to match her pace. Chloe's face pale and dreaming as we pass under street light. "You're wondering, Rae, I know—and the answer is yes, Medea wants Garth, most of them do. They see his intense power only as sexual. It's both physical and intellectual. And yes, I'm staying with him."

"I'm going to sound like my own mother or a fussy sister, but I worry about you."

She smiles, swinging along. Maybe she needs someone caring about her. I go right on telling her what magazines are saying. The counterculture movement has turned into "hedonism."

She squeezes my cold hand. "They're looking from the outside."

Yet she starts telling me how the movement is changing, like a wild rose garden of hope getting crushed into a tangle of thorns. How most are giving up on "forcing sociological change." And those like Garth becoming more angry.

We walk faster in the cold night, Chloe sounding sad talking about those who are staying drugged-out, zombies, some of them kids who came out expecting free sex and escape from any authority. But something else is happening, too. Communes.

So many she knows are leaving Haight to get back to the earth in open rural places to set up "authentic ways" to live. Grow organic gardens. Create free schools. "That's what I would do now, Rae, but—"

"Garth won't go?"

"He wants to move up to Santa Cruz, he's involved in plans. I'm going with him. He won't say so but he needs me."

"You could go home to Boston, get back in school, finish your degree."

"Home?" Her profile is pale ivory in the street light. "Rae, I grew up in a house that never knew any love. An overly ornate museum of a place my grandparents built, and my mother inherited. Probably why my clever father married her.

Since her deb days, no earlier, my mother had no identity of her own, and since, no spirit. As a child, I've known my mother as this cold person preserved by Martinis, my father a womanizer and now my brother Norman wants his hippie sister disowned."

"Oh, I'm sorry, Chloe." We track on. Maybe this is why she cares to be friends with me, somebody with an ordinary family.

"I've decided . . ." She pulls me on past a bunch of chanting Krishnas trying to hand out papers. Some spill along underfoot, colorful pictures of strange gods.

". . . one's intended home may not be the place you're born into. It is the place you're meant to be, that feels right to your inner being, so you can do what you're in this world to do. Your purpose for being alive. And we have to find that place for ourselves."

"I bet Santa Cruz isn't it. Or a commune?"

"No. Only stops on the path. Who knows how many stops."

To find the place, she means. My feet are numb against the cold pavement, but we're almost at her building.

So quick she turns from solemn to quiet excitement. "About going to Santa Cruz with Garth. I have something else to tell you no one else knows."

Climbing the stairs, I'm thinking how she must love him. Makes me feel lonely, chest so tight it hurts. Charley and I were in love since senior high, what we called love. Married, I realized right off we were two different people, but thought, well, that's the way it happens and you just hide the fact inside. Maybe Charley didn't even wonder.

Inside the dark room, Chloe lights the candles again. The bare walls dance with light and shadows. So what's the secret? She catches me shivering, hugs me a minute, hands me a towel and a robe. "The water's cold in there, but it'll warm you up."

When I come back out in a gown from my bag and Chloe's thin Chinese robe, weird Eastern music is curling from a little radio on the floor. Sitar, she says, stirring something over a hot plate that smells of curry.

We sit facing, cross-legged on the water mattress, with bowls of curried rice and wine bottle in reach. Chloe has a funny pipe like something out of Arabian Nights. I don't say anything. This isn't Birmingham with mother watching. This is *Be Here Now*, title of a funny shaped blue book lying there on the floor.

"What about people like Medea when you go to that house in Santa Cruz, or some commune?"

"Hear my news, Rae. I waited till you came to tell you. I'm pregnant, two months. On purpose. Garth doesn't know yet. No one does, yet. When they do, they'll realize he's mine."

She sounds as happy as any girl back home, only back home the girl would be married. I gulp down wine. "Well, if you're happy. But I'm going to worry about you. Oh my, I sound like my own mother."

She hands me the pipe. I've never smoked a Lucky Strike, but I take the thing. Tastes sweet then burns. Hand it back, coughing. Have to drink wine to cool my throat.

Chloe knows how to draw it in. Her voice becomes dreamy, telling me she let it happen, she wants a child. Garth needs the focus a child will give him. He can connect with a crowd, ignite their imagination, yet he'll end up dead or in jail for twenty years unless that fire is directed toward the future. She intends to save him from destructing by staying by him, giving him an image of himself, and responsibility to the immediate future.

I accept the stupid pipe again, listening to Chloe being glad she's pregnant. She's rocking on the sloshing mattress, her arms around her middle, grimacing one minute, smiling the next. I try the crazy pipe, feeling nothing but lonely. All those caught tears and maybe a scream still caught in my chest. Not as ice because it's not melting. More like crushed glass. Dizzy on top of that.

Chloe is a blonde Buddha sitting in front of me, cross-legged, candlelight making a white aura around her head, telling me, "Rae, it's time to talk about yourself and what happened." Voice dreamy, telling me I'm hurting, yes she knows, but it's safe now to let out the pain from this calm viewing place. Telling me the real self is never wounded, is always whole. "To find that place, Rae, you have to step out of ordinary consciousness where the pain is so real."

The pipe again. More wine on my burning throat.

Stories about Charley start pouring out from where I've held them down. About the wives on the base . . . and about taps at the funeral and the folded flag . . . and on to how everyone at home is watching me and waiting for me to cry . . . all of it tumbling out until there's nothing left to say, as if I'd come to a cliff that drops off into a dark abyss echoing my own voice.

I stop, look at candlelight dancing on the walls and back to her waiting face. I haven't cried or screamed. My chest has a different feel. Not crushed ice or glass now but a solid cold stone of dismay I'll have to live with forever.

"See, you're mellow now. You've let it out. Are you sure Charley didn't leave you pregnant?"

"No. . . . Didn't happen . . . even when I forgot the diaphragm . . . So no."

I don't feel mellow at all, just drunk for the first time in my life on wine and sitar music and pot and so weary I don't care. Have to lean back on the pillows, head swimming, watching candle light flicker. The music is red and yellow now . . . dancing with the shadows.

The water bed sloshes as she gets off to go to the bathroom. I float on . . . now she's back . . . no, off and gone again. I wake up with somebody crying out. Chloe? Now back again, whispering, "Rae, I'm bleeding, I'm loosing it."

I pull myself up. Her face, against the Indian spread looks like wet white marble. "Oh, God, Chloe, what can I do?"

"Clinic . . . Have to get to the free clinic." She stumbles back toward the bathroom.

Garth walks in, looming over me, the smell of the night on him, asking who's the extra female in his bed.

"Chloe's in terrible pain, she's bleeding."

His face darkens and he's gone. Comes back, carrying her in his arms, her blonde head against his chest, towel around her waist, her bare legs dangling. He's taking her to the free clinic. Chloe murmurs, "You stay here, Rae." And they're gone.

Leaving me on the waterbed . . . in Indian print, lost in unreal time and space. Wanting to stay there.

I'm hunting for Charley . . . yes, see him swaggering toward me, grinning . . . then he's gone when I try to open my eyes to flickering walls . . . No, Charley stay. I sink back into the dream.

He's here again, now on the waterbed. Must stay with the dream. Need his warm body to hold me. . . .

Yes, moving so close, my heart's racing, don't let me wake up, must not wake up to keep him here. . . .

A hand pulls up my gown, warm breath on my face . . .

My eyes fly open scattering the dream. Flickering candlelight backs his shaggy head, a dark face close over mine, only his eyes catching the light. . . . hands moving on me. Not Charley. Not a dream. But Garth, the man Chloe loves.

I push at the arms, at the moving hands, but they're claiming, triggering needs . . . banked-up needs . . . a sweet hot coil of need awake and spreading. . . .

Give up pushing away . . . have to cling instead to this wirey hot body on me, smelling of night and danger . . . Have to hold on as the fire spreads, rising into my chest, ripping through every blocked need and grief hiding there . . . rising to rip from my throat with a scream.

The sloshing bed is still. I'm floating alone in dark place. Candlelight out. The man gone. Silence. I must not think, wake, must sink back into sleep, stay there forever forgetting this unreal place and night.

In gray morning light, the bare room is cold and ugly.

I don't look into the cracked bathroom mirror. Oh God, blood all over the floor. Try to clean it up, the bloody towels like guilt on my hands. A spot of red on the hem of the white cotton wedding dress, hanging from a hook on the bathroom door. Force myself to stand in the yellowed tub, shivering with cold and dismay under the cold stream of water.

Put on the dumb blue suit, run out, down to windy streets, asking where to find the free clinic.

In a hall, Chloe lies on a narrow cot, damp hair spread on the pillow, face pale as the dull white sheet pulled close around her. They will be keeping her for two days. She looks up with a flicker of smile, murmuring apologies. "Rae, I'm sorry. Come back another time, because we are meant to be friends, always."

I kiss the damp forehead and run out of there. Find a dirty cab and let the silent driver take me back to the air terminal. The crowd a blur this time. Change my ticket, eat a revolting candy bar, wait hours, eyes shut to this noisy place, screaming silent orders to myself. Don't think. But the body remembers. No, don't, don't. I must go home, start classes, forget ever going to Berkeley.

&

Birmingham
December 9, 1968
Journal:

Been staying in my room pretending to read. Nobody knows I went to San Francisco. They think I went to MacDill. Can't let Chloe know why I ran away. Last thing she said was how we were destined to be friends. I couldn't say anything just ran out of there.

I have to forget, forget.

&

December 12, 1968

Want to die with this horrible cold. Even told mother to leave me alone when she came in to take my temperature. She doesn't cry but sniffles like a martyr. Now she'll have one of her sick headaches and I'll be the blame. I always have to hide what goes on inside of me.

December 26, 1968

Worse Christmas in my life. Couldn't eat Mother's turkey or Aunt May's Eagle Brand lemon pie. They think I'm sick on sadness, staying here in my room this way. Forgive me, forgive me God, for what happened. Have to stop thinking about any of it. Freshman classes start next week. I'll get out of the house early, walk to the campus, do nothing but study, study.

January 5, 1969

Journal:

Don't feel like writing but who else can I talk to? Journal, this is the only place I can get things off my conscience.

Went with old high school friends to the play "Our Town." Dead Emily in that play was happier than I am. My girlfriends are married now and having babies. With me, they look smug and act apologetic. Makes me want to scream or crawl away and hide, but that would give Mother one of her "sick headaches." Less trouble to tell her I'm all right. I just want to scream with Mother and all the aunts and neighbors watching me with their worried little smiles.

When I think of Charley, he seems to be off flying somewhere and happy. I don't know who I am or supposed to be anymore. I didn't want to write this down but I will:

Worry keeps buzzing in the back of my mind too awful to name. I keep studying the calendar, counting and wondering. Guilty conscious, I tell myself.

ॐ

January 20, 1969

I'm happy in class until I go to the bathroom again to check and hope. Did I have a period before the funeral? And not since? I try not to think of Berkeley. That whole trip seems unreal. Chloe wrote they're moving to that house in Santa Cruz. I wrote back a post card saying, "Good luck, I'm busy now, studying hard."

February 1, 1969

Want to study but can't concentrate on a page. Fear must lock up the body. I keep looking at the calendar, and going to the bathroom, praying, God, let me see a show of pink, a promise. Nothing happens. Just a sick feeling. How can a few minutes of letting go take your life out of your own hands? Was it ever in my hands?

Still nothing. What's holding on inside is more powerful than all my praying and hoping and running to make it let go. When I stop, all that happens is my heart keeps roaring, imagination scaring the sense out of me. If it's true, I'll have to leave Birmingham. I can never face my folks. Oh, God, I'm so miserable.

February 7, 1969

At the table. Supper time. Hate the sight of the pork chops.

"You're not eating a thing, Amy Rae," Mother says.

"I've been thinking. I can't study here. I'd like to go to Huntington. I could stay with Aunt Vyola."

"Well I never. This is your home. You've always wanted to go to East Lake."

I can see her worry building. Can't let that happen. I make myself swallow food. My hand shakes lifting the fork. "Daddy? I need to get away, you know. . . ."

He clears his rumbling voice. "Martha, it might be good for her."

I go out walking, half running to the drug store, find a pay phone, call Vyola. Tell her I need to come down there, to the cottage, go to Huntington if I can. She hears fear in me, doesn't ask questions. I'm so thankful I cry in the phone.

"Rae, I'll call your folks, invite you."

I walk home making myself calm down, and planning. Once I'm in Montgomery, maybe a week, I'll call back home and say I went too a doctor and found out I was pregnant all the time and didn't know it. Tell them Charley flew in on night before he went back and crashed. Oh God, I'm so scared of anyone wondering.

How strange to discover you don't own your body, that something going on inside has invisible strings to whatever is out there ahead, a future you don't know about.

Montgomery

1969–1972

April / The Cottage

The words are stiff in my mouth, repeating my news as Vyola comes in from her late class. ". . . so if you'll take me down to the bus station first thing in the morning."

"Of course. Rae, don't start blaming yourself for not knowing." She hugs me, gently, my round stomach between us.

It's like some bad fate for my sins, being pregnant, not going up to Birmingham all this time. "I didn't know," I moan. "Mother was calling all those nights as usual. She sounded tired, but that wasn't unusual. I didn't know what was happening."

"You told me they didn't know."

I drop in the chair by the kitchen window, stare out to a cold spring night. "When Daddy called this afternoon, he sounded strange, but then we never talk much on the phone. Before, when he answered he'd say, 'here's your Mother.' This time, he told me she'd gone to the hospital two days ago and was already back. I held on the phone, waiting, hoping he'd say she was all right. He just said I should come home quick as I can."

"Of course. I'll drive you." Vyola is still in her suit, and stocking feet standing in the kitchen. "Right now lets heat up that vegetable beef soup. I know you have to eat."

"Don't want you to drive me up there." I don't want her to have to go. "I'll take the first bus in the morning. Why did this happen to my poor Mother. To punish me?"

"You're punishing yourself."

Uncle Will and Aunt Meg are waiting at the bus station. Driving out to the house, he stays hunched over the steering wheel not saying anything while Aunt Meg goes on and on about how they'd opened Mother and sewed her right back up. "The uterus," she whispered as if a man shouldn't hear a word that private.

I listen, numb, imagining that dark place turned bad inside my mother, the place I was made and born. A baby in mine right now. We're special creatures having that, and for the same reason we inherit being vulnerable.

The house looks the same as we pull up, yellow forsythia blooming in the yard like any spring. Except the shade is pulled down on the white organdy curtains in the front bedroom. Make myself walk in to that darkened room with its flower sweetness and strange smells, Aunt Sarah and neighbor women standing back from the bed, hugging their arms, murmuring. Aunt Sara wraps her big arms around me and cries against my cheek, talking in my ear.

Flowers on the bureau are dying more slowly than my Mother. She lies here in the big oak four poster, so still under the counterpane, making little whimpers. A neighbor nurse bends over, giving her a shot of morphine.

I sit beside the bed like a hurting lump, restless stomach heavy against my lap. Reach for her veiny cold hand and watch her face. I want her eyes to open, focus, see me. We need to say so much that we've never said. Her dry lips smile just barely. It's not the old worried mama smile. Have to grit my teeth to stay quiet. Too many people watching.

In the dining room, hushed, fussy voices insist I have to eat. I can't look at the table of berry pies and macaroni casseroles. Can't bear their bemoaning how poor Martha would never get to see her grandchild, "left for us here by poor dead Charley." Have to get out of there, go stand in my old room and shut the door. This is no good either. I'm not the person who lived here.

Night comes. Back in the room, lit only from the hall, everyone so quiet now, waiting. Preacher there. Now the doctor for his final visit, but just a visit. I stop him in the hall, ask for a sedative pill. Not for me. I want to hand it to my father, he'll take it without question, before they tell him it's over. I know he'll need that help because he has to do his suffering inside of himself. That's the way Calhouns do.

By eleven, my mother's gone. Neighbors stay. Daddy sits in the living room, not his chair, like a silent visitor. He took the pill.

Three days go by somehow. Again a cemetery. Too many faces. Sometimes at the house it's like a hushed party, talking and greeting and watching pregnant me.

"I need to get back to Montgomery," I tell them. "Have to see my doctor." Daddy doesn't say anything. What could he do with me?

I'll always hate the bus ride, going back to Montgomery, remembering, the baby beginning to move in me, a terrible terrible guilty thought going through me. Mother will never see this baby, to guess he's not Charley's, she'll never know where and how it happened and if she had, it would have killed her in a way no morphine could have blocked.

***

April

Journal:

I've written Chloe at the Santa Cruz address from a card she sent back in January. Decided I had to let her know I'm expecting a baby. Told her the same story I told everyone else but Vyola. That I was too upset to know at the time, but I was newly pregnant when I went out there. And that Charley had come back one night before he flew back out to the desert where they were testing that plane.

Didn't have anything else to tell her but I'm living here with Aunt Vyola, reading, reading, walking for an hour at night around this neighborhood. Told her about our garden and about my cooking because my aunt is this busy teacher. How dumb all that will sound when she's out there living with counterculture people. I remember how she looked so beautiful and special even in her black sweaters and so calm, dealing with those messed up people I saw. At the library I read about the hippies turning "anarchists and druggies." I've also read, "Haight has gone ugly. The dream is dead." So I write back with questions, because I'm worried about her.

July

A hot July night. Vyola and I are eating ice cream with peaches watching a scene on television, grainy black and white as some early movie. Only it's real. Neil Armstrong there, standing on the moon, in his bulky white gear. We listen to his raspy words—"One giant step for mankind" coming from the moon to Houston to our own living room.

"Like a miracle," I murmur.

"You're handling one now," Vyola says.

"I'm not doing it, though. It's doing me." The baby is filling me up, kicking against my ribs.

"More the miracle. You're creating life without having to know how cells divide and create a new being." Vyola's husky voice softer than I've ever heard.

We watch the astronaut, listen to the voices. "Will we ever look up at the moon the same?" Vyola says.

Then it's over. I sigh, thinking of something I'd forgotten. "It was stars I used to look for when I was this dreamy kid about nine, summer before Molly died. Did I ever tell you about me and stars?"

"Tell me."

"On clear summer nights, dark, no moon, I'd lie on my back in the yard, flat out, to stare up to the sky. No one knew but our dog Randy. He'd lie close, head between his paws, watching me. I'd do this nights when so many stars could be up there, shining, blinking against that dark purplish blue, taking my breath. I'd think how people walk around, never really looking up at such mysterious flickering stars or glowing planets."

"You were looking."

"For a shooting star as a sign—"

"Yes?"

"Well, a message that the power that put the stars in orbit, the Source of the whole universe including my back yard, would know I'm down here watching. Give me a little sign. Does that sound like the foolish, dreamy child you knew?"

"Sounds like a lovely memory, coming from the innate wisdom a child has until thwarted by the world we live in. You've always been a seeker after answers, Rae. I wrote that in your journal if you remember."

I nod and gather up our ice cream dishes. "Know who I'm remembering now? That red headed Loren Shaw from next door who told me he was going to the moon someday. He must be watching this now, feeling trapped on earth. 'Course nobody's more trapped than I am."

August

Journal:

Sweet old journal, waiting for me. I am back in my room with a flat front and feeling empty.

He's pink and perfect, twenty days old. Crying and kicking in the crib Vyola brought in, a big basket, padded. Charles Ryan Kendall. I'm going to call him Ryan. The name came to me out of nowhere. Well, he did, too. Feels strange and good to have my body back, but it won't be the same life.

Bertie stayed a whole day, bringing a baby buggy and more gifts. Brought chicken salad as if Vyola and I are on a desert here. Bertie cried a lot and rocked him and called him Little Charley. Took pictures to send Louella in Texas and show Kendalls back in Birmingham. I asked her to take one over to Daddy who is now living in this boarding house. Everything changes.

Bertie is pushy and gushy, but I feel bad for her and the Kendalls. And guilty. In the pictures he'll be a little fussy face deep in the baby buggy. Later—that's the worry.

❧

September

Vyola works late up in her attic library, but stops in my room to say good night. "Look at him, more awake than you," she says, touching his head with a long cautious finger.

"I hate to hear him cry. You have to sleep too." I'm rocking slowly by the open window, holding him close, hoping he won't start up again when I put him down. When I nurse him, his face is so possessive against my breast. Pulls at my nipples until I wince. I have to give him a bottle nights.

"The doctor said he'd find his own schedule in time. I wonder."

"This phase won't last forever."

"And what comes next? Vyola, I've got to find a job and pay you board, you feed me so well."

"We've settled that. You're my guest, you and baby."

I rock and sigh. "My immediate worry, you know, is Bertie. She keeps calling, asking when I'm bringing him up to Birmingham."

"You have to, of course," Vyola says. She knows why I'm worried.

"The Kendalls are old and sick and yes, they have to see Little Charley. Daddy, too. I'll go. Oh, I hate that bus ride."

She steps out of her shoes, holds them looking tired but sounding gentle. "Babies inherit genes from grandparents. He can have dark curly hair and still be Charles Ryan Kendall."

When she goes I rock and croon against his head, Ryan, baby mine, I'm doing best I can.

❧

October

Journal:

Love the color and smell outside. Makes me wish I were on campus, a real student, not one reading when I get the chance.

Mornings, when I bath Ryan in the sink, he fusses and kicks. His body is a wonder, such firm perfect flesh, round belly, the little penis floating in soapy water. If I sing out loud, he'll stop and look up at me, really look with those dark brown irises, too wise for a baby's face.

Oh, I love him so much. Do I have the right? I don't say that aloud even to Vyola.

❧

In the mail today, a letter from California. Tear it open, baby struggling in my arms, and here is Chloe, back in my life. I hold my breath. How did she take my news of being pregnant?

❧

Dear Rae:

A happy day! I found your lost letter hidden in a book. It's difficult to keep up with anything personal in this house where everybody claims the space. Oh, your news! Do write and tell me everything is all right, tell me what it's like to hold a new life in your arms.

Garth has been in jail. Out again, teaching alternative politics in a small college.

Women are into their own revolution here. I go to a place called the Sacred Seed, a co-op store. Ten of us meet there to talk about our bodies, masturbation, lovers and claiming the sexual freedoms the men have always assumed as theirs. They challenge my choice, berate me for being loyal to Garth, say I'm out of my mind to get pregnant again. They don't know my heart and my intentions. Rae, send me pictures. Tell me how it feels to have your own child in your arms.

Your friend, Chloe.

How wistful she sounds. I shudder to think what she might know, looking at Ryan. It would be so cruel, it would make everything about me false. I'll send one snapshot of Ryan in the buggy, a cap hiding his curly brown hair. I will never ever hurt her by letting her know. She must never never know. Vyola is the only person in the world who knows and we don't talk about it.

"This child is here and he's yours," Vyola says.

December

Letter from Josey today.

Hi Cuz,

Mother and I are invited, as well as your Dad, to the Kendall family Christmas, so I'll be seeing you. Warning in advance: your dad is a sick man, but silent about it.

I'm looking forward to seeing you as little mother and what you've produced. Babies are sweet things, I hear. They become little monsters by twelve in the sixth grade.

At home I do duty listening to Mother recount the first thirty of her past seventy years. So to get away, I'm teaching a night course for women at the YWCA called "Assertive does not mean Aggressive." A lot of women need that.

Now where in that range of assertive-aggressive would you put women like your sister-in-law? Bertie was born to be the bossy matriarch if never a bride. Also, as if you didn't know, Bertie wants you to move back home—her home of course. Be prepared. See you Christmas, for all that food and gift swapping. Let's be different and skip that gift routine. I could bring you a baby blanket but there's no need for you to find me a sexy nightgown.

Josey

January 1970

Dear Journal:

Recovering from the family Christmas. All those Kendalls filling that overheated house with family talk. Everybody having to see and hold "Little Charley." Glad cousin Josey was there and my poor sick Daddy, too. They saw a beautiful six months old Charles Ryan Kendall. Everyone said his dark curls must be from the Hinson side of the family. I pointed out I had something to do with it, oh, did I, but did speak up to say the Calhouns are brunettes and mine gets curly in the rain.

It's true. Bertie wants me to move in with the Kendalls so they can help raise Little Charley. That would positively ruin my life as they would run my life.

ॐ

April

Ryan finally asleep, reread the last two letters from Chloe. Beautiful flowing handwriting like her special voice. Writes on all sorts of odd papers. Calls us "soul sisters" because we have the "same inner questions even if our lives are different." Always begs to know about my baby.

I wish she'd get away from Garth. I hate the thought of him. He gets in my dreams and I'm so ashamed. Maybe she has her own life along with getting him out of jail. She rides an old bus to some Zen colony in the mountains and once took a bus down to Esalen Institute on Big Sur. Wants me to read Hermann Hesse. Said he writes: "The true profession of man is to find the way to himself." I wrote back how that speaks to me all right, though right now my inner self is foggy as my future.

Ryan is so big now. So full of determined energy. I chase after him, have to keep the back screen locked good, and keep him from crawling up the steps to the attic library. Won't eat what he doesn't want, screams for what he does want. Asleep, he's a rosy cheek angel. I don't look in the mirror at myself anymore.

November

Short note from Chloe today. She's PG again. Makes me angry for her and sad. She's trying to give Garth a child. A son, I bet, so "he can see himself in that child." She wants him to realize "the new generations have to be taught love and peace rather than just fight the entrenched politicians." The women at the Sacred Seed came down hard on her for getting pregnant again.

Chloe keeps asking about Ryan. I write funny things and add babies are a lot of work. I swallow back my awful secret: this child is the one that should have been hers.

I sent her a page out of *Look Magazine* called a "Vision of the Human Revolution." This must be the kind of thing Garth says in his speeches. The lines keep going through my head. . . .

> *"Up quick, if you can. It's long past time to go . . . The good life grown blind, bland, banal and numb . . . passionless tedium turning living souls into solid state circuitry . . . it's time to go, thaw out the blood, prance high. . . ."*

When Vyola came in to say goodnight, I showed her those lines. Watched her read them over. She knows about Chloe and about Garth. Knows I read this kind of stuff.

"What do I think? This rebellion began with students who saw their parents and professors as hypocritical. Many are. Do they also want to throw out annoying establishment traffic lights? We'd have a lot of collisions. I'd ask this Garth, what new vision do you have beyond the shouts for change?"

She handed back the magazine looking weary. "New visions are needed, I grant them that. Only it takes time and clear minds and patience to make changes. Now with that sober thought, I'm going to the kitchen and chop vegetables. See you when you get Ryan asleep."

I know what those lines do to me. Makes me want to march down town announcing I'm here, give me a job! How do you do that pushing a baby buggy?

January, 1971

Journal:

Real life hurts. Poor Daddy, ending up forty years with Prudential, so old and sick now. Spent time with him when I went up with Ryan for another Christmas at Bertie's. Sat with him in that nursing home. Awful. We didn't have a lot to say, but then we should have said more years earlier. He did pat Ryan's head and say, "Reminds me of Molly." We never did talk about it when little sister got killed by the car. Just kept it inside, all of us hurting. But when Daddy said that about Molly, we both broke down and cried. So I guess we did communicate.

❧

March

I hang in the doorway, watching Vyola close her old Gladstone bag. She straightens, draws on her cigarette, douses it in a tray, gives me her level look.

"You knew I had this student tour coming up. If I treated you as helpless, it would take longer for you to find out you're not."

I know, but I'm miserable being left, even if the cupboard is stocked and I don't have to push the buggy to the store unless I want to get out, for a reason, any reason. Ten lucky girls will be following her around in Oxford and Cambridge for two weeks and here I am, stuck.

Back in my room, I rock with silent fury, not to wake up Ryan. What do I want? To be on my own. To get out of this house and into the world, support myself and Ryan. The allotment won't do it. I need a job, a real one, not some dumb clerking job behind a blouse counter at the Montgomery Fair. Or making twenty dollars a week typing in some lawyer's office. I've found out that much.

May

Cooking Vyola's breakfast, I can't wait to tell my news. Had to hold it last night when she got in so late from her London trip, with a cold, heading for bed. Coughing in there now. I take in the tray, butter melting in hot grits, a soft boiled egg in a cup, toast and her little pitcher of tea. "I'm treating. So wake up, traveler. I have news."

"Won-der-ful," Vyola rasps, climbing back in bed, propping up her pillows. "Ah, look at that. I'm blessed. Ah, this hot tea. Sit down over there, but keep your distance. Can't have you and the baby catching this."

"We don't smoke Pall Malls and run around in London rain. Ready? You were right, my wise Auntie. I'm not helpless. While you were gone I found a job, a real one."

She smiles over the teacup. "Tell me."

"Mrs. Shaw next door kept Ryan while I walked downtown to look for a job. Didn't have a bit of luck. Then I sat in the coffee shop of the Jefferson Davis, treating myself and thinking, now here's a place I'd love to work, in a real hotel, in the office or greeting people."

I wait till she stops coughing.

"A nice bald-domed man behind the front desk let me talk to the manager. He looked me over, asked if I could handle the switchboard afternoons and early evenings."

"And? You look happy this morning. You've cut your hair shorter."

"I hurried home, talked with Mrs. Shaw to be sure and yes, she can look after Ryan over at her house. The job is one o'clock until seven. I've started. I'm on the switchboard, then handle the front desk when the others take lunch and dinner breaks. Oh, Vyola, this has to work."

Evan

1972

July / Montgomery

Journal:

This isn't a secret gripe or a question. It's a discovery. Having this job, I feel new. l love walking the ten blocks to the Square, along Court or High Street, down sidewalks lined with old oaks and magnolias, past gabled houses with wide front porches. The grand one, white with columns, sitting far back on a perfect lawn is the Governor's mansion where George Wallace lives. Blocks down, the Jefferson Davis Hotel is around the corner from the Square. Some nights I get a ride back home, but I like the night walk, too. Passing couples with their arms around each other's waist. People waving from their dark front porches, Cape jasmine so sweet in the night air.

Different world here from the one Chloe knows, though this is where the bus boycott happened and Martin Luther King started the civil rights marches. People here still don't talk about him as a hero, not even since he was assassinated like Robert Kennedy. Chloe's friends talk and cry about it, though. Some of them marched with King when he was the young preacher from here.

The whole world is changing, though, even here in Alabama. One of the waitresses in the dining room tells me she's living with her boyfriend and not about to get married and stuck.

Busy as I am with Ryan all day then working late, which I like, still I'm so lonely. Don't complain to Vyola. She's busy with her students and papers. The only chance we get to talk is at breakfast and supper.

⁂

July

Dear Josey:

Thanks again for being family for me during Daddy's funeral. The Kendalls don't understand why I didn't go back to the cemetery before I left. I don't think Mother and Daddy's spirits are there and that's what counts. I hope they're somewhere happier than they were here.

Write, Love, Rae

⁂

In bed tonight, thinking about what happened today.

I'm behind the desk all this afternoon, manager away, the lobby busy. Three Eastern Star ladies come up to complain about their meeting room, like bossy, gushy aunts, big bosoms heaving under their fancy white gowns.

I listen and nod and explain things as if I'm their favorite niece. Send them off chattering and satisfied. Then two old sisters at the desk indignant that the bellhop made a face at their tip. I get them talking about who they're visiting until they go off looking justified.

Then this impatient salesman type came up, lecturing me for making him wait. Men can treat me like I'm some little girl in a navy blue dress behind the desk. With a day like that I expected the other type to show up, the kind who leans over close to ask where a sweet little thing like me would like to go to dinner. I have an answer for them. Say my husband is picking me up from the base, but he might try the Elite Café two blocks down. Strangely enough, when I do that I'm not even thinking about poor Charley.

This trim nice looking man sitting in the lobby, waiting on something, must have been watching. When the lobby got quiet he came over to say in the most sincere voice, "You handle situations quite well."

I can spot an honest smile when I get one. He smelled nice, just out-of-a-hot-shower nice, wet blond hair combed from an exacting part, smooth tanned skin. Standing there with a lonely look in his brown eyes that was kind of sweet. He was in town for his company, looking for property. He had noticed a piano in the dining room and asked if there might be a time this evening he could go in there to entertain himself, since the dining room seems to close at eight.

Told him Mrs. Mavis plays in there for dinner, does her waltzes and Stephen Foster melodies and the like, and I'd find out if he could use the piano when the tables were being cleared, and maybe stay longer if the night manager didn't mind. Hallson will be coming in at seven-thirty when I'm leaving.

I didn't leave. Called Mrs. Shaw who goes to bed at nine. Asked if Ryan could stay, I needed to work later.

The dining room was dim, the tables cleared and empty when I slipped back in to listen. Stood there looking at a man immersed in making music. His slim fingers floated over the keys doing my favorite song, *Tenderly*. I moved closer, sat on the carpeted platform near the piano, listening to the sound of such love and longing, feelings I have hidden inside. He went on, doing *September Song* . . . then *Laura* . . . melodies that give me goose bumps and make my eyes water.

He smiled down at me, said he's from the Fifties, but knows some music my generation is doing. Played and sang softly for a minute a jumpy, *Need Somebody to Love* . . . explaining, "Grace Slick, without Jefferson Airplane," then he went back to songs like Sinatra's *Cottage for Sale*.

I sat on the platform at his feet, listening, with closed eyes and tight throat, wanting somebody to love.

Later, he sat down on the platform with me in that quiet dim room of tables set up for breakfast, our voices like muted echoes of the music. Talking the way two strangers can talk, sharing a small pocket of time, feeling safe to say things in your heart out loud to another. Even a stranger? Especially a stranger.

I let him drive me home up Court Street. We turned silent then. It wasn't the same. But before I got out, he gave me his card. Evan LeMarr, representing Sterling Resorts. Told me I handle people with "intelligence and grace." If I'm serious about hotel work, he could help. Then he was gone, driving away down the street.

December 5, 1972

"No," I tell Bertie, on the phone. "I'll bring Ryan up for Christmas, but no, Bertie don't expect me to move up there."

"Why on earth are you being so stubborn, Rae? We have this big house and a perfectly lovely bedroom empty since Mother passed. Father's getting absent-minded, but he loves that baby, believes he's Charley. Rae, you make me wonder what's going on down there with you."

I bristle all over with that. They'd never let me have a life of my own if I lived there, or anywhere in town. But I keep my voice even. "Bertie, what's going on is me trying to make a life so I can take care of Ryan."

"Even with Vyola going off again with her students?"

Why did I let that slip? "I have to go now. Goodbye."

I hang up on her snort of disapproval.

What if she knew Mrs. Shaw was going to leave, too? Going up north to Cornell to stay with her son for awhile.

Vyola waits at the kitchen table. I sit down and report. "I'm facing a stone wall."

"There are always choices around stone walls."

"I know only one."

"Sarasota? The resort man who comes through?"

The piano player with Sterling Resorts, yes. He's been bringing me little gifts for months. A book of poems, a tiny bottle of perfume, a compact. He gets an hour at the piano and tells me about Sterling Resort buying up old hotels, redoing, expanding and about their trainee program down in Sarasota. If I want to come down for an interview, he'll set it up. Says the program offers a start on a future in the hospitality industry.

"Wait a minute, let me show you the card about Sterling." I come back with it and read: Sterling Resorts, Milton Hargrove, president; Sheila Hargrove LeMarr, vice-president, Evan LeMarr, sales representative.

I look at Vyola. "Last month when he came through I asked if they were family. He gave me a sweet pale smile and said, "More or less." Milton Hargrove is his brother-in-law. Sheila is his wife. And a few minutes before, I was ready to hug and kiss his smooth face."

Vyola is smiling. "Romantic notions aside, what are you going to do?"

"Go down there for the interview. It's my best chance for a real job. A career. They're accepting more trainees in February. Only it won't work unless I can find a Mrs. Shaw down there who would handle my rambunctious child."

***

January 15, 1973

Journal:

Needles and pins. Waiting to hear from Evan LeMarr to set up an interview in Sarasota before I lose Mrs. Shaw. Vyola leaves with her student group in two weeks. Had to give up my job at the hotel to be able to get away to Sarasota.

A letter today from Chloe. She's seven months pregnant this time and they're leaving Santa Cruz for the

Freedom Farm commune in Georgia, the one started by a professor at UCLA who's become a spiritual leader with an Indian name. What a time for her to travel. But she sounds happy, relieved. Why didn't Garth agree to go earlier? I hate that man! He must be in trouble again to be willing to go to this Freedom Farm in Georgia.

She wants me to come visit them there. That's Chloe, thinking everything is possible.

Sarasota

1973

February

Every mile on this bus to Florida, I've been thinking: this is jumping into deep water where I'll sink or swim and I intend to swim like mad.

Here's Evan waiting for me in Sarasota's bright sun. Evan in his true element, I guess, white slacks, blue shirt, Panama hat on the back of his head, standing by a yellow convertible, top down.

He looks me over. Already my navy blue skirt and knit shirt are hot. He says, "Rae," with that pensive smile, "you should have flown, but you're here." Gives me a quick kiss on the cheek. I was ready for a long soulful hug, but what the heck.

We head across a causeway, bay waters rippling blue, the wind smelling of sea. "That's the beach ahead," he says nodding to low horizon, green fringed under expanse of blue sky.

This moment I'm happy. Next moment he's warning me about Sheila, what to expect.

"Now you tell me?"

"Clueing you in, Rae. So the interview won't throw you. Sheila will impress you first with her degrees from Penn State, her summer in Switzerland at the Hotel School les Roches. Where we met. Father and I spent some time over there." He shrugs with that, looking straight ahead.

"Sheila will tell you that entering the hospitality industry with any plans to go into management or sales and marketing calls for four years of a BA, at least. Once she has you feeling humble, she'll explain a year of supervisory experience and training can be an alternative start, for someone with the right aptitudes—attention to detail and the right communication skills."

He looks over with a real smile. "And my dear Rae, you do have that."

I settle back down in the hot leather seats, holding on to my small bag and hopes. This place is for me. This chance. Has to be. I've cut my bridges. Given up my job. Told Bertie I'll bring Ryan up after I'm accepted for this training program. Counting on it, to be sure.

I have no intention of being afraid of Sheila. I know how to appear confident while hiding every doubt. We're rolling along the beach road now, past pink and white motels set back into palmy landscaping. Behind the motels, sure enough, the gulf glitters in afternoon sun, rippling in from that far horizon.

I love this moment. I want this.

"Sterling Crown headquarters," Evan announces dryly as we whip into a front drive of a sprawling stucco place lined with giant bougainvillea bushes. He stops at the entrance. Gets out, opens the door for me, hands me my bag. "Turn right from the lobby, go past the dining room on down to Sheila's office and good luck." Just like that, leaves me there, walks back to the yellow convertible and whips away.

Well, okay. Clearly, he isn't interested in going in to see his wife. So he doesn't love her, doesn't even like her. Yet she's the one I have to please here. Sterling, here I come.

Sheila LeMarr looks up from behind a loaded desk, lit by high sunny windows in back. A round-faced plump woman enveloped in green flowered muu-muu, half glasses perched on top of her short carrot red hair. I'm guessing she's a few years older than Evan, and a real in-charge person, looking me over now as if she's ready to throw out one more kid looking for an easy job on the beach.

I stare right back. "I'm—"

"Kendall from Alabama, the one who knows her Southern manners behind a hotel desk. Well, sit down." She talks clipped and sure of herself, going into some of the stuff Evan predicted.

"Sterling is expanding, marketing for small, specialized convention groups. Guests will expect a great deal. Not that a new trainee will be dealing with them right away—if we both agree this field is right for you. To do that, this visit has to be your look of what goes on behind the scenes."

Some "look," I tell the trainee I bunked with for three nights. I've folded sheets in housekeeping, worked in the kitchen, filed in a back office, but mostly bused tables in the big dining room.

"Giving you the acid test," Millie says, sprawled on the other narrow bed. The "dorm" here, an old motel across the road, on the bayside from Sterling Crown. "She'll look over the comments you got before you go home."

"What's Sheila like to work for?"

"Tough. A task master. The big boss around here. Evan? Oh, they're married but everybody knows they don't live together. Hey, if Sheila takes you on, look out for her brother, old Milton Hargrove. He looks grim, but when he gets you alone he tries to get a feel."

Only once have I glimpsed Evan, in the dining room, playing the big grand. Shock. I believe that dear man really is just the piano player here when he's not on the road looking for property or convention business. Another girl let me know Sheila has her apartment in the Crown and he has his down at his "studio," an old unit at the far end of the building.

Poor Evan. I had the idea it was his money, well his rich father's money behind Sterling expansion.

Monday morning, I'm back in Sheila's office with my bus ticket and bag, ready for the verdict. She's studying the reports on me. Looks up with her cross-examining gaze. "Kendall, to come on board here means six months of job training at minimum wage and six more advanced with a raise. You live in the dorm with the others, kitchen staff and ground keepers. Any reason you can't handle that?" She leans back eyeing me over the half glasses.

I have a flash picture of Ryan, in one of his tantrums and no Mrs. Shaw around. Hope sinks like a kick in the stomach. I could never bring him down here to that dorm, couldn't afford an apartment and baby-sitter until how long after six months? Even then?

Sheila leans forward, arms folded on her desk. She'd make a good judge on a bench. "I should let you know you have shown good aptitude in handling details and response to guests. You could be right for this field. A serious young person like yourself could look forward to a good future in the hospitality industry. Advancement without a degree, with our training. You have to decide if you can handle it. I'm filling my new trainee group in the next ten days."

My mind races. Nothing waits in Montgomery. I've tried. What else can I do? I say yes, I want the job.

March / Montgomery

Vyola's left for England. I sit here tonight rocking myself, dealing with hope and uncertainty, Ryan asleep like an angel after his sobs. To take this training means letting Bertie win. Let her keep Ryan for six months at least. She doesn't want me up there anyway. Just my baby. When I told Ryan he's going to visit with his Aunt Bertie, he jumped up and down on the bed screaming no, Bertie has wet kisses. My baby's going to hate me.

On the phone, Bertie purred, "You go on to Florida," sounding noble as if she's letting me go down there and lie on a beach while she takes care of my child.

Keep telling myself: What else can I do?

Freedom Farm

1973

All the way to Birmingham Ryan sleeps in my arms, warm body against me like some precious package I'm giving up to Bertie.

There she is, waiting. A solid-bodied thirty-two-year-old woman looking the matron in her fur trimmed coat, trying not to come in contact with anything in the tired old waiting room. Her pink face lights up when she sees us. I put him down and she scoops up my boy, promising ice cream without much of a hello to me.

I try to explain how I'll get back up every chance I can, even if it has to be a round trip. She doesn't care, holding him now, delivering the wet kisses. Has she even listened on the phone when I explained about this being a school, a training program? I'm not going down there to be a waitress.

"Tell Mama good-bye," she coos, not even asking if I'm coming out to the house with them as I'd expected. I watch them go out to her big old town car, Ryan's little feet going fast, pulled along by doting Bertie.

I drop back on the bench, feeling so empty, totally alone.

Six days now until I'm due in Sarasota. The cottage will be so lonely, Vyola and Ryan gone. I could go early to Florida, look around, but that would take motel money.

An idea blooms all through me. I study the schedules on the board. Ask about that little town Pikings in Georgia where Freedom Farm is. Yes, if I catch a bus in three hours, ride all night, I'd be there in the morning. Have a day and night to visit Chloe before busing back to Montgomery, then to Florida. Yes, my only chance I'd have to look into her life, tell her mine, face to face, and do it without Ryan.

I walk downtown to Loveman's, buy some jeans I need anyway, underpants, and toothbrush, change in the rest room, stuff my skirt in my tote bag and head back to the bus station. My sweater will do for two days if Georgia woods aren't too cold in April. The little book I always carry in my purse can be my gift.

Am I doing another crazy thing? No, but eating a bus station hot dog is crazy, when you're excited and worried and missing your baby.

Bus out of Birmingham smells of boiled peanuts and oily gears. Old man next to me watches when I sniff back tears. I lean against the window telling my old hometown good-bye. My childhood, rather. Movies at Alabama Theater, with its brass banisters and fancy dark red alcoves, and handsome lovers being tragic on the screen, Charley with his arm around me, tracing the edge of my breast. What an innocent kid I'd been then, after the movie, getting kissed in a shadowy car at Vulcan Park, worrying about Charley's busy hands, but so thrilled with vague expectations, waiting ahead.

Out of the city we're humming along open highway, sun going down. A song comes to mind that Uncle Vance used to sing in his baritone, "*Look down, look down, that lone-some ro-ad, be-fore you travel on. . . .*"

Morning after that awful night, half sleeping on the bus, rumbling now through worn little towns, past open pastures, sun shining on beautiful brown horses. The diner stop for breakfast—ugh, the greasy smells. Sat by myself reading the little book I'm going to give Chloe. I've memorized the line I love best in *Golden Precepts, a Guide to Enlightened Living.*

The pathway is you, your own being, your own nature, your spiritual self. You follow that pathway to your Higher Self to reach all the mysteries and wonders of the boundless Infinitude.

Worrying as we get closer. What if Chloe takes drugs now? Communes are supposed to be spiritual ways to live, but they think drugs are spiritual too. I've read about the Jesus Freaks who go to churches now and beat drums and say they're off drugs.

The bus driver hollers back to me: "Your stop's coming up. Guess you know those folks you asked about are a bunch of squatters, hippies, that's come in."

Bus leaves me at a country store beside a dusty road, three old men sitting on a bench in front like crows on a fence. I must look like an incoming hippie in my jeans and sweater, clutching my Loveman's bag, hair a windblown mess under the twisted scarf, asking about Freedom Farm. They steady-eye me, their wrinkles twitching a little.

"I'm looking for my sister who's at the farm," I say. That's not a lie. Chloe says we are sister-souls.

"Ain't no farm, Miss, just some half-naked people claiming they're gonna live on the land."

The second old crow says, "Smart-ass city kids, ever one of them. Don't know a damn thing about farming. My quail dog'd be smarter."

The third offers, "Place is five, six miles, but Judson could haul you for five dollars if you're a mind to ride in his pick-up."

This Judson comes out, banging the creaking screen door behind him. A rusty-faced fellow with a slit-eyed grin. One of the bench sitters says, "You watch it, Judson."

I need the ride. I get in. We barrel down a country road, past open pastures and woods, the stinging wind hitting me with Judson's tobacco and sweat smell. I lean against the open window away from his oily right hand, brown as rough leather on the gearshift between us.

Judson shouts over the noise, something about not feeling right taking five dollars from a sweet thing like me. His hand clamps down on my knee and squeezes. I shout, stop that, and jerk away, dig into my canvas bag, throw a five dollar bill onto the dusty dashboard. I shout back at him over the roar, "I'm a nun."

He sits back, stiff-necked, hands on the wheel, muttering about being a Free Will Baptist himself and how I am walking into the devil's campground.

Going slower he starts telling me about sneaking up there. "Saw them bathing in the river, then one full moon night watched them dance around a fire, beating bongos, waving their arms like a bunch of Indians, or witches. A hippie orgy, I reckon."

I figure that must be a full moon festival Chloe wrote about once.

He goes on how the women look like dancing witches, in long nightgowns, bodies jerking. Stoned, all of them because he knows they have more kinds of dope than the grass he grows. He drives out here now and then, parks just inside and deals. "Easiest cash I ever made. Their money comes easier, in the mail, in checks from mama or the old man back home."

Just like that, telling me he goes out there and sells marijuana. "Them hippies can all go to hell for all I care."

He stomps the brakes, stops the truck in a whirl of red dust to growl, "You go in that path and you'll start seeing them. They live in tents, teepees, old buses scattered around in there. Farther in, look for a big old barn they call the heart center."

I get out, clutching my bag. He spins the truck around, and speeds away.

The path is a narrow dirt road with pot holes, going into the deeper woods. First thing I see, sunk in high weeds, is the rounded shape of an old silver Airstream van, with someone peering out the open door.

A bearded fellow steps out, looking like a gnome or a short Santa Claus with bushy white head, arms crossed on his big chest, khaki shorts showing knobby brown knees. I shout out, “Is this way to the main house?” He ambles toward the path, grinning out of his shaggy beard. “All paths lead to the heart. Permit me to show the way.”

I feel like Red Riding Hood or Alice in a crazy fairy tale, but I follow. He huffs alongside, talking nonstop like a man who hasn’t had the chance lately. Tells me, like a joke on himself: “Call me Ishmael, Ish for short.” Came here a year ago looking for his wife. She’d taken off with some woman. He’s stayed, figuring he might as well hang out here, teach little kids to read, rather than go back to Ohio and pay taxes and sit around with boring fellow retirees bemoaning the youth culture.

“My generation doesn’t know a fire’s been lit under the old assumptions. I have my own hopes for the power structure to wise up, give up some greed for the working stiff but figured that’s a young man’s mission. Way thing’s have gone, I’m not at all sure this crop of anarchists and idealists are going to do it.”

“But you’re here,” I say, keeping up with him.

“Yeah.” He asks me, chipper as anything, “You came to check out us hippies? This place has had all sorts of folks showing up, looking for drugs or just curious. One reporter is here now, hanging around.”

He grins over at me as he hops along. “Truth is in the eye of the beholder, different beholders, different truths. And you, young lady?”

Came to see a friend, I tell him. Does he know Chloe? And is Garth McCullough here too? Asking that makes my pulse go funny.

“Ah, Chloe, Venus with a mellowed Boston accent. That’s what I call her. Garth’s from a different side of the moon . . . has a hard bright intellect, that boy, only slightly skewed in his rationales. He’s an egotist, ambitious as any the Washington politicos he hates. McCullough’s one faction here. The other is a professor fellow from California, turned Buddhist. Everything’s in flux now.”

We tromp on down the dirt road, I have to ask, “Are Chloe and Garth still together?”

“Venus and Saturn, yeah. Chloe got Garth here to save his ass, after some trouble back in Marin County, a trio of them arrested, like the Chicago Seven. The jury acquitted, in their way voting against the war.” Ish does an impish grin. “I don’t think that vote of confidence from the establishment pleased Garth McCullough all that much. But she got him here. Say, we’re at the Heart.”

It’s a big faded red barn, wide doors open, set in a clearing, painted with peace symbols and orange yin and yang signs. Ish says, “You’ll find Chloe inside. The females cook for the men and children the way their great grandmas back on a farm had to do. One reason my wife took off. Don’t blame her. Salude.”

Heart pounding, I walk in. The big open barn hums with voices and smells like curry. Toddlers and leggy kids are running around the rough wood tables. Along one sidewall, at a crude wood counter, women are chopping vegetables, dumping them into a huge boiling pot. I stand rooted, staring, remembering the Golden Gate park, girls wearing gypsy colors and bells on their ankles. Now they look like poor country women, ones I remembered seeing as a kid, in flour sack dresses.

I scan faces. Further down, a tall thin girl with pale blond hair to her waist puts down a child who scrambles away. Chloe. When she straightens up, and sees me, her face lights up with true pleasure.

She runs toward me, arms open, enfolding me and hugging hard. Oh, how thin she is under the long cotton dress. Dark circles under those sea green eyes, but her face warms with color. We stand back, nodding at each other, laughing. She’s telling me in that clear bell voice how that very morning she’d promised herself there would be surprise of joy that day and “here you are, coming to see me.” Not even surprised I’d come.

Not even wondering about me traveling all this way to stay a single night.

"Come look at my daughter."

How pleased she is, leading me toward the back wall to a row of basket cribs where babies kick or sleep or cry, watched by a skinny young girl with a sullen face. Chloe reaches into the third basket and brings up her baby, a fragile looking three-month-old who'd arrived early. Named Emily after her grandmother which surprises me. In this place, the tiny little thing is called "Emilybird." I watch Chloe cradle that baby in her arms, thinking how much this child had cost her, she'd tried so many times. With a glowing face, even says she wants another.

It's food time. Chloe has to help herd children to their bowls of thick soup. I stand back, out of the way, afraid to see Garth. No, have to look in his face, have to find out if he remembers me.

In the clatter and hum of the food scene, we eat the same curried vegetables and Chloe tells me I'll be sleeping in the cabin where some of the women bunk and she'd stay with me. I wander outside while she helps collect bowls.

There he is, leaning against a tree, alone, smoking. It's been more than three years, yet I know that tousled dark head, the lean muscled shape of him, standing there defiant, imperious, restless. I walk right up, say hello, and wait.

He takes a long minute, the dark gaze flickering over me, into me the way it can. His smile is condescendingly amused. "Why, here is Sweet Chile, Chloe's friend from Alabamy. The pen pal." I see no other recognition. None, none. I want to beat my fists in his chest. No, I'm glad he doesn't remember and I'll never ever let him know he has a son, a bright, healthy handsome little boy who would be able to tell him what's what in a few years. No, I will never let him know.

"I'm Chloe's friend all right so I worry for her health. She shouldn't get pregnant again."

"Earth Mother Chloe? You want me to stop laying my girl?"

I walk away feeling stupid, seething inside, chilled outside. Have to keep thinking: *I have your son and you'll never ever know. He's mine.*

Finally, I head toward the women's cabin and showers in the long wooden shack. Water will be icy, but I'm too angry to care. On a slope above the clearing and the lighted barn I have to stop. A low bonfire glows down there. A bunch of men sitting around in the flickering light, listening to the one who's pacing, gesturing.

Garth McCullough is the silhouette, his determined voice echoing in this damp chill night. Watching, I see what Chloe believes in—the thwarted leader, an Aquarius high priest, eloquent in his rage at a lost cause.

In the women's place, cold moonlight steams across a row of cots. In my sweater and jeans I crawl under a scratchy wool blanket, my cot close to Chloe's. Her long hair spills across the gray pillow, eyes bright in a shadowed face, tiny Emilybird nursing at her thin breast. I reach over, trace a finger across the soft fuzz of the baby's head. Chloe smiles but the special glow she used to have seems more like a fever now from a fierce will.

I lean closer to whisper what I have to say. How could she let Garth rule her life when she's so passionate about women's rights and powers? She's quiet for long minutes. I feel terrible. Finally she tucks Emilybird into the basket, secured at the foot of her cot. Curls back up under the blanket, leaning close. "I know how it looks. Trust me."

Her face catches the pale light, telling me what she believes. That nurturing is a strength, an innate endowment, an inate wisdom a woman has. Not a lesser gift, but a divine one, not a role of servitude that history has made it. Men have used this, freeing them of responsibility. They have to learn better to be fully human for themselves. Have to be taught, but not with hate for an enemy. "My sisters in the movement don't agree. But there it is for me."

She reaches over, presses my hand. "The whole world needs nurturing, people, children, the planet. Women have to know that gift and refuse to call it weakness. I want to help teach that."

"Then why don't you go, take Emilybird and leave here?"

She lets out a long sigh. "That's my mission, but I have another right now. Saving Garth for what he could do later. It will take voices like Garth's, a political animal with intellectual fire, to wake people in power to make changes. To be heard, I know he must be part of that power, a lawyer in a three piece suit."

"You still love him that much?"

"Garth is . . . the personal mission right now. We share beliefs about the ills of our society. He's the objective thrust. I have to work in the trenches, in a more personal way. Even so, I'll need some letters behind my name, only to satisfy the powers that be. There's a women's studies program at Wellesley—but right now, yes, I'm staying with him."

"Wellesley means home, Boston. What's happening with your family?"

Leaning close, "I don't dwell on it. Mother lives with a nurse now. Father left home with a young woman. Norman has taken over the estate, the business and the house. He's not about to let go of any funds to his hippie sister here or there."

I lie still under that scratchy blanket, thinking, love can blind a person, even someone special as Chloe. Believing she's found love when she's had none from her family.

She lies back, telling me why she had to get him out of Santa Cruz. "He would have self-destructed. I've seen others do that, the ones who really believed in the movement. Some have gone underground. Others stay stoned. Some of those you saw at the co-op were disasters from the start. Kids who left home to kick over the traces, get with the action. I escaped to Zen and Esalen and any guru who seemed to emit a kind of peace. But wouldn't leave California without Garth."

"But do you trust him? Is he worth—?"

She props up on a skinny elbow to look at me. "Faithful you mean? Rae, he needs me. He trusts my views. I know you hate him. Please don't. Hate is toxic to your inner being." With a sleepy sigh, "I draw protection around him. You can't do that unless you direct love to that person first. Resentment would block any flow of energy."

In the faintest whisper, "What is faithful anyway? You have to be faithful to yourself, your cause. When Garth took off for three weeks back in Santa Cruz, I accepted comfort. A friend who used to be a UCLA professor. He's here now. But Garth came back. He always does. He needs me, I keep him balanced."

Silent a minute, then, "You haven't told me about your little boy and your new job. I want to hear everything."

I whisper back a quick report, praising Bertie's care, my plans. I'm glad she lies back down, eyes closed. The room is quiet except for sighs and whimpers of the other sleepers, and now a wind blowing through Georgia woods.

Chloe, I decide, is a misplaced angel on this earth while I am this ordinary person, looking out for myself and can't wait to get away from here tomorrow.

Long Boat Key

1974–1975

August / Sarasota

Dear Vyola:

I can just see you pedaling around Cambridge on those narrow curving streets crowded with little cars and students. Proud of you, my Anglophile auntie. Also glad you're back at the cottage. That's home.

If you'd been there a week earlier, I would have stopped by the cottage for one night, with Ryan. Yes, on my way to take him back to Bertie's.

I had him here for four months. Ran out of teenage baby sitters who would show up. Those girls would walk in that little apartment with a smirky look of pity for what they saw. I'd be in this rush to do the dinner hour, floor covered with toys, Ryan crying, mad because I'd brought him in from the beach.

Also ran out of friends who would fill in for me when the sitter didn't show. So I gave up the place, gave up on having him here and took him back to Birmingham. Moved back into the dorm.

If we could have stopped by the cottage, you would have seen what a wild hellion my son is. Demands his way. In Birmingham he rules Bertie who bosses everyone else. Vyola, he is so bright and so much to handle. I wanted you to see how handsome he is. He'll be going into kindergarten in Montgomery, so that's for his good. The doctor says he's hyper, needs directed activity not babysitters.

We did have some good hours on the beach before I had to go to work. He'd run along the surf like a little brown Indian and bring me back some special shell. Even gave me a sandy hug now and then. Have to treasure that memory. Middle of the night sometimes I wake up and wonder again if I've made a terrible choice about this training. But I've invested so much time and study here, it has to pay off. Back to work now.

Love, Rae

❧

September 3. 1974

Dear Chloe,

Did you try to reach me on the dorm phone last night? It wasn't my aunt, so bet I missed you. Wanted to tell you I'm glad you decided to go ahead and accept living in the carriage house on your brother's property. I know you can't stand to be in his presence, but it gets you out of that small apartment Emily hated. Garth must have hated it, too. Are you alone, Chloe? I keep thinking about you using what money you had from your grandmother to help him get into Harvard. What about your own plans? You tell me about your retreat week at Omega, but what about Wellesley?

Your friend Rae

❧

Sterling Crown Management Training Program

1973 Class

Welcome New Trainees:

Your fi... he
ho... g
y...

rem...
dini...
joyab... the
...earn with the

...o sessions with T...
...ri...

As trainees...
properly withi... r assigned...
and in free hour... munity. Below you
will find your fi...

Boston

Dear Rae

What a treasure, that snapshot of Ryan running down the beach! Enlarge it and keep it by your desk. As for taking him back to the aunt, think care and patience, not guilt. Surprised at me saying so?

It is strange but we each are having to lend our children to another woman. Something in this I've yet to understand.

Some lesson yet to discover. Is it that we don't own other people, even our own children? Is it reminding me to live, be in the moment, not focus on loss?

Yes, I finally accepted moving into the carriage house on Norman's estate because my little Emily begged for this. I resisted for reasons you know. Garth wouldn't go near anything belonging to Norman Payne. Garth sees my brother as the epitome of the self-serving insulated conservative allowing travesties between the powerful and powerless. Yes, he has his own place near Harvard.

You know how I dislike thinking of money as a reason for anything, but my costs are less by living on Norman's property. He doesn't charge me and probably has some grim satisfaction that his hippie sister lives in his back grounds. I haven't told you much about this but I shall now. Norman's wife, Jean, who has no children, has a ruffly room for my child, and a closet of clothes to match. Emily loves the place I think of as the mausoleum, void of love. My petite daughter thinks it's a castle. Jean showed up often, taking her from what she called the miserable little apartment. Took her for the day and night. I was having bronchitis and allowed it.

Bringing her back, Jean would report how Emily skips through that house, pretending to be a princess. My daughter loves all that with as much fierce determination as she hated the retreats and the meetings where I've taken her along. She loves ruffles and looking at Jean's jewelry more than being with grass and sky.

I have given in for another reason. My little Emily has asthma. Jean has her room with a perfect climate and wants to take her to special camps for asthmatic children. I can't hate Jean. She's married to an empty-souled man and needs to focus on something pretty that's also alive, my child.

I comfort myself by believing Emily still lives with me, only visits Jean in the big house. Also, I never have to come in contact with Norman. Jean points out she's allowing me freedom for my classes. Yes, I'm into Wellesley for the long haul. I already know what my thesis should be. The Nurturing Feminist. More on that later.

We must get together soon and have an eye-to-eye meeting. Meanwhile, keep writing. Don't worry about me. I don't give energy to the negative by focusing on it. I find groups here who meditate together. I release negative thoughts, to ride above them, move ahead.

Your soul-sister,
Chloe McCullough

October

Tonight, I'm working the dining room as hostess. Evan, at the grand, plays *Tenderly*. The melody turns on chills, romantic or challenge, maybe both. It's been our cue for two months now. I'm so careful, nobody guesses. Oh God, I hope they don't. Even if the crew does complain about task master Sheila, somebody would make sure she knew.

Tell myself, no don't go tonight. Just walk the beach, look for stars. Yeah, and run into my roommate and her boyfriend making out in the seaoats.

Back in the room at eleven.

Everybody else gone. They're partying at the beach bars.

Ryan's picture looks at me from the wall. A running child who doesn't see me, thinks Mama is someone who visits, takes candy away, and leaves.

I brush my teeth. Brush my hair that's long now to my shoulders. Look at my lonesome self in the small mirror.

Cross the road to the Sterling Crown to walk the beach. Half moon tonight, shadowed sands. The surf rolls in and pulls back with a moaning sound, leaving white foam.

His door is way down at the end of the building, past the laundry room, almost hidden by heavy bushes of bougainvillea. He'll be at the piano, in shorts and expensive sport shirt, smoking, cussing under his breath, drinking wine and working on his composition. I always pretend it's good. He needs the encouragement.

Evan looks up, nods, keeps on playing with a new flourish. I get a Coke from the lighted wet bar alcove. The only light in the room. He's still playing, as I go to the couch to watch and listen. Nothing wrong to visit, I tell myself. Need company. He needs an audience who cares.

His fingers race over the keys, with a theme from Grieg. He starts his own composition again, plays a few bars. Ends with a discordant chord, sound of anguish, protest. I know what's coming. Another story about doing the major concert at seventeen in Switzerland, how arrogant reviewers can ruin what should have been the start of a career.

"And look how my life has turned out, playing piano bar music for rude, sunburned tourists." More chords. Minor key. Sadness.

"I say that to no one else but you, Rae, because you see, you understand."

Is this a compliment? Is that what I come to hear?

I know more about him now. What he doesn't say is his father was buying him a part of Sterling Resorts when the concert career didn't work out. Did the father also talk Evan into marrying Sheila? Or Sheila into marrying his son? Don't know. But I feel sorry for this man who is the reason I'm here. He's like a crown prince who was kicked out of the kingdom by his father and told to go to work.

So I watch and listen. In the half light from the recessed bar, he could be a handsome actor at the piano in a sad movie about a rejected composer.

He stops playing. Comes over to the couch and stretches out, his blond head in my lap. I trace his even features with a forefinger. His eyes quiver under the closed lids.

We don't talk, not really. Maybe he says, "You're the one person, Rae, who sees the situation here."

It's always the same. I try to pretend it just happens naturally.

He sits up to draw me into his arms, kisses me lightly over my face, my neck. My own eyes closed, head against his chest, the hum of his heart, smell of his cologne. It starts like that, sweet and quiet. I think of hugging him back and getting up and saying 'bye and walking out. But I don't. For these minutes I'm needed. I have needs, too, buried deep but coming alive, insistent with his touch.

What happens doesn't remind me of those months with Charley. Or that one night in my life at Berkeley. This is silent and deliberate. We don't talk. We're two lonely people exchanging needs.

He's asleep on the couch when I gather myself up, hurry out of there, crossing the dark road and going back to the dorm, already trying to block it out.

❧

December

Dear Vyola:

Meeting you there in Montgomery for a stopover on the way to Birmingham was to be my big gulp of fresh confidence before another Christmas at Bertie's. Even before your unbelievable gift, I was so happy to walk through the cottage again. So when we got in your familiar gray VW and rode down to the Chevy place, I was still talking away about Sterling Crown. And there was your new blue Chevy waiting, and you handed me the keys and registration to the VW. I could have melted with gratitude.

I drove up to Birmingham, still thrilled. Now I can see Ryan when I have the chance, without waiting on buses. I hugged you hard, but was so choked up I couldn't even say how wonderful. Driving up I felt like your confidence was riding with me.Thanks a million times from my heart,

Love, Rae

March

Journal:

I must never forget tonight so I want to write it down.

It's midnight, I'm back in the dorm room, roommate still out. Tonight was the Greek Feast in Ringling Museum's courtyard catered by Sterling. Our crew set up and served, but were part of the show, too. Boys in white tee shirts and bathing trunks under short white skirts, being Greek runners with torches, lighting the candles and serving that awful tasting retsina. We girls looking Grecian enough in long cotton dresses tied high waisted. Sheila got them from the beach shops.

What a scene. Long tables set up in the courtyard centered with ice carvings, raised platters of whole fish, glazed, gleaming under the lights. The formal dressed crowd streaming in set up a party hum along with the Greek music. Once they were seated, dinner going, our crew stood around on the open loggias looking down on the lighted courtyard and tables. Here's the thing.

I watched alone from the terrace next to the statue of David in all his naked bronze glory. Behind me, the Gulf coloring everything in a pink glow and made silhouettes of tall royal palms against the sky, first a violet sky then turning this magical dark blue.

I spotted Evan down there next to Sheila, watched him being so animated and charming to everyone at their table. Really playing a part. And there was Sheila, being the quiet one, letting him shine.

Wow. It hit me—Evan is always acting a part in some self-centered way. Maybe my tough boss Sheila knows that, but really loves him. Well, not me. That minute I was finished with fooling myself Evan could be any comfort to me. Why had I been such a stupe? Just because of loneliness, not seeing anything ahead.

Standing up there watching a magic night, looking on to other people's lives like I usually do, I decided it was time to get on with it. Be somebody in this business. I'd worked at slave pay long enough. I would walk into Sheila's office and demand to know where I stand, when would I start a job that pays. I need to bring my boy down, all of that.

I'll sleep on that like a settled vow.

❧

Wouldn't you know? Sheila is too busy with some visiting Importants to be seen this whole week. Tonight, Evan played *Tenderly* looking up with quizzical hurt when I passed the piano. I paused an instant to tell him to play *Fools Rush In Where Angels Fear to Tread*. Should have thought up something worse.

I'm in bed when somebody shouts,"Hey, Rae, have a call out in the hall."

It's Josey on the other end of the line. "You'd better get up here, Rae. Bertie is talking to her lawyer about claiming full custody of Ryan, leaving you out of the picture."

My roommate warns: "You leaving? Better wait until morning and get Sheila's okay."

I can't wait. I'm in the VW, barreling up the highway by midnight. Drinking coffee to stay awake. Near Birmingham sunlight closes my eyes. Have to stop in a parking lot behind a motel and sleep two cramped hours before driving on to the big Kendall house.

It's two in the morning when I pull back into Sarasota three days later, cross over the causeway and onto Long Boat Key. At the dorm, fall in bed, too exhausted to care about the note that's waiting. "See me in my office first thing in the morning. Sheila." What morning did that mean? Yesterday? Day before?

Wake to harsh sunlight and that note. She has to be faced. This tough boss who has driven me every day on the job, whose best compliments can be a nod or a "doing okay, Alabama" is going to fire me. I stand under a cold shower, feeling nothing. What would Chloe do? Think positive? Ha.

She waits behind the desk like a one-woman judge in a purple muu-muu. Sun from those windows hurts my eyes.

I don't wait for the questions. "I was in Birmingham. Had to go."

"What was the hurry?" Sheila, being cool.

I make it brief. "Sister-in-law Bertie Kendall in Birmingham was ready to seek legal custody of my son. Had to drive up there non-stop to face them and their lawyer."

"And what happened?" Sheila, arms crossed against her amble chest, listening.

I bite out a short version of the meeting in the Kendall living room. Their lawyer saying yes, as mother, I have rights and I'm not a callous unfit mother because job training has kept me away, as long as there has been adequate family care here with the Kendalls, as long as the job training promised results. Also, turning over to the Kendalls the Air Force allotment for Ryan, as I'd done, meant cooperation, not giving up my child.

That said, the lawyer had turned to me, the accused, to ask: what is best for your boy's welfare? Isn't this the main issue? Ryan has started first grade at five-and-a half. He's a bright restless child who needs that stimulus. His aunt here is giving him a secure home. Could the mother afford time and circumstances to provide such care? Not at present, right? No, not at present . . .

"And how did it end?"

My eyes want to close, facing the sunny windows behind her red head. "This was my sister-in-law's way of punishing me for not moving up there, for staying down here working for you. Well, the legal thing was dropped. In return, my son stays there until I can afford to have him with me."

Weary anger in my voice, telling this, Sheila listening calm as you please. "So what do I have to tell them now? That you're going to fire me?" Have to close my eyes to the sun.

"Sorry about your trouble, Kendall. I asked you in to hear the news."

For a minute I still can't open my eyes, listening to how Sterling is being bought out, real estate, logos, everything, but not the training program. Excel Institute has its own big deal training program.

"Are you staying? What happens to me? "

Sheila looks pleased, leaning back now, saying she's staying on for a couple months, going to buy the most elegant penthouse condo on this coast, put her feet up and read. Her brother is retiring. Evan is going to a dining room on the east coast, to the grand piano there.

My heart is racing. Hope fighting apprehension.

"You can stop hiding the panic, Kendall, there's something in this for you."

She goes on with the rest of it: Excel Associates does employee training for more vocational fields than the hospitality industry. "They don't spell it out in the pretty brochures, but the training focuses on motivating employees to work in harmony with one another. It's time whites, blacks, Hispanics and whomever get the word. You've seen it here so you know that includes the egotists and the insecure types who show up in any group, as well as the passive-aggressives. Right, Alabama? I had you sit in with me on some of those cases. You have a quiet way of sharing empathy, bringing them around."

I'm waiting, breathing hard.

"I've talked to Excel folks about you going to Atlanta, corporate offices where they start you. Am I about to see you cry for the first time? Toughen up. You're ready to move on. You do need a hellava lot more self-assurance under that calm Southern exterior, but you have an unobtrusive way of dealing with others having problems."

She goes on, "With Excel, you can get their training in spades from their big-deal facilitators before they put you anywhere in the organization."

Adrenaline pumps. "In front of an audience?"

"It's a big operation. You'll fit in somewhere. They also need advance people to check out hotel space, book dates for their sessions. You know your way around a property. I've promised them you're ready to start there."

"They agreed, not seeing me?"

"Ever heard me waste my time promising? They'll be here tomorrow for in-the-face interviews. Be ready."

I sit there, numb and relieved.

"I know of your situation, Alabama. Tough, but don't expect any big company to give consideration to a woman because she happens to be a single mother with a kid to look after. The accountants call the shots no matter who is sitting in the boss's chair."

I pull myself up. Sleep now will be delicious.

She gives me the softest look I've ever seen on her determined face. "Go buy one of those books about dress-for- success. Looks are the facade, but appearance helps. Shorten that mess of curly hair. Main thing, tread water, Kendall, look confident, until you feel it. You'll make it to solid shore with these folks."

I go around the desk and hug her shoulders, something I'd never dreamed I'd do.

At the door she stops me. "Another word of advice, Alabama, about men you'll find in the real world. Don't let the males out there intimidate you, in the office or behind the office door. And don't mistake any male's sense of lordship for love. Most men are controlling bastards. You're stronger than you allow yourself to believe. Strong without being a tough bitch like me. You came here an unsure babe, but you had staying power. And made some other choices, didn't you?"

At the door I'm hoping my warm face isn't flushed with guilt. She has something else to say, I can tell.

"Also, Rae Kendall, don't take on the opposite kind— a charming man with more sensitivity than balls. They stray, looking for sympathy. With one of those, you have to play forgiving mama and wait until he wants to come home."

I bolt out of there.

Flights

1975–1978

May / Atlanta

From deep couches in the atrium lobby of the Hyatt Regency, Josey and I sip our wine and watch glass elevators glide up the inside floors.

"Maybe I'll move to Atlanta, too," she says, sounding pensive, un-Josey like. "Sixth graders here couldn't be any worse than mine at pummeling and double-daring each other, hormones kicking up, ready for a worse stage."

"It's big city pace here." We both know she won't move away from her mother. Or the married school principal with the school board wife.

We're resting now after stalking around Rich's, where I bought my first good suit so I could look like a professional. The whole lollygagging day has been a celebration, coming up for air after three months of Excel training and moving out of one room into a real apartment. Josey, bless her, listened with respectful belief while I related the training. "Equal to a cram-condensed college year in social psychology and conflict management," I boasted.

"So you'll be flying a lot," she says, in a faraway voice, looking at one of my new business cards, the dignified gold print against maroon saying *Rae Kendall, Field Representative, Excel Associates, Success Management Training.*

"To hotels like this, booking space for Excel sessions. It pays more than the desk jobs here in Atlanta, doing session schedules."

"What about Ryan?"

"Oh, Josey, you know how to make me worry. I have to make myself solid with the company before I can bring him here. He's satisfied at Bertie's, well he gets his way there. This assignment gives me some leeway time to fly on to Birmingham sometime before showing back up in Atlanta."

"You used to be my cousin the dreamer. Look at you now. Turned tenacious working woman."

"It's called survival. Without a degree, you have to act the part, dress the part and hope the pay follows. They promise—"

"Don't trust promises from men," Josey says looking grim.

We're silent, sipping our wine. I confess, "The money isn't great right now, true. I could make more if I went for more training to work with a facilitator on stage, backing him up. The win-win sessions are for employees sent by the company. They're our captive audience. I don't care to bounce around on stage and through the crowd with a mike, doing the rah, rah encouragement. That's show business."

"Because?"

"Some of them out there may feel as I do. Prefer to consider and accept advice in one's own private head."

"I hear the dreamer again. Afraid to hurt anyone's feelings? Or expose your own?"

I swallow a sigh. "Well don't tell anybody, okay?"

I look out over the lobby sluffing that off. "Do me a favor, Josey. Will you talk to Ryan's teacher? He was a first grader she'll remember. Bertie got sniffy with her, which didn't help Ryan. I have to dig in with this company before I can afford to have him here with me and in a good private boarding school when I'm not home. Baby sitters don't work. I shudder at memories."

Josey nods, looking around. "Who's the sharpie couple heading over here as if they know you? The guy anyway."

"Mel Myrick, one of Excel's hot-shot motivators. You should see him working a crowd—smooth, glib, like a charming salesman who knows he has you hooked. Off stage, impatient chain smoker, thinks he's sexy. Be glad he's with a disapproving female now. She'll pull him away."

❧

August / Chicago

Dear Vyola,

It's too late to call tonight, but I long to talk to you. I'm at the Chicago Regency, still awake at midnight. A pleasant enough room, but hotels, like air terminals, are alike after the first fifty.

For four hours today, I handled the registration tables outside the meeting rooms. Later stepped inside to watch Mel Merrick work the crowd, an audience of junior-level managers aspiring to climb their corporate ladders. I look at those blow- dried heads and wonder if any were shaggy-haired protesters not too long ago. So many smart looking women in the sessions now with their crisp suits and challenging rebuttals at the mike. They're determined and "dressed for success," as the book says. Crisp mannish suits. Am I too stubborn to conform, or too female to want to pretend I'm a man?

Yes, I'm still in touch with Chloe. We visit late nights on the phone. She's getting her degree at Wellesley and working at an agency. Has been doing volunteer work, too, at a shelter for women. I sense Garth is still in her life though she says he has a U.N. girlfriend.

I'll try to drop in for a day when possible if you aren't in Cambridge again. Glad you found friends there, but don't let anything happen to the cottage.

Love from lonely, busy Rae

ꕥ

September / Cleveland

Packing now to leave in the morning. If Mel knocks on my door again tonight, will I let him in? If I do it's to practice holding my own with a dogmatic, arrogantly confident male. Or lonely for a one-to-one conversation in a quiet room, even his self-assured confrontation? Watched him on stage before a session of mid-level executives. Saw him take one smart-ass fellow apart and put the guy back the Excel way.

Maybe he won't come up. Gloated earlier he might stay down at the bar tonight and get lucky since I'm playing the Southern working girl. Good luck, I told him.

Standing under a pounding shower like this is my five minute meditation. No, cross-examination time, wondering where I'm going with this job. Showers aren't enough. I should get myself a journal again.

Looking at this woman in the mirror. Tired face, fresh, vulnerable-looking without make-up. Damp curling hair. Okay, add lipstick. Zip up a robe. Turn on TV, but sit in a chair, away from the bed. Click through channels. Gad, I hate canned laughter. Click it dark.

He's out there, with the quick tap. Open the door for Mel, the manipulator. He breezes in, smelling of cigarettes and hyper with energy, followed by a room service fellow carrying a tray. Mel pays, spins a fast joke for the boy, closes the door, hands me a Manhattan on the rocks, and with his Scotch, drops on the bed as if his presence is unquestioned. Stretches out, with a comic groan for the long day.

I sip my sweet Manhattan, listening to his bitchy recounts. "Did you hear that last guy, that arrogant little s–o–b, trying to tell me what works?" Shop talk, mixed with come-ons, his polished Italian loafers restless on the spread like tapping fingers. No, Mel, I'm not going to ask you to take off your shoes.

He picks up my book off the nightstand. *Conscious Person's Guide to Relationships* by Ken Keyes. "Hey, look at this, what kind of crap do you read lonely nights in your room?"

"Something from a busman's holiday I gave myself last week."

"Yeah? What?" The cocksure voice can be snide.

I sip my drink. "His session followed ours, so I took it in. Keyes is a little man in a wheel chair who teaches about love. Don't laugh."

"Honeychile, forget the poetry. Action is what counts."

"That book is about staying on a higher level of consciousness where you don't have to be victim or vengeful. He says you can kick someone out of your life if necessary, but not out of your heart so you can go on from there—"

"What a bunch of crap. Marketplace psychology."

I say calmly, "Whereas our win-win dictum is—"

"Teaching the climbers how to win, training the hired help not to fight with each other, as you know. Today you watched our fledgling male predators pay their own tab to learn how to act with power. All those serious-faced babes, too, trying to be men."

"No, they're women, learning to play the game. It's the others, the employee groups, I wonder about. Making them role-play their interaction on the job. They need it, but behind their hesitance or belligerence, I see personal needs, doubts, personal stuff going on in their lives, besides the job."

"You're a bleeding heart for the hired help because you have to handhold when they walk out of a session."

"I talk to them. Part of my job, I know. I hear concerns, banked underneath."

Mel groans. "Not our problem. Let them find a shrink."

He gives me the Direct Confrontation look. "When are you going to let me teach you how to be my back-up at the mikes? I'm willing to take you on—"

"Thanks, but no thanks."

"Willing to take you on, Southern accent, calm demeanor and all. The up-tight ones would feel you're on their side."

"I know of two at Excel who'd like to stage with you."

A grimace. "I need a back-up girl who is not trying out for a TV anchor job. Wise up, Rae. There's more money working the sessions on stage than booking space and sitting out there like secretary who can handhold when necessary."

"I like my job all right. Flights give me a tiny bit of freedom."

He's into his own sales pitch, enjoying himself. I drink down the Manhattan, rattle the ice, imagining a debate of beliefs between Chloe and this brash man. Sound of a pure flute solo drowned out by caustic rock beat. No, Chloe wouldn't try. She'd look serene and murmur, "So that's your chosen belief."

Mel pauses, demanding an answer. I've stopped listening. He says again, "You worrying about their poor troubled souls, for God's sake? We're training for company efficiency."

"I know. I was expressing a personal belief. That for a person to function well, he, she, needs the two selves in sync. The inner and outer."

"You talking religion to me? My Southern child, I don't see you floating around in a glow. Didn't take you as a member of the self-righteous who boast they've booked space in heaven and I haven't."

"No, I don't gloat." And I'm not in sync.

Mel gives me his best stage smile. "Hey, come over here and let's practice some role-play that counts."

"Get your shoes off my bed, Mel. It's been a long day. Go sleep it off. I need to do the same."

"What? Okay. Pass up your chance again." He yawns, gets up. "See you in Philly in two weeks.

January / Boston

A cold bright day in Boston. Handing the cab driver the address to vegetarian restaurant close to where Chloe lives reminds me of San Francisco, another cab ride ages ago. Still in my senses if I allow. No, I won't allow. Instead, remember it's been three months since I was here and Chloe met me in the Delta terminal for a fast-talking hour before my flight.

Today, there's time for lunch and maybe a look at where she lives. I take a booth, wait with mellow anticipation, looking at the place. Baskets of fern hang against windows above crystals that flash in pale winter sun. Subtle Windham Hill music in the background, suits this pleasant place. The warmth carries the good aroma of some kind of soup. Assorted patrons stand at the serving bar, waiting for their orders.

Here's Chloe, swinging in, flushed with the cold, wearing a long great coat, knitted red band holding back loose pale hair. Sweeps toward me, smiling, arms open. Against the unbuttoned coat, the usual black turtle neck sweater, I feel her thinness, her beating heart. The long pale hair is wheat color now not Rapunzel blonde.

"My friend, the traveling business woman." she says.

"My friend with a Wellesley degree," I counter.

She slides into her side of the booth, dropping the coat back, and laughing at the cold. "I'm an ice maiden with a warm heart, getting eye-to-eye with my friend who writes short letters answering my long ones."

The sea green eyes are still lively, inquiring, lilac-shadowed but not from make-up. Does the perfect ivory skin have a hint of pallor? She should be past the bronchitis, but Garth's defection?

"I love your letters. They're keepers. They could go in a journal like Re-Vision. What about the book you're writing?"

"First, we collect our veggie chili and watercress salad."

Back in the booth, we dip into the food, tear into the crusty bread, stirring lemon in hot herbal tea, exclaiming about the place, the warmth, our various adventures getting here. She's taken a cab, doesn't have a car. "I cab to the shelter six days and can walk from there to the agency." A pause. "Emily is with Jean during the week."

"Sounds like a brutal week. I live in hotels. Spend my nights with Johnny Carson."

"Rae, I'm so proud of you."

"For looking like a traveling rep? It's the suit, ultra suede. What about Chloe herself? Your letters skip over that."

"I told you about the bronchitis. I can breathe again." She holds up a forkful of salad, eyes sparkling again. "Life is in this bite of green—sun, air, earth, water."

A couple saunters up, nods at my introduction then focuses on Chloe to talk about holistic health programs coming up and Ram Dass coming to town.

I sip tea and watch her profile, serene yet responsive. Watch the pair's obvious respect tinged with curiosity. They must know her as a one time Boston deb, rich family and all, later hippie, now trying to mother the world as volunteer at the crisis shelter plus her job as agency therapist. They must know Garth who isn't around anymore, but working for some politico in Washington. I think they see an earthy woman who is somehow ethereal, too. Like the crystals in the window, still one moment, flashing subtle light the next.

They leave and Chloe turns back, eyes full on me, asking her questions. Yes, my job keeps me on the move. Yes, I see Ryan often. Still plan to bring him to Atlanta, but he's doing better in school now, don't want to disrupt that, and his grandfather lives to see Little Charley. Subject of Ryan makes me nervous. Guilty. Stirs up the old fear she might see him, recognize Garth in his face.

"And your writing?" I insist.

"On hold. Unless all those letters I write to you are going to be part of it. I'm using you for a sounding board because your rebuttals are honest, from a women dealing with marketplace realities. At present, the Nurturing Feminist is a loose-leaf book of notes and questions and impressions from the shelter and the agency."

"Chloe and her missions. What's the priority now?"

The fine lines around her eyes tighten. "My concerns? Pregnant teens I see at the agency. They don't know where to turn. They can be rich kids or poverty bred, but if they've had no nurturing examples in their own lives, they have no values to pass on to these infants. The poor ones turn too often to the next boyfriend. And that, as you'd guess, can be a disaster for both child and mother."

"You're still between pro-life and pro-choice?"

"Oh, Rae, the answer has to be somewhere in the center, not either extreme. So much grief comes from either extreme. Unwanted babies or unwanted guilts. A woman has a right to her body, but it begins by valuing the body. How can the impressionable young girl learn that in a culture that sexualizes every product? They're taught to flaunt their bodies and follow the Pied Pipers of whatever's new, like lemmings." Chloe looks into the empty teacup, silent a moment before looking up.

"Rae, you know how it is being young and alone with a child. But you had values and family behind you. You had a place to go. And had family to help. Even if it is your bossy sister-in-law."

That digs into my guilt. "It's hard anytime to do it right. Hey, do we have time to see your place? Where you write those letters?"

We look at watches. Yes, if we get a cab now.

All the way out we talk of Watergate-Nixon, teens, children, and carefully about our own who seem to have a life beyond us. Is there any man in my life?

A month ago I would have said she was looking at a lonely, uptight, celibate woman. Now I say, "No one who means anything to me. I see a lot of men during a day. A passing parade. I've wondered if I wear an invisible shield that holds men back because they guess I need love, not just sex."

We swing out of the city. "I've started seeing one of our facilitators. A bright man in whom I have nothing in common, but the job. Distraction for now. Why? Skin hunger, as you said once? It's the Excel me who does this. My real self looks on."

"That helps skin hunger, but confuses the real self."

I have to ask, "Do you still allow Garth to come by, practice his speeches?" I watch her face, see a flash of patience.

"I did tell you that, didn't I? He's invited places to speak as a former radical, then A.C.L.U. lawyer and political aide. And yes, he goes back to his U.N. girlfriend."

"He doesn't deserve any help from you."

"Garth respects my views. I keep him from being caustic. Rae, we are veterans of the same Sixties' war."

"So you finally got him into a three piece lawyer suit."

She laughs. "Here we are."

The cab whips into the driveway of a huge baronial stone house. Yes, it could be forbidding. The drive continues on around to a back drive and her carriage house, set in a ragged winter garden with a few bare maples. Inside there's comfort and warmth I expected. A beautiful dark oak desk, tapestry covered couch and chairs, a small table by a window, an efficiency kitchen. The bedroom is tiny.

I say honestly, "It's small, but pleasantly English and bookish. Is this it, the place where you know you're meant to be? A coming home, after all?"

Watching her face, I regret asking.

"It's where I need to be for now. Emily is up at the house. I wanted you to see her, let her know her mother has friends in ultra-suede suits and heels, with airline tickets in a leather purse. Her uncle has taught her to see me as the hippie mother. But she's away with Jean."

I realize with a jolt. "Chloe, you are lonely. Don't pretend to me you aren't."

"No pretense. I'm finding it takes longer to get where you're intended to go. Meanwhile, I don't focus on the negative, give it power. I choose to live above disappointment."

She calls me a cab. Outside in the chill air we do a quick hug. "You're thin enough for a runway model," I say.

"You look like the one who manages the show or owns the store," she says. "Oh yes, wanted to tell you about Omega, the place upstate New York where I go to sloff off stress, find my center again. I'm mailing you the next brochure. Try to save the second week in June, join me there even for a day. I want you to experience that place, the quiet, the people, the ideas."

"No promises. My life belongs to Excel." I laugh and wave as the cab pulls out but I hate what I've just said.

March / New York

At LaGuardia, waiting on my Delta flight, I dial Chloe and get a faint hello. "Did I wake you? You okay?"

"Hi," she says, sounding sleepy or lonely or both.

"I've been thinking, you can send the Omega brochure. I'll try, and I just dropped in the mail, one for you. Happened on a program yesterday at the New York Statler. You would have loved the mind-boggling session I heard."

I rush on. "The conference was called 'New Dimensions of Consciousness—a convocation of visionary men and women pioneering this new evolution of scientific knowledge and spiritual realization.' Get that? I managed to hear one afternoon session along with a huge audience. You listening?"

"I am. Chest is congested tonight but the ears are good."

"I heard two famous theoretical physicists I read about in that Re-Vision Journal you sent me last year. Fritjof Capra and Englishman, David Bohn. The core message from each one was: 'we are each connected to the universe.' What do you think of that?"

"We thought so all the time, didn't we? The problem is believing and listening in. Thanks, my friend in flight, I was feeling like a lone creature tonight."

June / D.C.

A Washington spring. Cherry blossoms gone, but abundant pink roses outside the restaurant windows tonight.

Back in the room now. Lonely. Couldn't reach Chloe. Did reach Bertie who fussed I'd waked her and she'd had a tiring day. No, of course she wouldn't wake Ryan. I'd even talk to Mel tonight, no, glad that's over. Glad he's working a different schedule.

The day at the registration desk still pumps in me. Can't focus on reading and don't want to watch Johnny Carson. I shall get up, dress, go downstairs, have a Manhattan. Alcohol doesn't turn me into a party person, it makes me sleepy. I'll settle for that.

Downstairs, a convention group and some of our Excel mid-management types crowd the lounge. I find a seat at the packeded bar. I know this scene. Lonely women being busy with their cigarettes. Loud guys thinking they are funny.

Find a single empty stool, order a Manhattan, take one swallow. The balding Yuppie-type to my left leans my way, moist face, bloodshot eyes, looking me over. Okay, will this be the morose male muttering surly put-downs . . . or some drunk goon ready to play verbal ping pong of inanities . . . or an ego expectinging a rapt, adoring listener.

Whatever, just ignore.

I give this one the grim smile that says I'm not playing and turn away. This bleary-eyed creep moves closer to slur some information to prove he's "a great lover."

Groan. One of those too drunk to get the message. I finish my Manhattan fast as a kid sucking a Coke, push a five to the bartender, turn my back, slip from my stool, tell the woman to my right—"Watch it. This one is a bore about his penis needs." Couldn't help it. Had to be said.

He looks stung and bleats his protest. "You have a problem with that, bitch?"

Loud and clear I say, "No, you do."

He clamps a thick hand on my arm. Some other guy lays a restraining arm on the jerk. I walk away, get into the elevator, race down the hall and back into my room, locking the door, shaking with anger at that jerk, at all men who still see female reps as rabbits in their own hunting fields.

Don't I usually move away, ignore? Tonight I tried bitchy. Tonight I hate myself and this job. There must be other choices. I have to ask for, demand a desk job in Atlanta. Get Ryan with me. No more waiting. This isn't a life. It's a lousy job.

Ryan

1977–1980

Atlanta / 1977

Have to let everyone know. Want to call Chloe first.

"Chloe? Glad I caught you. Tried the agency earlier, then the shelter. Do they really call you the blonde Mother Teresa there? This has to be quick, I'm here in my office using the Watts line and up to my ears in work. New job, tedious details. Took off a week to get Ryan home. . . .

"Yes, knew you wanted to know. . .

"Hard to answer that now but we'll work things out. It's an adjustment for mother and son, believe me. . .

"Well, he's non-committal at this point. We go shopping this weekend for his room, to get wall stuff and bedspreads, whatever nine-year-olds-going-on-fifteen like to live with. His room at Bertie's was kid stuff he probably ignored. I've told him about Woodridge Academy but haven't pushed it. . .

"I'm being patient, as you wanted me to be. And loving? My way, quietly. I can't gush like Bertie. He needs to accept this change on his own. . .

"About that Pasadena thing you mailed—haven't had a chance to look at it . . . . Yes, I promise . . . have to go now. Chloe, don't work so hard . . . Bye."

❧

Dear Josey,

Well I've done it. Brought Ryan to Atlanta. Help!—send me an intelligence report on what goes on in the head of a boy almost ten. He looks at me and this place with narrowed eyes, as if plotting to announce he's decided to chuck it all. Yet I'm sure he's glad to get away from Bertie and that covey of dotting relatives. You've seen how they treat him, like the poor crown prince left an orphan.

Our departure was wrenching for Bertie and for me, couldn't tell about Ryan. Did I thank the woman? Of course. She has treated me with disdain all this time, yet I know it hurt her to see Ryan go. She's aged. Is this my fault, or dealing with Ryan, or her diabetes? Whatever, add her red- rimmed eyes and weight to my guilts. Look in on Bertie for me and keep me posted.

From your cousin learning to act like a mother at this late date.

Rae

❧

Dear Vyola,

Quick note as I didn't find you on the phone. I'm letting you know Ryan and I got home with no casualties after our one day visit with you. Thanks for talking to him as if he were an intelligent fifteen-year-old, not a wary nine-going-on-ten, being uprooted. I even saw a flicker of respect in him.

Handsome isn't he? You can imagine how I feel looking at those dark brows, eloquent eyes, and determined mouth, as if impatient to be a man and tell the world where to get off. You didn't hear, but when I told him he had taken his first steps here in your house, he gave me a look that cut to the quick. Sardonic or pained, I don't know. He said, "Guess you had to live with Vyola cause you didn't have a husband."

Arrow to the heart, with that remark. Told him again I came here because Charley Kendall was gone. He must have heard endlessly about Charley those years with Bertie. I know he didn't care about the picture she gave him, Charley in his Air Force uniform.

I have him in a summer day camp here. And take him to a restaurant most every night. In our little breakfast room, I seem to do most of the talking. So far he keeps himself in his room watching TV. He'll also have a room at Woodridge Academy by August. Now—if we can make it through the summer.

If you're going back to England, don't forget to come home. It did my heart good to see the wisteria is still shading the arbor.

Hugs, Rae

Atlanta / 1978

"Ryan, look. It's this way. You're the son and I'm the mother. It's my responsibility to decide the best school for you."

The restaurant is a noisy place, but it's one he likes. I keep my voice down, face calm so no one notices I'm gritting my teeth at my ten-year-old. He's digging a fork into the steak he ordered, showing his disapproval. A fourteen dollar waste.

"I hate Woodbridge. It's a place for parents to dump kids while they're getting a divorce or going off to Europe."

"Neither applies to us." I pretend to be calm. Have to swallow chicken salad down over the block of frustration.

"You don't want me here."

"Haven't we gotten past that line? You're repeating Bertie. I couldn't afford bringing you with me before."

"Yeah? Living in ritzy hotels."

"Ryan, you're too bright not to know better. The job required travel. I've given that assignment up for this one to be home most of the time. So you can be here with me in Atlanta. Woodbridge means you have a room and roomate there when I do have to fly out of town. At the apartment you have your own room. This summer you'll be swimming again at the camp. Then the junior debaters camp, if you like. . . ."

It goes on, my private dismay covered by cajoling. "Do you really want to see *Saturday Night Fever* again?"

His surly replies go on. How long will he hold out as the unloved child? "Bertie said . . ."

"I am not Bertie. I am your mother. And listen here, Bud, we've got to make this work. You may not realize it now, but you have a life ahead and your education is the way you get there prepared to make your own choices."

I keep telling myself it has to get better.

On the phone today, I ask Josey again how to deal with an adamant, defiant ten year old. She laughs. "They grow up and on. Well, out of my class, anyway."

"I go to my boring job now as relief. Keep smiling as my way of self-defense. Learned at my mother's knee, as I used to tell Vyola. If you don't let a person know you're hurt, if you appear calm, you walk away like a winner to swallow the hurt when no one's looking."

"I like my turnip greens same as you, Cuz, but I don't buy that. I've always fought back. Hey, speaking of sad facts . . . what about Elvis dying?"

Atlanta / 1979

I'm excited. Get Chloe on the phone late tonight to tell her what I might do. Crazy, but I need crazy right now.

"Guess what? I have two weeks off and I'm taking Ryan up to summer camp near Boone, North Carolina. I'd planned to find a little place and look out at peaceful woods and sky. But then this bright idea hit, looking at the date and folder you sent me. I'm willing to take a few days to fly out there and see you at this Pasadena thing."

"Wonderful. I've been sending you vibes. They worked. We'll room together and talk all night. We're overdue for an eye-to-eye."

"Maybe I'm hungry for those miserable little inflight meals. What's this World Symposium on Humanity thing?"

"It's not the peaceful retreat you missed at Omega. It's an idea the Canadian sponsors have worked for a year, mortgaged their houses to finance satellite plans and get key people there. I'm giving myself a four day break to go. Rae, I'm so happy you'll be there, even for a couple of days."

Pasadena / 1979

Crowds are already in evidence when my cab pulls in to the Pasadena Convention Center. Indian teepees cover much of the sprawling parking area. Assorted people, family groups, spill out of RV vans. Is this a hippie convention in 1979—twenty years after Golden Gate Park?

I claim a key to our room, go up, get out of suit and heels and into jeans and shirt and loafers. Chloe's already hung up the sweaters and pants she wears. Note says: "Can't wait to see you. Find me in the exhibition hall."

I go looking. The spacious hall is draped with bobbing helium balloons and hung with banners. "No more Nukes" and "No More Three Mile Islands" and "Solarize America." Exuberant music blasts over the milling crowd.

At last, here's Chloe, face glowing, wearing a blue flowing caftan for a change, serving tiny cups of green wheat grass tea.

She greets me over the clamor, makes me drink the bitter green liquid. "It's life, remember."

Tiers of seats are filling up when we walk into the huge convention center auditorium. With Rabbi Carlbach on stage

at the mike now, waves of energy rise with so many voices singing along with his lusty baritone: "*God wants us to heal the world; first clear the air of hate.*"

On it goes, from nutritionist Paavo Airola to writer Norman Cousins to architect Paola Soleri, psychologist Carl Rogers, the death-and-dying lady Kubler-Ross and more, voices speaking like twentieth century prophets about saving the planet. At the mike now, Physicist Karl Pribram is saying, "Our consciousness extends into the universe in a way we have not previously thought."

A few voices from the crowd scream down to the stage: "Science has polluted my world."

Pribram shoots back, "Not our science. That's technology."

A brooding dark-haired Ralph Nader at the mike now delivers his solemn warnings of corporate power. A chorus of audience voices start chanting: "Nader for President."

Late in the exhibition hall, the colorful garb comes out as Paul Horn and jazz combo supply the beat. At invitation, the crowd banks the sides of the darkened hall, to move out as individuals, free-form dancing into the lighted center, settling in a pile of languid poses.

I watch from the sidelines. Chloe moves out, long hair flowing past her shoulders, blue gown fluttering against her tall slim body, arms open, settling in the light with the others.

Much later, each stretched out in our beds, we're ready to swap opinions. I start because I'm surprised Chloe seems pensive, no exhilerated from the exuberant beat downstairs. "So tell me, is this New Age a new version of the Sixties' intentions, the early ones to make love not war?"

Chloe sighs. "Some came hoping so, I'm sure. Maybe looking for what they missed out back there, when they were too old or too young to drop out."

I say, "Some came looking for a weekend soul mate. Like the handsome in the silk shirt and gold chains who picked up the blonde before our own cool eyes."

A faint laugh from the other bed. "You can see that in any big crowd. Yes, of course, I loved hearing those responsible people on stage who really know the Sixties' warnings are still true. That the planet is a living entity and we're draining it with greedy consumerism."

"What would Chloe McCullough have added at the mike?"

"They said that well, too. Change has to start in individual minds and hearts. That's why I go to retreats, Rae. Go to be quiet and back in touch, connected with the source of strength that's both beyond and part of me. To you, it looks like I'm running away from realities. No, I'm getting renewed to handle them."

"I know." We're quiet for minutes. I envy Chloe's source of serenity. She knows I get turned off by dashboard preachers and the opposite, gurus with a string of Cadillacs and the kind of preachment I used to get from Bertie. She still calls us "soul sisters" and we are.

"I want to get a newspaper in the morning," I say. "See what they say about the World Symposium."

"Don't expect much. The media covers what's new because Americans have to sample what's new. But it gets written with raised eyebrows and a hidden smirk. The far out and kooks get the attention."

"New Age is getting attention."

"It's only a new label. The core ideas are timeless as Plato or Christ or Emerson and mystics before and since. It's about ones spirit recognizing its connection with the Intelligence that made us all, rather than some remote God. That brings in the living planet, too."

I'm quiet thinking of what I heard today. "Are you wary of movements now?"

"I am. They become distorted, misused, distrusted. You know what I believe. Environmental needs can be explained. But spiritual ideas don't fit in a headline. Dogma can be reported, but not the ineffable. Spiritual experience is personal, subjective."

"On that we agree."

"I know you do," Chloe says sleepily. "You keep your own beliefs like something cherished from childhood saved on a shelf. But not to use."

How true. "Groan, groan. I guess you're right about that."

In a crowded breakfast scene, before I leave, we swap the eye-to-eye personals.

Chloe looks out over the crows and reports quietly. She's loosing Emily to her sister-in-law. Her mother is living with a nurse-keeper. Garth is getting married. "Those are the current and on-going items. I don't deny their reality. I have to believe someday my daughter will listen to someone else than Norman Paynes and understand what drives her mother. Now you must tell me about Ryan."

Mid-morning, I tread past the Indian teepees to find a cab to the airport, fly back to Asheville, to pick up my car and drive up to Boone. Once back at my new desk job in Atlanta, will I try to describe the World Symposium? If I did the response would be: *You mean you went to one of those kooky California things?*

Impass

1980–1986

~

Atlanta / January
Journal:

Have to write this down for my own eyes.
Must pretend calm.
Not fight with Ryan.
Hate the sound of it.
He wins and the failure stays in me like a weight.
Must hold on to the hope:
When he's older, it might get better.

~

I'm not the only person banging my head against a stone wall. Friend Maria who books our flights has confided she's pregnant. She's panicky. The man is a rep with Air-France and seldom in town. She has to get an abortion, yet it's against her religion.

Then here comes scarier news, worse than Maria's. The new "exotic illness" called AIDS. The *New York Time*'s headline on the science page: "The Price of Promiscuity is Premature Death."

Makes a woman shudder, even when she's celibate again by choice and necessity, with a son in the next room. Glad it's over with Mel. Men like that only know about sex. Love is the verboten word. Not that I expected anything real from him. Must I confess the need for sex is not only a male thing?

Postponed question: Will I ever know how it is to love a man wholly, and be loved that way in return? Love his body and enjoy his mind? I need both. Why hasn't that happened? File that question away for now. It's my time to be a mother, try to make up for lost time.

Looking into Ryan's face I see Garth McCullough.

August / 1986

"I'm not going back there this semester. I'll finish at the high school with my real friends or I'm outa here. I'll look for a good beach. California, maybe. Or Hawaii. I could stop by Montgomery and get some dough from Bertie."

My tall son, just turned seventeen, stands at the fridge, gulping down a bottle of chocolate milk for breakfast.

I haven't let him go to the crowded high school to be with his mall hang-out friends. I couldn't stop him from leaving one semester. At least he showed up at Bertie's. Got him back with the car he'd bargained for.

I make toast for myself, take vitamins and sip coffee, holding onto false calm. Does that infuriate him even as it exhausts me? I go on with how great he's doing with the debate club, wanting to say how proud I am watching him on stage. His silent antagonism stops me.

"Barney Reish tells me how well you're doing in the debate group."

"Barney has the hots for you."

His disdain cuts where I breathe. Maybe he thinks I have no feeling because I show so little? To tell him what's going on inside would sound . . . no.

"Don't gimme that look. He's always calling you, having you come to his office."

"To talk about you. Barney Reish is trying to be your friend as well as debate coach. You're a natural, he says. I knew you would be. Don't fight me, Ryan, just to prove you can. There's so much ahead of you."

"What do you care?"

"Oh, for God's sakes, Ryan. Let you visit Bertie a couple days and you come back repeating that old line. You're not changing schools. Final. You finish next year. We'll find some other junior college or prep school for you then."

The coffee is vile in my throat as he goes out, slamming the door behind him. I hear him roar the motor of the car I'd hoped would be a bid for peace. How angry he is. And lonely? That makes two lonely people in this apartment, and we can't bridge the gap between us.

Atlanta Journal

November, 1986

Three Atlanta youths were taken into custody last night, another treated at the hospital and released, in what officers say was a fight over a sixteen-year-old girl in the Hilltop apartments. Residents there complained to police of frequent drug parties in one apartment. Two of the juveniles, seniors at local private school, were placed on probation.

Home tonight. In the quiet. I need to speak to someone. No good to upset Bertie. Don't want to tell Chloe. Vyola is in England.

I go out to walk in the early night, reliving the courtroom scene. Ryan walking out with his back to me. The girl he fought over leaving her mother's side, rushing to join him. A stringy haired waif of a girl whirling back to me for one second to say, "Thanks for the lawyer and all . . ." Then running to catch him at the elevator. I followed to see them disappear.

Out of my life. I felt it then. Not surprised now that he never came home.

He hasn't gone alone. That skinny girl clasped his arm possessively or for comfort. I walk streets, thinking even sixteen-year-old females who look like malnourished children can have more depth of feeling than angry boys at seventeen, man-sized or not.

The girl's mother had sat in the courtroom, huddled and silent, unwilling to speak up. The woman must have accepted helplessness long ago. No father there for either of those adamant, troubled children.

Atlanta Journal

February 10, 1987

Further handling of the Hilltop Apartments complaints are on hold as the two 17-year-old youths involved in the fracas there, released on probation, have left the country, friends of the two have told police. They say the 16-year- old girl is with them. They are believed to have flown to California in a private plane, with the intention of going to Hawaii. Parents of the girl have made no comment and declined to make charges.

❧

Journal:

I have to tell someone, even a white page.

Having to go to work as usual helps. The women around me are kind, don't push for details. I'm grateful.

Coming back here to the apartment is difficult. No rock music blaring, no raucous voices from Ryan's room. This silence is a rebuke, its message: To hell with you, I'm gone. Not coming back.

I have finished a difficult letter to Bertie, just the fact Ryan has run away with some friends. As difficult, the letter to Chloe. But then she's had her own problems with her haughty Emily. Vyola called from Cambridge, giving me her kind of courage. "This is happening, but not the end of the story."

I have to see the lawyer who represented Ryan. Have to learn what jeopardy he's in, leaving the country.

Searching

1987

Atlanta / March

In the hushed and elegant reception room for Aylesworth, Pyle, Wells and Reese, I wait for some attention from a cool-faced young woman deep in her phone conversation. She whispers good-bye and looks up with a set smile. No, Attorney Pyle is still away, but would I care to see Whitney Wells? She taps a button on her desk and announces my name.

A gray haired woman comes out to usher me in, asks would I care for coffee?

I want nothing but advice, comfort, hope, information as to the danger my son has put himself in by running away. I follow the woman's suited back into the private office of another attorney.

Waiting for me, Whitney Wells stands behind his polished desk, a spare man in tailored brown suit, thin pale hair color of his skin. He studies me from behind gold-rimmed glasses and a scrutinizing smile. Gestures to the waiting chair, sits down as quickly in his high back chair, expanding the smile. "My partner Pyle has spoken to me about you, Mrs. Kendall. Please sit down."

I comply. The china cup of coffee I don't want appears in front of me on the shiny desk. My questions burst out. I hate my own breathy sound.

He leans back, fingertips together, pinning me with his pale brown gaze. "Rebellious juveniles are not my area of concern, thankfully. I can only advise you to realize that your son at seventeen is not a child and is apparently determined to go his way. So let him. You have your own life to consider."

My anger flares like a tired flame and as quickly gives in to fatigue. He apparently thinks I accept this because I sit here leaden in the chair. Clicking polished nails on the desk's smooth surface, he talks on, but not about Ryan. He's offering me a job. I listen like a trapped person.

"My partner Pyle mentioned to me your employment with Excel and the fact you might want to change. I'm looking for the right person to work with my clients. Adjunct guardian services to the legal ones I provide as their estate attorney. They're elderly women with absent family who need someone to accompany them to doctors, deal with their medical insurance, say, as a thoughtful daughter might do."

I don't move, only stare at the gold stripes in his tie. He goes on, looking pleased.

"They need attention, these clients. I understand your professional experience with Excel has meant dealing with individuals as a sympathetic corporate representative. This would be excellent experience for the services my clients need."

I look away from this assured person to paneled walls and a dull print, handsomely framed. Reach for the china cup, something to hold, or throw at his carpet. The cup rattles in the saucer. The black-suited woman appears and quickly whisks it away.

"I am not here to talk about changing jobs," I say with surprising calm. I stand, looking for the door. Have to get out of here.

He follows, cupped hand light under my elbow, the voice meant to be pleasantly cajoling. "This does need discussing, of course. May we do so over dinner some evening?"

Once out, down the corridor, grateful for an empty elevator, I throw myself in the car, lock the door, sit here disoriented. Deep breathing helps. Carefully, not to hyperventilate.

At the apartment, I call police and private investigators, grumpy voices disturbed at eight o'clock. Someone finally gives me a name and a suggestion, a private investigator I can call in Hawaii.

April

A Friday night. I'm the lone woman in the far booth, unfinished dinner plate pushed away. Have to read my letter again.

Independent Personal Investigators

Oahu, Hawaii

Dear Mrs. Kendall:

I have made all possible attempts to find your son, with no results. The best I can do for you is to explain why finding him is unlikely, until he wants to be located.

Your son has obviously changed his name, so he doesn't want to be found. It is easy to do that here. On most of the islands, we have a mixed group of Haoles (non-Hawaiians) and people of all races who camp on the land, in tent groups, or in shacks. They live well and are not looked down upon, generally. The way of life is to fish for food and forage for fruit and make use of the facilities of beach parks. It is also known they plant a "cash crop" of marijuana in the jungle-like overgrowth on some neighboring property.

There are also part-time low-paid jobs and some money to be made selling harvested fruit to tourists. All this is to say, your son must be one of many (young to old) persons who have chosen, for whatever reasons, to step out of whatever life they had, to live this way here.

Actually, they live pretty well. The Hawaiian way is that no one goes hungry. This is the best information I can give you. May it somewhat assuage your worry.

Sincerely, A. L. Malon

"Hope is restorative, takes you to a different place," Chloe has written me. So I hope he's well, doing what he wanted to do. Finding his beach in Hawaii. Becoming a man there by whatever name. Vyola has told me: drop the failed mother cross. He'll become a man there, on his own terms.

I can't go home tonight to that silent place.

I start driving. The streets glistens from an earlier rain. I drive too slow, impatient lights behind. Speed up, window down, accepting mist, trying to pull into my lungs the intangible promise of this spring evening.

Some nights, like this one, I think of driving miles to Montgomery, to walk into the cottage, sit with Vyola across the kitchen table. No, the office expects me within hours. Fortunately. The women there are kind, knowing about Ryan. Sometimes three of us, women without lovers or husbands, go to a movie. My life.

I pull into this lighted strip of stores, an excuse to move around like a shopper with purpose in her life.

Get out, walk past a drug store, a pizza place, a second hand bookstore with its windows stacked with worn romances. Next a long windowed place, softly lit from behind its heavy tan curtains, a placard in front saying this is the Atlanta Yoga and Health Center. Welcome. Sitar music seeps from within.

Adam

1987

Seeping from inside the curtained store front, the sitar's other worldly chords trigger memory of Chloe's candlelit room, Berkley. Is that eighteen years ago?

No matter, the plaintive sounds pull me in. Here's a place I can sign up for yoga sessions, a way to physically relax.

Inside, obeying the sign, I slip off my shoes, and stand looking at six pairs of floor sitters, facing one another, waiting for instructions from the low, soft-lit platform. Three people are poised there, a little round man in orange, then the young sitar player.

The third is an imperious looking woman in black leotards, hair coiled up like a bronze gold crown, shoulders erect, wearing blue glasses. The sitar strains fade. The player bows his head, instrument silent on his lap.

Waiting at the doorway, I listen to the woman's eloquent, assured voice telling the seated pairs this is White Tantric Yoga. "A non-sexual, interpersonal mediation, in which you will allow pervading cosmic energy to expand, bringing both energy fields together into one."

The visiting pundit who is to lead this sees me and whispers to the woman behind the blue glasses. She calls someone from where he sits in the shadows, his dark head bent to a pad, sketching. "Adam, we need a partner."

I sit on the floor at the end of the line. The man coming toward me could be Fiddler on the Roof in jeans, heavy chested as a roustabout. With quick ease, he settles into instant stillness in front of me, in yoga position, sandaled feet tucked under his thighs.

We swap faint smiles, hands on our own knees, eye meeting. His brown pupils sparkle like dark quartz. The gaze reaches into me, yet I feel warmed, recognized, not invaded. His strong face is shaped by close curly beard and cap of dark hair. I break my gaze to search heavy shoulders, relaxed muscled arms. I imagine this man is capable of passion not mere lust.

The pundit's soft instructions draw me back to meet my partner's eyes. They're waiting. I believe I am looking into a man's soul and being seen in return. In that gleam equanimity, and some kind of strength that is unattached, independent of these surroundings in which this man seems to be a player.

The sing-song voice of the little Indian man on stage continues to lift and fall, but I don't need it.

I want to know what's inside my partner's head. Put my head against that live chest, ask and listen and swim in the answers. I believe his strength would add to, not take away my own.

Then it's over. Nothing further than my own hand briefly pressed in his big warm grip.

On the lighted sidewalk outside, a teenager tells me with gossipy pleasure, "Aren't the Rosens a pair? Christine used to be this California actress, he was an important artist, until some accident. She's almost sightless behind those blue glasses, but you're supposed to grandly ignore the fact."

And another: "Her thing now is collecting gurus, you know these East Indian ones traveling the country. She claims Adam's total time. Because of the accident, you know, her sight gone. You saw tonight."

A weird spring somehow becomes summer, Ryan's disappearance a hard fact, a rock of guilt swallowed down, kept out of sight.

The Yoga Center is a place to go nights after work and Saturday afternoons. I show up with my leotards to do yoga with Jenny, my new friend. Jenny with her honest rosy face, telling me, "If only you would learn to breathe, Rae."

I go to sit patiently in front of Christine, listening with others to her talk of macorbiotics and herbs. Or listen to some visiting yogi doing his chants and meditations in his sing-song voice.

Saturday mornings six of us women, sometimes ten, gather around Jenny, exchanging talk of where our lives are going at the moment. We began with adamant opinions until more personal frustrations begin to slip out. Dealing with a teenage step-daughter. An older husband's depression. Office rivalries. An affair going bad. A breast cancer fear.

I offer, without explanation, "My seventeen-year-old son has run away. I accept the fact I've totally failed as a mother." I shake away their protestations.

Wednesday nights I am back for Adam Rosen's Kabalah classes. Ten of us earnest Gentiles sit on folding chairs willing to grasp some understanding of this ancient Jewish mysticism about the Tree of Life. Adam tells us how it proposes, "God projected Himself in ten rays of light to help make the divine cause and effect perceptible." We listen entranced by his quiet baritone pronouncing those magical old words like Sephiroth and Mulkuth and Yesod and Kether.

When he looks at me, I feel it.

Saturday afternoons Adam demonstrates body's pressure points to the group. I am jealous of his hands moving, pressing on willing thighs, and backs, and arms stretched out on the massage table. At my chance, in front of a class, I lie still, eyes closed, the firm pressure of his fingers alive as magnets against my tight jeans, and back of my neck.

Saturday nights and Sundays are empty. I try a proper Episcopal church and meet face to face with Whitney Wells. Accept his invitation to join him the next Saturday night at the Bar Association dinner. I am touched by his obvious need to have a partner. Apparently there are no women in his life, not since the first Mrs. Wells.

On this proper date night, another wife imparts the gossip about dignified Whitney Wells. The wife left him for the guy who put in their pool five years ago. His mother lived with him for two years until she passed on. I feel sorry for the man who doesn't tell me any of this. It's just as well he doesn't want to hear about my missing son.

The yoga center was once a store front church. A large and spartan kitchen is behind the big room with its low platform and pillows against the wall, and the small massage room and office to one side.

This August night I am alone with Adam in the kitchen, helping prepare the tea to be served. He's wearing a faded orange tee-shirt with Yin Yang symbols while setting out cups and telling me about a world away from this place, the politics of art shows in the past, of his disinterest in catering to the gallery owners. It was creating the canvas he had lived for, not the rest.

"You should have been a rabbi," I tell him. "One who paints," I add.

"That was my mother's wish, not mine." He's amused, setting out the herb teas on a tray with the sesame cookies I've arranged.

With a shot of nerve, I say what I'm thinking. "Now you only sketch. When she isn't keeping you busy."

"True."

"I shouldn't have—"

"But you wondered. Before the accident, Christine was a magnificent figure on stage. Had the presence and the driving ego necessary behind those lights. A controller, yes. The night it happened, I was angry and speeding on a dark road. Swerved to avoid another car parked on the shoulder. She was thrown from the convertible. I was pinned. Amazing that either of us lived."

His big hands gripping the tray of cups. He looks at me with those deep brown eyes, his voice low, even. "I talked her back to life. Reminded her of her power, made her believe there was some destiny she obviously had yet to fill." With a wry, slow smile, "I made what you see. So I live with what I have created."

"Just like that?" We stand, close, the two of us in this kitchen, tray between us.

"At first it was penitence. These eight years later, I'm beyond that. The harder the experience, the greater the lesson, if you choose to use it. I found there's no relief in fighting against circumstance even if your bitterness is kept silent."

"You just accepted . . .?" I wait for more.

"Accepted the outer situation as one to be lived with, yes, but not as a victim. One has a choice. You can tap into a private resilience that means a different level of freedon."

"Freedom? From what?"

"From anger, resentment. I look on the whole passing parade with some amusement. Including my own situation."

The door swings open. Jenny says, "Hey there. We're ready."

Her honest face must be reading what she sees. That I'm in love with a man married to a woman who owns every minute of his life.

July now. These Saturday nights I meet Whitney at hotel dining rooms and restaurants he selects. My own choice is to meet there, not that I think he'd get personal at my place. His obvious hesitance to make any approach keeps me patient with him, relieves any guilt of accepting this dinner as a way to fill the evening, away from work, away from a quiet apartment that means nothing to me. Once we even take in a Sunday afternoon concert.

I listen with a polite face to this man who selects wine as if he's studied how, and directs the server with an edge of superiority I don't like. Waiting for dinner, he teaches me about investments by way of showing how I'm getting nowhere with Excel. I admit my lack of attention to that part of my life, my single excuse is the cost of a private school. Whitney only frowns at a mention of Ryan.

Instead, I listen to his description and attitudes of his elderly clients. He expects me to take the job he's offering.

His voice is different when he speaks of the brother. "Now my brother, Wylie . . ."

I've come to think of Wylie Wells as the Rich Brother, younger, but making his second million in property out there in Los Angeles. They grew up with a determined mother and no father. I wonder: Are you so proud of Rich Brother or jealous? The question would startle him, would be unkind, so I don't ask it. I don't think Whitney has even wondered.

A September night at the center. I sit among the pillows, close enough to hear Adam's murmured comments as he bends to his sketching of the action. Ten barefoot women are weaving and turning to soft Eastern music, Christine in a purple leotard among them. Behind her blue glasses, is she aware of the heat between this man and myself?

"I need to say something. It will sound rude and righteously arrogant," I tell him, looking straight ahead at the dancers.

"Listening. Say it without excuses."

"What about these yogis, these people Christine brings in. Are they for real or enjoying their attraction to us? Westerners looking for an easy sample try for Nirvana?"

Adam sketching hands keep flying on the pad. "Christine is an entrepreneur. She also needs to perform and this you see is her new stage. This is the purpose she found. I think she also falls in love, in her way, with some of these pundits."

I make myself go on. "This is what bothers me. The so-called spiritual men I read about who collect Cadillacs and have sex with their followers. It makes me angry. "

"This world, my dear, is not a perfect place. Too much power corrupts the would-be saints as well as politicians."

"There's something else I wanted to say but they're breaking up now. I have to go help Jenny with the tea."

"We'll find that opportunity," Adam says.

The dancers drop to the floor in relaxed poses. Only Christine stands. "Adam? The tape must be changed." The imperious stage voice. He puts down the pad and goes to her without loking back.

Yogi Bahan is expected tonight, preparations going on inside the center. Adam and I sit on the back steps from the kitchen looking out on a darkening asphalt, behind these stores. When you only want privacy with one other person, any place is beautiful. We only have minutes.

"I'll sound like somebody at a priest's window," I warn him.

"I'm no priest and I'm listening."

Should I tell him first how since a child I've carried around, if hidden, my belief in God, as a caring, unfathomable universal intelligence, a power I might call on and perceive an answer? No, I don't need that preamble.

"Adam—well, here it is. I've decided I don't believe in anything. It makes me feel so damn empty."

I steal a look at his strong profile and wait.

His big hand closes over mine for a moment. Finally, "You're lonely."

The shadows deepen on these cement steps. He sits without moving, sighing from his depths. "I wish I could hand you comfort. I'm hurting now with the need to do that. Rae, no one can give another anything but words. And you know the words. The ones that say belief has to happen within. And the promises that this difficult time will pass. But you don't want words. You have to find it's true within your own being. There are times when we have to wait for that."

We can hear them inside the kitchen. The back kitchen door bursts open. Jenny again. "Hey you two. Yogi Bahan's here. Handsome as his pictures. Better get in."

A rainy Sunday afternoon. I come by for the massage I've booked with husky Alice. His car, alone, is parked in front. Christine is being driven to the airport to pick up the night's speaker.

He lets me into the quiet place. Searches my face. Do I still want the massage? I murmur yes, go in the curtained room, pull off my shirt and bra and slip out of my slacks. Lay on the table under the towel, trembling.

How dangerous a needy woman can be, breaking through caution. We have no shame. I lie still, open to the pleasure of his strong kneading hands before I pull him to me. His hands clutch my shoulders. He burrows his face in my neck, moves to my breasts. I float on the table, perhaps I whimper. He gives me his magic hands, not himself, but I take them, need them, love him for it. Still standing by the table, he rocks me in his arms to calm me back down.

Saturday morning, I bring a bowl of fruit into the yoga kitchen. Find Adam alone preparing food for the veggie feast to follow. We work at the table silent for moments. I tell him, "I have to make a trip. I have to fill in for our advance rep, job I used to have. I'm flying to Boston next week."

He puts down the avocados, wipes his hands, and draws me in to his arms against the solid chest. Holds me close, my face buried in his warm neck against the crisp dark beard. He smells of soap and garlic and maleness. He whispers words few men would know to say. I am nourished by his arms these seconds before we know to move apart. The door swings open. Others sail in carrying salad bowls.

"I wrote you a poem," I say, stuffing the small paper in his pocket.

Adam. . .
Hands of an artist
blunt but strong
face sculpted heavy, bold
yet gentle,
eyes shooting brown bolts
of meaning unsaid
even as he embraces this
later destiny
the role of service accepted
with the gentleness
of the strong. A man
whose healing touch
feels like love.
from your
pupil on the
back steps

October / Boston

My week here finished, I wait in the terminal for one more visit with Chloe. She emerges from the crowd of hurrying travelers, face bright, still without any make-up but lipstick, still thin in a tunic sweater and pants, color of her long pale hair. We find two seats near the bright glare of plate glass for our hurried, eye-to-eye visit. She's still doing agency as well as volunteer work and waves away any mention of the progress on her book.

I tell her about Whitney Wells, who is insisting that I come to work for him. I tell her about loving another woman's husband, love his mind and body though there is absolutely no future in this. It's something I need now.

"You're being tested by these two men in your life," she says, sympathetic. "What's the lawyer like?"

"Whitney is part of a good firm. Compulsive about order, records. Has this big two story Colonial outside of Atlanta. I've acted as his hostess once at a very proper cocktail party. Lawyers and wives there, doing polite chit-chat. Men don't slap Whitney on the shoulder and tell a joke. Actually, he's an enigma."

Chloe shakes her head. "Slept with him?"

"Once . . . he's no lover, he's an uptight male who hasn't had a woman in his bed for awhile, I'm sure. He's not comfortable with the subject. His first wife left with the pool man. No pool there now. No evidence of the lady, even in his conversation."

I tell her about Adam Rosen.

"He sounds like an old soul. This Whitney sounds like a newly minted one. Meditate before you do anything you regret."

Chloe is more eager to talk about Ryan. "Please, Garth has connections. He could possibly find out—"

"No, I've tried, Chloe. Don't involve Garth. I hate to hear you still let him come by. Look, I have to go. They're calling my flight."

We hug. I watch her walk away, this willowy woman who stays too busy to be lonely I suppose. She turns, waves good-bye.

It's ten days before I pull up at the yoga center again, eager but wary. Is this insane, coming here this often, for moments of seeing love in the man's eyes? A sign is posted behind the glass—Closed—but the light is on. Door open. Inside, Jenny has finished her last yoga class. Five women stand around her, talking,

"Rae! Thank heaven you got here before I closed up. Adam and Christine have left. They've gone back to California." Her face shows she understands mine. The other women come closer, wanting to hear.

"They left all the books from the rack for members to take. Adam asked me to give you this one. "She hands me a small Yoga Center envelope. "Rae, I'm going to be at the Y. Look me up. We can talk."

I thank her. Clutch what she hands me and get out of there. Sit in the car open the package. It's a little Alan Watts book, *Wisdom of Insecurity*. Read the note tucked inside.

⁂

My dear Rae,

So much I wish to say but time and situation make it necessary to confine this to a slip of paper.

Leaving Atlanta is a choice forced on me, but in the greater scheme of things, one I've delayed too long. I am returning to California and to my art, which fuels my passion for being alive. I am taking Christine with me, reversing the situation here. I'm going back to what I can give to, and be nourished by.

An Englishman named Pater once said a counted number of pulses are given to us. We can spend each

interval in listlessness—he might have said anger—or we can use it with passion. Loosing oneself in the passion for a certain calling expands our pulsation. Mine was to put beauty on canvas, with apologies to no one.

My dear Rae, your honest intensity, hidden inside that lovely, quiet self, has nourished back to life that passion I'd lost.

You are mired in a difficult personal time at present, I know. This is not a perfect world, as we've agreed. We can't control others, only our own focus. True seekers are always troubled until they find what is right for them. The finding might come as a surprise, when least expected. Never regret that our paths crossed. You reminded me that love is always possible. You will find that is true for you, if you live forward with no regrets.

With a lasting and silent love,
Adam

❧

I read it, fighting tears and chagrin. Did I cause them to leave? Is Christine going to make him pay for whatever she guessed? His note is a validation, a love letter. Yet he's gone. I expected nothing, but I'm left knowing I've made one more mistake.

Whitney

1988–1992

From the back of the YWCA gym I watch Jenny up there in blue leotards, finishing a session for twenty supine bodies lying on their mats. She spies me in the doorway, squints and waves with vigor without breaking her concluding spiel. Lights come up. Bodies stretch and rise, start rolling up their pads, ready to leave.

Jenny hurries over. “Rae Kendall. Where have you been? Not at Excel. No phone. I tried.”

“New address. New job.” I don’t say, yet, married.

“That’s a somber annoucement. Give me ten minutes. Meet me next door at Denny’s, okay?”

I order coffee and wait. Jenny comes in, all bustling energy, firm curvy body in sweat pants and shirt. An uncomplicated up-beat woman, married twenty years. How do some people do it?

She slides into the booth facing me. “Rae Kendall, I’ve wanted to talk to you since that last night at the yoga center. Gad, how long has it been? A year? No, longer. What’s happened to you?”

“A lot. Or not much, however you look at it. I need your breathing and stretching directions again.” Meant as a joke but it comes out flat. “I spend a lot of time with Whitney’s clients, mostly lonely grand dames, fingers crusted with diamonds, who tell me their lives and complain about their fifty-year-old children. I think Whitney hopes they'll decide to leave some of the diamonds to me."

Her brows go up. "Who?"

"Whitney Wells. My Saturday night dinner date, remember? The lawyer? You're looking at Mrs. Wells."

"You're kidding. No, I mean, really?" Jenny's pale blue eyes study me from under stubby blonde lashes. "Life's full of surprises. Well. You look good, great suit there, but yes, I advise some yoga sessions."

"I just found out you were at the Y."

She leans forward, intent. "Rae, that night I was closing the center, I had more to tell you, but you ran out so—so stricken, and those others were chattering around me."

"About Adam?" Saying the name sets up a familiar vibration of longing and hurt I have to reject. "I put that behind me. I admit being a fool back there. My own fault. What hurts is knowing I caused Adam trouble. Christine must have yanked them out of there and moved on to set up her tent somewhere else, because of me."

Jenny gives the server bringing her coffee an absent minded nod. "I saw what was smoldering between you and Adam. You know that. Unconsumated, I bet, more's the pity."

I nod, trying to blank out memory.

She goes on. "There's more to it. It won't help, but if you insist on suffering you might as well know the truth. You took off and disappeared so fast I didn't have a chance to tell you what I knew."

I brace myself.

"Day after you left on that trip, Adam had to go into the hospital. He'd had treatment for prostate cancer some time before. His count was up, it might be coming back."

I swallow down black coffee.

"While the man was under sedation, the surgeon came in, told Christine a radical was advised if they wanted to be positive the cancer hadn't returned. Or, they could wait six months and do chemo if the count went higher."

Oh, Adam.

"They did the radical. When Christine came back, she told us that earlier they had both vowed never to allow chemo. I believe she didn't wait until Adam was awake to tell them what he wanted. That woman let them cut his balls off."

"I did that to him?"

"No, Christine did," quiet disgust on her pink face. "You had to know, because you loved the man. I'm not telling you this to make you lash yourself to some mast."

She drops back again the booth. "It happened. It was done. Christine's choice. You don't have to claim every guilt as yours only. I'm sorry, kiddo, but you're a big girl and should know the full story."

"I should know, yes."

"And this too. We don't have to worry about Adam. He's a rare case of man who can ride the tide without shaking his fist at God, or at us. We all loved him for that. We just didn't get it coming back to us as personal as you did."

I close my eyes on the Denny's scene, trying to imagine Adam.

"Don't know what he said to you in the note but he told all of us he was going back to a studio somewhere near Ojai, but he didn't leave an address or invitation to find him. Oh yes, she went with him but don't think she'll be ordering him around."

The woman with the coffee pot is back. "What the heck," Jenny says, "let's divide one of their apple pies with a disgusting heap of vanilla ice cream. You haven't told me your news, marrying the Saturday night dinner date."

I make myself talk. It helps. "I decided to be practical, give up hoping for inspired direction and love that doesn't leave you abandoned."

"And?"

"So much for practical logic. I work for my pragmatic husband whose interest and tension is focused on making money. Making love, that euphenism for sex, is more or less a scheduled exercise. I have a house beautiful on approach, decorated throughout in blue velvet by his mother ten years ago, and I can't change it. Lost the urge from the first. We have a social life built around the bar association and the appropriate banquets."

"So, you've concluded. . . .?"

"It was my choice, like taking a new job to get away from the last one. My life has been shaped by jobs, so what's different. I'm stuck with the situation. That's the last complaint you'll hear from me."

Jenny threw up her hands. "Lordy, lordy. You're going to live with that?"

"When's your next yoga night?"

A rainy November evening. I am expecting a call from Chloe out in some desert place in New Mexico. Her voice is faint. There is so much distance between us.

I come back into the living room into the reality of my ongoing present that has no pulse.

Whitney is waiting. "Yes? Can we get back to this?" The guest list he means. When the phone rang, we had been working on the Christmas open house.

I hung up the phone here wondering if he had bothered to pick it up when I ran to the kitchen to answer, expecting Chloe.

"That was my friend Chloe McCullough. I had a card earlier she would be calling. They're on the road, Chloe and three others traveling in one small RV, speaking to different retreats."

"Retreats from reality, I assume."

"They are three professional therapists and one Navaho woman poet. They invite women to share their stories."

"What used to be called gossip?" He's looking over the guest list.

"There is such a thing. But that's not what they're doing." Thinking out loud, I say that every woman's life is an involved private story that's being worked out and it helps to talk about it in certain circumstances of trust."

"You're not still into that touchy-feely stuff are you? Your yoga nights?"

"That's body conditioning. I spend my time being touchy feely with Mrs. Hawthrone and old Lila Miller and sweet old Harold."

Whitney looks impatient. "Can we get back to the issue at hand?" The guest list for the open house calls for some names dropped and some added.

Last year I handled the elaborate party with a bride's determination to please. This year the thought of the thing waits ahead like a charade to get through. Whitney's pleasure is real, looking successful in his home, building clients, the cost a business deduction.

I intend to invite Jenny and her husband Milt, who runs a Jewish deli. I don't mention it now.

I look up from my list at this large room of heavy pieces and ten year old blue velvet. The staidness mocks my disinclination to change anything here. A lethargy of emotion blocks that desire. Certainly Whitney sees no reason to change.

On the phone with Chloe tonight, in the kitchen studying the duckie wall paper I hate, I avoided her questions about this house, my life, "Let's say it's not your definition of home, right for spirit and body."

"We're always making stops along the way, aren't we?" Chloe says with a soft laugh. "Neither is this cramped fifth wheel trailer, shared by three other women."

"When are you coming back? I need to see you for real."

"I don't know. Rae, if you've made a mistake, you have a right to change it."

May

Thank goodness for Jenny. We meet for lunch in the mall. I'm satisfied to listen to a daughter's wedding I missed. Anything but talk about myself.

"That's Gret for you," Jenny says about her daughter who doesn't want to be called Margaret. "Strong minded as her dad. Gret warned me she didn't want any 'ethnic' stuff' at the wedding. Not from this Baptist mother or Jewish father or her new in-laws, Catholics. Well, once the reception and dancing got under way, I had the band play that Jewish dance, then some wildly Italian beat. You should have seen the dance floor. Jumping. Everybody loved that party. Can't forgive you for not coming, but thanks for the gifts. I would have pulled Whitney Wells out on that floor."

"How do you do it? Without making a big failure like some of us do?"

She shrugs. "I love them both. My independent daughter. My Milt who can't walk into a protestant church without getting hives. I give in just enough to Gret and I let Milt be himself, knowing he loves me. Works both ways."

"When there's love."

"Egad, Rae, don't be some martyr to a mistake."

"Do I sound like that? The thought sickens. You don't hear me complaining."

"No, you're having migraines instead. You've accepted being stuck. How long have you been doing this? Four years? If you're waiting for Whitney being unfaithful as an excuse, forget it. That man has what fits in his life. You're working for him, for God's sake. You've being one of those noble women who believe they need to suffer longer before having the right to make a move."

June / Montgomery

Dear Rae

You know I don't intrude in your life, but I recognize your silence in your otherwise lovely birthday card. If you were here at my kitchen table you'd probably tell me more. And I'd say this. A woman has more body clocks than the menopausal one. We know when we need to stay in a situation and when it's time to leave. We have to listen well to know when, but the message is there.

Your aunt Vyola

~

August

A sultry hot day under white sky. At a service station counter paying for my gas I look up to recognize a young face. Mike, the boy who left with Ryan and the girl four years ago. He blinks at my rush of questions but tells me what he can.

Mike says he left Hawaii three years ago to come back to Atlanta. Ryan was moving on from Kauai to another island. Just months ago Lisa had stopped by his station here asking where she could get in touch with me. He couldn't tell her. She paid for gas and left.

"Probably wanted to hit you for some money," Mike says, "Lisa was pregnant when I last saw them three years ago. She was coming home and he was going on. I don't know more than that. Except that she works in a lounge at some hotel near the airport."

I drive off, stunned with a new desire. There are too many hotels near the airport, but I have to find that girl. See that child. Ryan's.

By dialing all morning, I find the bar, claim I'm an aunt, get the girl's address. Break appointments by phone, drive across town to a scrubby neighborhood. When I find it, I know this Lisa needs help. A dusty Camero sits in the rutty front yard of this duplex, a child's cheap plastic tricycle at the steps. Ring the doorbell, tense with anticipation. I am going to see Ryan again, as he was at whatever the age of this child. I want that. When have I wanted anything so devoutly?

The young woman who opens the door is not the stringy-haired sixteen-year-old Lisa who fled with Ryan to Hawaii. Frowning, she looks me over from under mascara black lashes, streaked blonde hair piled high. The midriff sweater above the tight shorts shows she's still thin.

"Lisa, I'm Ryan's mother. May I come in?"

She grimaces. "I'm getting ready to leave for work."

"Please."

"Well. For a minute."

I follow her into the small living room, dark, littered, noisy with a window air conditioner. Two plastic leather love seats, a coffee table cluttered with magazines. A toy truck lies on top.

We sit facing one another, Lisa fishing in the depths of her open purse, coming up with a compact and lipstick, proceeding to draw full purple lips on her own thin pale ones.

"I'm due at the lounge in thirty minutes. Traffic's a bitch. But since you're here, well, I'm glad, if we make it quick. I did have something to tell you, Mrs. Kendall."

"Where is he?" I mean the child. Anticipation roars in my pulse. A boy, I think, or a little girl maybe, waiting at this moment down that narrow hall. I have to see, feel that child's body in my arms. The desire is so strong it surprises me, sweeps everything else away, even Whitney who would never allow a child in the periphery of his life.

I ask her again, "Where is he?"

"I knew you'd be asking me that." She snaps the mirror shut drops the compact in her purse, looks at the cheap watch on her thin wrist. "Believe me, I honestly don't know. When I left Ryan in Hilo, he was moving on. He didn't like tourists and he'd hooked up with some native growers. Macadamia nuts, I think. I told him way back he should write to you, at least to thank you for helping us get out of that mess. But you don't tell Ryan what to do."

My impatience is greater than hers. "How old are you, Lisa? Twenty, twenty-one? You could go to business school or college. I can help you. I want to."

"Hey, that's cool of you to offer. But no thanks. I'm in a hurry, like I said." She stands stretching her thin frame like a weary person. "Gotta go."

"You had something to tell me, Lisa. Your baby, Ryan's child. Let me see him." At this moment, I want this more than I've wanted anything for so very long. Like a purpose that's been waiting for me. Not to take her child away from her but to love him, care for him, long enough for this Lisa to get a foothold. How well I know that situation, that need.

"Please, I have to hold that child, Lisa."

She drops back onto the couch, looking as if I'd struck her before answering through tight red lips. "I don't have a child. Never said I had one."

Hiding him, I think. I say with such calm, "Four years ago, you were pregnant. Showing. I know this, Lisa, and I also know how tough it is, having a child to raise when you feel you're on your own. But I can help you. Don't shake your head. I can, I want to. We must talk about it."

She shoots me a stricken look from under those heavy black lashes. "No. Stop it."

I pick up the toy truck. "Please, Lisa, I must see him."

"No." She looks around at the cluttered hot room. Gets up, turns off a window fan.

"Lisa, please."

Her voice is flat, "I had an abortion."

I believe her face. I sit, numb with loss. I had loved a child that didn't exist.

"Sorry, but that's the way it was," she says, faintly, looking away. "I was coming back without Ryan. Wasn't going to bring home any baby. Not to Mama's with Daddy still there. Wouldn't do that to any kid."

She picks up the toy I'd dropped and flips it to the couch. "My sister's boy from next door. I look after him when they're working. And I'm taking computer science on my nights off if you wanna know." She picks up her purse again. In a flat voice, "Gotta go."

With effort, I follow her out. Into the glare of the hot afternoon she has the bleak look of a sad child with too much make-up.

Lisa jiggles her car keys. "Sorry if I was abrupt, but you see I don't like thinking about it, and you sort of took me by surprise."

I nod and turn to go.

"Wait—I did mean to tell you this if ever I saw you again. Ryan doesn't hate you the way you probably think. He says you two never got to agree on anything and that he probably was a bastard in making his own case. Ryan's a sharp thinker, brighter than anybody I know, Mrs. Kendall. I think the main thing he missed was knowing who he was—you know, not knowing his father and he took it out on you."

"Thank you, Lisa."

Back in my car, I sit for minutes, absorbing this. She gave me a gift for which I am grateful. A gift that leaves a larger debt, an old one. I withheld a father from Ryan. And I knew he never accepted the blond and grinning Charley Kendall as anything but a picture tacked on his wall.

I drive back to the house with disappointment I have to hide. What was I thinking of? No way could I have brought a child here.

September / Los Angeles

Early morning in Wylie's house above Malibu Beach. Five years of marriage and five visits here—one too many. I'm dressing to get out. A pajamed Whitney sits watching coldly. "What do you think you're doing?"

I tell him in a rush. Can't stay another day in this garish house that looks like his self-centered, egotist of a brother hired a madame to decorate. The collection of cars in the sweeping drive are his toys for show. I can no longer listen to Wylie brag about his affairs and lash out at his wife, this sister-in-law who takes the emotional battering with no more spunk than a trembling female in a silent movie. My God, doesn't she know she has power of her own if she'd use it? This must be the kind of emotionally battered woman Chloe sees from rich homes or poor. Afraid to contest him, take her small children and go. She'd be out on the street if California law didn't mean this impossible man would have to share the wealth he's piled up.

Whitney looks shaken. "I don't like the way Wylie lives . . . but he's my brother and don't try to cross him. You're in his home. He's invited us here."

"So we have to pretend not to see what he does, how he operates? What he's doing to his wife, his children?" I swallow back the rest, finish packing the bag, both of us silent.

Early in this marriage I'd felt compassion for his strange connection with this unconscionable asshole of a younger brother. Whatever came from their sibling past, I never tried to probe. Whitney probably doesn't know himself, if this is love or hate or envy, this hang-up he has with Wylie. He wouldn't look under his calculated dignity.

"You can't leave," he whispers now, dismayed. "We're staying here another week. Wylie has made plans."

I close the small bag. "I'll see you in San Francisco, at the plane Friday. I'm calling for a cab."

I can tell he's seething, disturbed. He calls the cab. I hurry downstairs to wait in the chill driveway to avoid any false good-byes. I have five days before our tickets call for flying out of San Francisco to Atlanta. Five days of freedom. I know two places to go. I've seen posters on a shop window here.

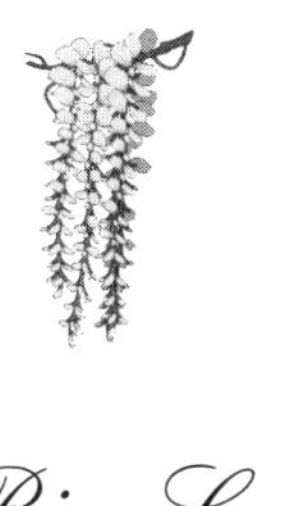

Big Sur

1992

It takes two buses to get to Big Sur, then Esalen further on. How many people must have escaped to this place on the side of the mountain, seeking some intangible other than the inner dialogue beating at their brains.

I get out on the highway, walk down to the cabins and lodges planted along the high cliff overlooking the Pacific. Yes, this is air remembered, aromatic with eucalyptus. I have no reservation only determination. They can't turn away a lone walk-in pilgrim.

Two days here is only a sampling of Esalen. Won't clear out my head, but it's a respite. In a gestalt session now, floor sitting with fifteen others, I'm the outsider watching each take turns by the leader, to beat pillows, hate mother or whomever. I hold back. I don't hate Whitney. I feel sorry for him and yes, for me, for all the stupid choices I've made in my life. Blaming anyone else doesn't help.

Afternoon: The air here is the payoff, even for a temporary escapee. The path follows the mountain rim, a hundred feet above a rolling blue-green Pacific, crashing on rocks below. Chloe should be here.

Ahead, a low shed is entrance to where mineral waters feed into cement basins, open to sky and sound of ocean. Following procedure, I slip out of my clothes, hang them on a hook and go into the baths. Other assorted males and females sit chest deep in the various steaming tubs. To stare at details of bodies would be gauche. The gauche are not expected here. I sink into the hot mineral water like a misplaced self, listening to others in their Esalen talk.

". . . the goal is to extricate the conscious mind from the subconscious . . ."

". . . the woman I'm with now, back in Chicago, is inhibited, repressed, unacceptable of change."

". . . You have a choice—resistance or acceptance . . ."

"This morning, I had a marvelous sense of becoming. . . ."

Dinner in the redwood lodge is a vegetarian's dream-spread of fruits, nuts, berries and sprouts. Late sun glitters on the rolling Pacific, but it's still light. I go alone down past the gardens, farther down to huge rocks above where the ocean roars into a cove. The wild beauty, the air alive with green growth and smell of the sea quiets me.

It takes minutes to realize I'm not alone. On a ledge farther down, a blond man from my Gestalt group sits, head in his hands, rounded shoulders shaking.

In this place, do you let someone cry alone or go offer comfort? I ease down, sit a few feet away, and wait. He glances sideways, wipes his face, tries to smile. I say, "A better release here than beating pillows, isn't it?"

He laughs. "Definitely." He's about my age, a tense looking blond fellow. We watch the waves roar in below, leap up and foam over the jagged rocks. Subsiding, they leave cool green pools for magical still minutes.

"I couldn't tell them up there," he says finally. "You weren't coming out with any confessions either."

"You noticed." We wait for another crashing, foaming wave.

I tell him what I haven't said in the sessions. "Sitting here, in this wild natural place, I'm looking at what is false in my life. Makes me hunger for what's real. What I'm going back to is supposed to be the real. It's acting out. Filling a role."

He looks hard at me, as if deciding to make his own confession. "Back home, in a very conservative suburb, at a very conservative church, I'm the minister."

"I don't imagine any of the members are here, checking up on you."

"Hardly." He's quiet again. Throws a pebble down onto the white foam. "I preach the Bible, as they expect me to. I believe much of it is inspired, much is parable, some is history. I preach to the converted who sit there, dozing off. Yet I'm aware of the many who never come into a church, who want, need to experience a personal contact with a living God. I want to reach out to them. But I don't feel adequate. Or courageous enough."

A wave crashes up and subsides. I wait for him to say what's working behind his face.

"When a person accepts Christ," he begins, "there is an experience of absolution, a new door entered. Yet—as long as one deals with this life, there are problems. I see so much trouble, so much bottled passions and questions hidden beneath the surface, even with my steady old parishioners."

Another wave foams below us.

He asks, "Have you heard of Transpersonal Psychology? This fourth arm of psychology deals with the connection between spirit and psychological understanding. If I could do some study there, immerse myself in this, I'd go back—this sounds like an egotistical fantasy—I'd go back home and start a church, avoiding labels. What I'm talking about is timeless, what mystics have known in every religion. Certainly Christian mystics, too."

"I know." I'm warmed to hear this man express my own beliefs I don't try to share with anyone else. Beliefs I still hold out from myself, don't really use.

I say lamely, "Sounds like you're waiting to give yourself permission."

"I have a wife who grew up in this church. I've given her hints, but . . ."

"Making a change like that is the ultimate challenge. I haven't made my own but I know what you mean."

He gets to his feet, looking out at an incoming wave. "Thanks. I agree." And he climbs up toward the lodge.

I follow eventually. Later that evening, the same fellow comes up to me, face shining. "When it happens, it will be something about Living Waters. Study center, maybe."

With one more day and night and morning before San Francisco, I find a ride going north with a fellow member of the gestalt group. "The woman with the red hair?" he tells me. "I think she comes down from Santa Cruz each year to get her kicks hating mama. Like a vacation."

I get out on the highway at the University of Northern California. Cross a campus that's strange to my Southern eyes. Open rolling land then woodland with stands of ancient redwoods. Here and there, buildings as contemporary as the trees are ancient.

Signs point to the gym, farther on. From that sprawling white building comes lovely chiming music. I know I will always remember this moment, this sound.

Inside, the entire gym floor is covered by a huge crowd sitting and sprawling on their jumble of wraps and bags. I creep along the edge, find a spot against the wall for my back and small bag. Someone in front of me turns to whisper, "Stephen Halprin," meaning the man at the vibes, doing his "Spectrum Suite" against a screen of changing colors.

Now a young woman in a long caftan is up there, careless dark hair framing the animated face, voice vibrant exhorting us to go beyond imagined limits. The man next to me—yellow sweater, strong profile—leans over with a conspirator's smile, "She's the witch, and we are her coven."

"But a white witch?" I counter.

We're watching Jean Houston, explorer of consciousness since she was a precocious child, daughter of a Jewish comedy writer, granddaughter of an Italian Catholic grandmother, with friendships with famous minds like DeChardin, Joseph Campbell and Margaret Mead.

Spinning stories, she is a comic actress one moment, a mythic wise crone the next, drawing her footnotes from a scholar's full range of reference to orchestrate the challenge she's about to deliver—her own new myth of the "possible human." Tells us that we sentient beings are primed with archtypical knowledge and innate gifts we don't allow ourselves to use fully—because we don't believe they are there.

I test my belief, shut away too long. For moments I feel my own possible self, purpose, destiny out there, yet to be discovered. I think of Chloe's belief in having a purpose and finding the right place to live that purpose.

How can I take this back to Atlanta with me? Moments of epiphany happen only to get packed away like crazy vacation clothes bought in exuberant moments, impractical once back to what seems to be the only realities—the job, the marriage, and next week's schedules.

Tonight, strangely content, open, musing, I sit alone on a low wall, watching others stand about under campus lights, talking in animated clusters.

Someone settles next to me. The man in the yellow sweater, voice pensive. We talk, the way strangers can when their ids and egos have been challenged, opened for inner inspection. Comfortable, honest talk because you'll never see one another again. He's driven down from Canada, alone, to hear Houston. He needs to understand some things going on in his life. He's Canada and I'm Atlanta, simple as that.

I tell him what I used to look for, what I must I still believe though I've made a mess of my life. Tell him I look for proof in others but seldom find it and how I know one wonderful spiritual friend who seems to float above her disappointments yet her life is one challenge after another.

Canada is listening, smiling in the dark. And what do I think of our "white witch" today, he asks.

"She's a mythic creature herself, isn't she? Most people you know in the workaday world will call her a kook. They'd miss the essence of what she's saying. And that's a shame."

"I have to catch a plane back to Atlanta tomorrow," I tell him. "Today had been a brief escape from a mordant marriage. Don't know whether to stay with it or end it."

"Then you will in time, Atlanta," he tells me.

He picks up my left hand, looks at my ring, turns it over on my finger. I meet his studying gaze, read its import, my body responding. Do I dare let the night happen as it might, like a shooting star, one flash in the heavens, then gone?

He drops my hand. "You will, but you're not ready," he says as if he has read it in my aura or my eyes. "I'm not quite ready myself," he adds softly.

We fall silent as others still murmur in the half light. He asks, do I need a ride to the bus station in Santa Cruz next morning? Yes, I'd appreciate that. Then, he'll be waiting at six. He leans down, kisses me lightly on the cheek and is gone.

Later, far into the night, I am awakened by a scream, echoing in the cool air from an open window. It is the unmistakable surrendering cry of a woman reaching organism. Then silence again. I lie there in a narrow dorm bed, crying too, but quietly, from loneliness.

Whitney is not on the plane leaving for Atlanta.

I walk into a silent house. Walk around these sedate blue rooms. Call LA, to Wylie's house. Whitney comes to the phone. He sounds diffident as a lawyer for the prosecution.

"I've changed my flight plans. I am staying another three days to give you time to find yourself an apartment. This marriage is not working. Wylie agrees. Find yourself a place, tell the office where you can be contacted. We'll meet there to discuss arrangements."

I listen, stunned. Something new slowly takes its place. Surprise. Gratitude. I'm being kicked out of this blue house and marriage.

I get up and walk around, looking for what is mine. Nothing really but clothes in the closet. Old stuff, papers, journal, packed away in the desk. I'll have to get them out. I have a year old Cutlass parked in the drive. And an open door leading where?

Stopover

1992

On this gusty October day, I leave Atlanta behind, singing to the dashboard's beat of country music pathos: *It's past, it's over, and don't look back.*

Back seat of the Cutlass holds all my earthly possessions, two suitcases packed with clothes, one small overnight bag and a carton of old personal papers, cleared out of the desk, dumped into the box, taped shut. I've called ahead to Vyola, but had to leave a message after her solemn taped invitation to leave a message after the beep.

By dusk, I'm nearing Montgomery. Don't take time to look at the shut down old town. Find my old street, nose the car up to the front of the little yellow house with a peaked roof. Jump out, ring the bell with more joy than felt in a long time.

Orange light floods the stoop. The door opens and here's Vyola, tall and lean in a zippered navy robe, dark eyebrows calmly lifted over the half-glasses. She arcs a lighted cigarette into the night and calls out her husky welcome. "You don't look like an unhappy divorcee. Come on in."

We hug on the stoop. "Wait. Have something to bring in." I go back to the car pull out the carton, the overnight bag balanced on top and follow Vyola inside.

This place. Memories flash, good and otherwise, just by walking into the hall. "Let me dump this box in my old bedroom."

"If you drove all day, you probably can use something hot. Kettle's on for tea and I have soup."

"I was hoping. For a school teacher you make good soup." My old joke.

I sit at the maple table by the window, watching Vyola heat the soup as vines rustle outside in the windy moonbright night. "Deja vu," I sigh, dipping into the blue willow bowl of beef broth swimming with finely cut vegetables. "You fed me this when I was carrying Ryan."

She joins me with her hot tea. I see deeper lines around the eyes, more white streaks threading the dark hair pulled tight in a bun at the neck. "Now, tell about what you're doing before I spring mine."

I sip my soup, watching the strong face, listening to the husky gentle voice finishing with, "So I don't leave for a month. Now, tell me. The marriage is over?"

"Over two days ago, papers signed around a polished table, done as coolly civil as, well, the marriage has been. Five years. A contract revoked. That's Whitney for you. He requires relationships to run as neatly as his schedules. He fired me the way he'd do a secretary. Made it easier I must admit. I'm a bit guilty he did it. I didn't have to."

Vyola reaches for her cigarettes in the pocket, but stuffs them back. "I've heard very little from you in these five years. Just pretty cards and an occasional picture taken at some banquet or cocktail party. He looks quite self-satisfied. Your smile was unconvincing."

"The pictures didn't lie. Whitney is a decent guy but avoids emotions by not allowing any. Or any discourse on the subject." I don't go into the Rich Brother hang-up which really did it. "He stays disconnected from vulnerability. I won't say robot. That's unkind. For whatever reason, he has to be that way. No woman could change that." I sigh remembering, "Maybe that's the safest way to go. Disconnect yourself."

"You don't believe that. You'd never disconnect from your emotions though you do a good job of keeping them hidden."

"I thought marrying him would mean structure, order in my life. My mistake. Let's say it was one more mistake I've made. Why the head shaking?"

"Rae Kendall, you really are a survivor, but you never give yourself that credit."

"Forget credit. I don't blame other people for what I do. Did you teach me that? Or does it come from Southern genes? 'Duty fulfilled or suffer the guilt' must be embroidered on old pillows. Yes, I feel guilty about poor Whitney for reasons I won't go into. Well! Subject at hand-what next? I came out of this with my name back, the car parked outside and not much else. Didn't stay to challenge why our mutual fund account wasn't mutual. But I have plans."

Vyola nods, still the sanguine good listener.

"I'm going to reinvent my life, as the saying goes. Slam the door on the past." I take a breath to judge her slow smile. "I have plans. On my way to that now."

"A quick decision? No pause, not even a few days here?"

"Chloe wanted me to wait, meet her at the retreat she goes to in upstate New York. Said I needed time to quiet myself inside, talk to some good counselors up there, then be open to some new direction."

"But you didn't."

"No . . . We used to talk about finding one's true purpose, the right place that would satisfy the inner self along with the outer. All that. Lovely belief. Suited the dreamer I used to be, remember? But at forty-two, on my own again, I'm choosing to be realistic. Hard-nosed. Unstoppable. All that." I laugh at my speech but I mean it.

"So?"

"I'm on my way to South Florida. Going to rent an efficiency, eat frozen dinners and study real estate non-stop until I am hired as an associate with the best broker on that coast. I've decided to make money for a change."

"Every job you've had," Vyola says, "you do with tenacity."

"I drove here from Atlanta to sit in this kitchen, tell you at this table. Once in Florida, I'm digging in. I'm in a hurry to get started. Tomorrow, I'm on my way."

"I wish you could stay." A momentary glint of loneliness. "But your feet are tapping under the table."

"Can't. I'm running on momentum. And that carton I brought in? It's a bunch of old personal papers cleared out of my desk and files in Atlanta. Old stuff I've saved, haven't looked at for ages. I couldn't leave it there for Whitney to look over and throw out. So do me the favor? Get rid of the box for me. Dump it. I won't be here to watch."

"All? You might have pictures in there."

"I didn't look. Wasn't a time for re-living my life, but getting on with it. My old journals probably. I'm leaving the past behind, but not for anyone else to read."

Vyola's gaze has an unspoken question.

"No, I still don't know where Ryan is and I've suffered about that long enough. Couldn't mention it to Whitney. All I know, Ryan's still in Hawaii using some other name."

"He's older now, maybe he's wiser too."

"Not to the extent of forgiving me for failing as a mother. Let's don't talk about it."

We're quiet a minute, listening to the wind outside.

"I'm leaving everything and everybody behind, except you, Vyola, and Chloe. I told her I'd be stopping by here. She'll be writing. So please forward when I have an address, before you leave for Cambridge."

"Chloe, is she still with Garth?"

"I gather he's always in her life somehow. Married to his U.N. girlfriend now. He may not be the only Sixties activist heading for a political career, but if he makes it, he has Chloe to thank. And it's cost her. Though she doesn't complain. I get so annoyed. He must still be part of her mission, as she calls it. Bright as she is, she's let that man be a drag on her own life."

"I know. You two have a special friendship. Garth the shadow in the background."

"I felt so bad for her a few years back. The sister-in-law was masterminding the Boston debut for daughter Emily. She had to be there in all that pompous society she finds depressing, people who know the family, her hippie years."

"The past."

"Yes, but those people know about the Paynes. Emily and the aunt insisted Chloe look presentable. She wouldn't go shopping. They had her go into that house she avoids, into the mother's room to find a dress, to be mother of the deb. Chloe's mother was long gone, living with a nurse, but the whole thing must have been trauma for Chloe. She told me about it with some very quiet laughs."

"You sound annoyed along with the sympathy."

"Right. I get angry at Chloe for giving so much of herself."

"Do you still hate Garth?"

"For Chloe's sake, and mine, yes. And Ryan's." *He never knew who he was, Lisa said.*

Vyola's husky voice goes gentle. "When you reinvent yourself, are you leaving that hate behind? It's a burden to pack along."

"You sound like Chloe sometimes. She says hate is toxic."

"True. Guilt or hate are burdens to pack along, even hidden behind the mental door you say you're slamming."

I meet her steady gaze. "I'm sure you must have left some hurt behind. You never would tell me about it."

"Told you enough. That I forgave that fate. It's the only way to survive and move on. Life has to be lived forward as the wise say, and understood in retrospect."

I reach over and squeeze her hand. "Vyola, you did it. Otherwise you wouldn't be the calmest, wisest woman I've known all these years. Only you still smoke too much."

"A bad choice of mine. One of the best known facts about human failings is how stubborn we can be with our bad choices." The wry smile fades to something more serious. "We all make our share. Rae, you never forgive yourself for yours."

I look out at vines in October moonlight. Get up and wash my soup bowl in the sink. "Vyola, I intend to be too busy to remember my secret guilts and bad choices. I'm giving up soul-searching. Decided it's time to make money and go for the advertised good-life."

The next morning, I roll out of the autumn colored street, heading east. At the first Welcome to Florida sign, start singing again to the dashboard beat, *I'm gonna do it, gonna do it, closed the door on what's gone before.*

Oceanviews

July 1995

❧

Fort Lauderdale

Dear Jenny:

You must come see me now. This fast-track place glitters under the sun, runs at its own pace, which is fast-forward. Caught in traffic you have a gloriously blonde old lady in a pink Caddie on one side and a tanned old sport in an open covertible on the other. Oh yes, behind, a kid in a daddy- bought sports car, blasting the air with his dashboard beat.

After my year in Boca Raton, I had enough contacts to move on with this new company in Lauderdale. Have done well enough here to get a good deal on one of their model condos. I'm six floors above Galt Ocean Mile. Upscale, Jenny. That's the operative word here.

I have a balcony outside. A clever little kitchen I use so far for coffee and bagels in the morning. I still feel like a visitor since I'm out most of the time. I'm enclosing a clip from an ad about my new company.

Burman Companies

one of South Florida's foremost real estate developers in the revitalization of Ft. Lauderdale, fulfilling real estate needs of a wide segment of Broward County with luxury residential conclaves, and Oceanview Towers along the Atlantic Ocean

Friends here are fellow realtors or women like a pushy new friend, Lily, who is a shopaholic by day and shops for a husband who can afford her at night at the club. I've joined one for dinner and contact reasons.

In my dreams I'm still doing sales speeches. They go like this:

> "Breathtaking view, isn't it? . . . This one, as you see, is furnished to be elegant and timeless, yet here in Fort Lauderdale's revitalized downtown. . . .Your neighbors will be successful retired individuals as yourselves."
>
> And for the younger ones, ". . . the ultimate comfort and location, for people like yourselves, young hi-techs and lawyers and entrepreneurs who want to be here in the heart of the action"

So come see.

Your busy friend, reporting from the heart of the action, Rae

❧

September

Dear Chloe:

You'd hate this money-driven, palmy paradise, but you must come to see me. There's a real ocean out there with a beach to walk except at spring break time when we'd have to step over bodies. Actually, I haven't been out there on the sands but once.

Wouldn't make you mall-walk in these glitzy emporiums, but we could make a salad in my own little kitchen or sit out on the balcony with Chinese food from little white boxes with the handle. Chloe, tell me how you are. I won't fuss about your health and schedule or ask about Garth. I do hope you see more of Emily. And do I dare ask how the book is coming?

Miss you, Rae.

October

Dear Vyola

I'm so disappointed you aren't planning to come see me here anytime soon. I want to show you there are areas of lush foliage and backyard yacht docks here as well as this mad commercial traffic.

Are you feeling okay, saying you need to be at home? I hope you've given up smoking, as you promised. I want you to see this place. Paid my dues with that smaller firm but working for the big developer now.

About my place. Oceanview's interior designer told me she used "a neutral palette, for sophisticated serenity, allowing the accents to be the touches of gold in the glass tables." Is there such a thing as sophisticated serenity? I want you to know I haven't added or changed anything, but I've done the bedroom in peach and lilac, remembering your garden back yard.

Love to you, Rae

Dear Josey,

Sorry it didn't work out with the principal. Don't let it make you hate all males as self-serving liars. Go have your hair done in champagne-red and come to see me. I'll take you to the club and show you a different variety of male natives here, only to observe for your entertainment. I've had some amusing offers but I stay the observer.

Your cuz, Rae

Atlanta / November

Hi Rae:

Milt will be coming down to Miami to do a major Kosher banquet next month, and you can bet I'm coming too, to see what you've done for yourself, my friend. Done it in three years, too. Using that Southern accent and still selling yuppie lawyers and retired CEOs. Don't forget how we Southern females are supposed to deliver our jibes. Just start with "Bless your heart"—before the dig.

No man in your life yet? Bless your heart, by now you should have found one among all those corporate types down there. Some must be ready for a new wife, a smart, honest, tender-hearted woman still young but old enough to have sense. I'll let you know more about our plans before I show up.

Hugs, Jenny.

December

I'm crawling into my lone and private bed late when the phone rings. "Rae Kendall? Brandon Price here. Didn't buy your Oceanview, but I want to see you again. What about lunch today? I'll pick you up at one. Tell me where."

As if I didn't remember that baritone from three weeks ago, I say, "Brandon Price? Remind me. Oh yes, the engineer with a Miami home he wants to sell."

"Not going to sell. But lunch?"

"I'm showing that penthouse today, the one you didn't want."

"With the copious gold accents and Italian marble. Overkill. You didn't waste much time with me when you saw I didn't go for it. Old world excess, South Florida version. But about lunch, you're missing a great repast at a new place along

Las Olas. I'm flying out tonight but I always come back. Have your card."

I hang up, snuggle down, smiling at the self assurance of these power players. Something other than Mel Merick's brittle arrogance. And nothing like Whitney Well's starchy dignity that was a protective veneer, a sham. Wouldn't mind if this Brandon Price surfaced again. A man of decision, obviously.

He'll call. Do I want to get involved?

Brandon

1997

June

The darkened restaurant is another glitsy retro place, decorated with crazy lights, throbbing beat and hum of diners. When I'm with Brandon, the dinnertime scenarios include table stoppers. The man standing there to talk golf plans, the woman to acknowledge me with an assessing quick smile before turning attention to my Brandon.

I smile back at the woman, veiling amusement at her begrudging fascination. She's studying Brandon, a tanned Sean Connery, thick, silvered hair, comparing him to the paunchy man she's with.

The table hoppers move on. Brandon turns back to me, taking up where he left off. "Have a meeting next week in California. Want to come with?" His first invitation a year ago was as blithe.

Our dinner arrives. Another crony stops by to talk. I dip my fork into salad, sip my wine, and let them talk.

That first date. Sitting across a table from Brandon. I had to laugh at the blithe invitation to "come with."

"You don't know yet if I have a lover, husband, or kids at home."

"I know you're single, lovely at forty—"

"Older and wiser."

"You don't chatter about yourself when you show property. You use all your wit and attention to play the game here—selling space pitched as lifestyle."

"I do the job my way. At first my broker thought I was too low-key to sell in this market. Now I get Steel Magnolia jokes."

Glowering, "I don't find many women who can be themselves and professional, too. Ones I deal with are officious and ambitious as men."

"I should counter that male bias, but I'm sure you've made up your mind. And I've had two glasses of wine. What takes you to California?"

"Aircraft fuel tank vulnerability, my focus since the Concorde disaster. American Institute of Aeronautics meeting. But you don't want to hear about systems engineering."

Dismissing that, he turned the charm back on with a quick flash of white teeth in the tanned face, and assessing gleam from the deep-set eyes. "I fly out next month to Boeing. I hate an empty hotel suite and I'm averse to the females I find in the lounge."

"You know, I felt the same way about the men I met when I traveled for a company."

He laughed. "Men are sons of bitches, aren't we?" His big hand reached over to inspect my left with it's simple pearl ring. Showed my right, with Charley's plain gold wedding band. "Not too long after my sweet sixteens, I had an Air Force husband whose plane crashed in the desert."

"You've survived I see. Some women turn bitches or complainers.

So, a controller. Doesn't want an emotional woman, but for different reasons than Whitney.

My first wife was an engineering student at Stanford. Sharp, but intractable. A second recent disaster was a conniving little bitch with a body that wouldn't quit. In love with a rock group before me. I shredded the file on both."

The confident smile came back on. "Never had a lady for a lady friend."

That first date.

Tonight by coffee time I glance out and see Lily. "Don't look now, but here comes a woman I know who will stand and coo as long as you allow."

"God forbid. The blonde rocking this way?"

"Lily Isbell. Wants me to sell the house she can't afford anymore." I don't add she's shopping for a new husband, too. He'll find out.

Lily undulates up to our table, flashing her smile. "Rae, honey, you're so busy all the time. I keep leaving messages. Hello," she says sweetly to Brandon.

❧

October

Dear Jenny:

How's Atlanta and when are you coming back to see me? Loved your pictures. Cute new grandbaby, but it was your beaming face I was happy to see. Thought it was time to get back to you and report:

I didn't come looking for a man, but one seems to have found me. I've been seeing him when he's in town. Four months now. MIT-type, fifty-two, in aeronautics engineering, a consultant now, flies out of South Florida, has a big house in Miami. He seems to be focusing in on this forty-seven-year-old realtor because he had a bad deal with one of the hazards for the rich males around here. You know, the trophy bride, ready to divorce her way up the ladder.

He isn't interested in my past lovers or marriages or children. Adament about staying in the present. Must be easier for men to do that. Okay, I came here to do the same, didn't I? Staying busy is the answer. I hope.

Brandon's once-grand waterfront place looks as you'd expect for a bachelor who is seldom home. Has an office there and doesn't know the cleaning people who come in.

Since you're going to ask, yes, I've over-nighted in the big house in Miami. At this point, I'm more or less watching my South Florida self go along with this very present arrangement. I keep my own apartment still as my private preserve, at least to sleep.

Try to get down here again. I need to be with real friends to remember the real self.

Bye, Rae

❧

November

Dear Vyola:

Did you get my flowers? You shocked me calling to say you were home from the hospital. Didn't let me know. Please bury those Pall Malls. Pneumonia is dangerous enough.

Please come visit when you feel like flying. Come sit in sunshine. It's blazing here, even in February. I'll actually cook your soup in my pristine kitchen. I've joined a club, place to entertain prospects and catch dinner without cooking, when I'm not dining in style with Brandon. Yes, that's still on. Vyola, I must tell you. We'll probably marry when he retires, if either of us don't pull back from the plan, arrived at unhurried and casually agreed. Call me soon as you feel like talking.

Love, Rae

❧

Something's wrong. With me, with that conversation tonight with Chloe.

We've missed our first of the month phone visits for how long? Then she calls back tonight. I'm blown away tired. "Where have you been?"

Her voice comes back, slow and sleepy. "I've been leading a group at Omega again. A break from the agency. Emily is in Europe with Jean. How are you, Rae? Still with the silvered engineer?"

"Yeah. I've just gotten in." And too tired to talk, but she's called and I figure I'll try to be cheery and make her laugh, too.

"Went to a wedding tonight. A client daughter's on the white satin carpet. You should have seen the reception. A six thousand dollar wedding cake, dinner reception for three hundred at the Boca Raton Country Club where white gloved security officers politely scrutinized anyone who didn't look rich. The cake tasted like cake, imagine."

"Imagine."

I describe some women in that handsome crowd. "Older women, tanned and face tightened, fingers coverd with diamonds from earlier connections. Young ones—"

"Rae, how do you keep in touch with your authentic self?"

That quiets me. "Sorry, the night is chattering in my head. What have you been doing? You sound too quiet."

"Spending some time sitting with my mother in a sanitarium. She doesn't know me. So I got away to Omega for five days."

I wait. "Did it help?"

"I wish you had heard Pir Vilayat Khan."

"I saw his picture in one of your brochures. The tall Sufi who looks like a Hollywood version of one. So beautifully handsomely grave." I hear my own impatience too late.

"Yes, he does. But he's real. I wish you could have heard Pir speak, a peaceful, nourishing experience."

"Chloe, right now all I want is a shower and oblivion between the sheets."

"I hear you. I've sent you a sketch someone did of me. Goodnight."

I hang up feeling like lead.

OMEGA
INSTITUTE
FOR HOLISTIC STUDIES
SUMMER

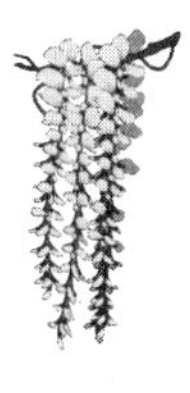

Messages

1997

April

In the windowed office for Oceanview Towers Properties, Big Sam Burman is pacing and pushing sales fever for Tower Four when ready to show when an emergency call comes in for me. A woman's Southern voice, hurried, stressed, tells me Vyola is in the hospital in Montgomery. An emergency lung operation. "She's been in trouble for a time. Didn't she let you know? She thinks of you as a daughter."

I call the hospital from my desk. No word yet. Have to sit through an afternoon closing with a German couple, buying a condo for when they're not somewhere else in the world. Back in my own place by four, I call again, and again. Finally, at six, the answer. She didn't come out of it.

For the rest of the evening, I sit alone, stranger to myself, looking at earned comforts that do not comfort.

Vyola, you leave me so lonely.

I fly to Montgomery for the memorial. Rent a car, check in to a new motel. Cannot bear to go to the locked and dark cottage, even to drive past. Tonight I wait in this generic room. A local brochure for visitors boasts of a civil rights memorial honoring everything that happened back here in the Sixties. Places to see: Martin Luther King's house on Dexter Avenue and a library named after Rosa Parks, as well as

Hank Williams' gravesite. A surprise. Sitting in the dark now, thinking of time and changes. Not ready to think of what they've done to me.

Huntington's grassy campus smells of southern spring. We stand, a group of ten, for words being said. Vyola's portrait waits on the stand, the strong face there with the wry smile. At moments like this, why does death seem more real than selling property, a filled DayTimer, buying yourself a Mercedes?

My turn to speak I look beyond the silent faces to say: *Vyola, you were my mentor and friend, a blessing in my life by showing me quiet strength and wisdom.*

Hugs now from soft-faced women I don't know. With one last deep breath of Montgomery spring, I'm behind the wheel, driving past banks of pink azaleas on my way out of town.

When the lawyer's envelope arrives later, with the deed and Vyola's letter, I read her words, grit my teeth, block tears, and file it all away in my alcove desk, out of sight.

May

South Florida days stay hot into the humid evenings now. Traffic as relentless always as the sun. Out of the glare, into the cooled lobby, I collect mail, studying a bulky envelope in the elevator going up to my floor. From Chloe, mailed from Taos, New Mexico. First word in two months since she sent a brief note about leaving in a RV with Luna, the Navaho poet, the feminist group leader she met at Omega and two other therapists.

"They left NOW politics to do this," she'd said in that first note. "I'm taking time off to go along. We invite women to share their stories. 'Feminism and Spirituality—being fully female, fully human.' That's our honest act."

Kicking off heels, I sink into a couch to read. Pages spill out, torn from a notebook, written at different times and different places. Topped with a brief explanation:

❧

Rae:

I've been writing notes to myself on this trip. Meant to collect ideas for my book, but these turned out like personal sighs. I was about to rip them out, send them blowing in the desert wind as confetti. Instead, mailing them to you to decipher what you care to, and then throw away.

From your hippie frined,
back on the road, Chloe.

❧

Alone on a plush couch in my artificial cool, I read:

Left today from Boston heading west. The camper is cramped with four personalities, our jeans, boots, caftans for the hot days, and some rations. This is no city tour. Gets me away from what I don't wish to deal with at present. The work on my desk. Emily's disapproval and distance.

In a rec hall yesterday we talked to teen girls from a local high school. First questions were about hippies. The young are enamored with the idea, they seem to believe this was a rockfest party they missed plus crazy fun clothes. How little they know. Did they hear what this veteran told them? That the counterculture Sixties set a grassroots fire of attention to society's ills. Also told them idealistic fire is potent psychic energy. Thwarted, it can become rage or the opposite, selling out to what was once the enemy. Didn't tell them lost causes can leave hidden ulcers in one's psyche. Did they care to hear any of that? Had they rather talk about Madonna? Not the figure in churches. Small town or not, their TVs teach the same consumer appetites. My own daughter, who considers herself the sophisticate, doesn't care to hear my version of the unfinished past.

Thinking of Rae tonight. We were once soul-sisters. What happened? She gets consumed by her jobs, as someone who almost drowned once so won't let go of the life savers.

Thirty women are expected tomorrow at a Unity Church. Luna opens with her powerful lines and meaningful myths. Then we share some of our unfinished stories and invite them to offer theirs. At first it's what they tell themselves. We are there to help them look beneath that surface. If a session works, I see shields drop, understanding shared between those different women, different lives.

By flashlight in the camper I have to write this down. Tonight we sat, four women in a booth in a roadside diner in Utah. Strangers to this strange landscape and to the faces watching us. We were seen as different, therefore suspect, therefore perceived as a danger. Even the two women behind the counter stared our way and muttered behind curled lips about lezzies because we traveled without men. Hate blew our way like the blast of chilled air hitting us from the vents.

We sat silent with our fried eggs and coffee, ignoring the chill, looking into one another's face for comfort. Only Luna muttered her rage as we left. Would the lidded gazes have eased had they known we were headed to an Indian reservation to be sisters for ten days to women there? Or do they hate Indians, too? Hate jabs me inside like a knife thrust.

I wanted to ask: What in yourselves are you guarding?

At our sessions, I talk of love and connection, yet here we were facing hate and I said nothing. Silence must be the grave marker over too many causes. Luna did speak her fearless mind as she paid our bill. They'll remember her. I'm dealing with this tonight, writing under this yellow ring of flashlight. . . .

Unbelievers don't need preachment. They need only to lie on an open desert on a night startling with stars, open to this infinity, to know there is a live intelligence behind this universe. The surreal quiet reaches into the body. These nights I send my troubled human questions into the silence.

Colin appeared at our camp last week. Shared food with us and his bed roll with me these nights under desert sky. I slept in the arms of a man who is 32 to my 49. How little that mattered. Or the fact his journey takes him back east to study as we continue west. I write this with a certain joy, sans logic. In this open place we have shared intimacy, both mind and body.

Wish Rae had heard his story. How back in Maryland someone "laid a Zen book on him." Began meditating, dropped drugs and a tech job, did fasting on weekends, read the Bible. The passages about "light" become real to him. Came out here to be alone in this openness for a month. Received his "break through." Says he's to do some teaching and believes it has to do with exploring the thought of Pierre Teilhard De Chardin, scientist, monk, intellectual, Christian.

No regrets tonight, crawling into my bedroll alone. With dawn, the light always enters me, registering as a soft physical thrill, a completeness and connection. Why doesn't it stay with me in bright sun of the day? No, to question validity of the expierience is to shut it out.

One need I can no longer shut out. To return to Boston to see my mother. It will mean sitting with a woman who doesn't know me. Hoping that deadened spirit inside that frail body can come alive long enough to call my name, a final recognition. Yet our group is expected in California. Then I'll fly back. If my Emily sees me she will be grimly sure her mother is still a hippie.

California. Yesterday, I sat in the Ojai oak grove with so many others, listening to Krishnamurti. This small-bodied man, silver hair, fine dark Indian features, old in years, ageless, quietly vital, sits there in shade of oaks, gazing out over the crowd of followers seated on blankets. With knowing eyes, and bristling, he says, "I am not your guru, and all that nonsense." Is he one of the last to be called a sage? He sounds like a rare intellect, yet he says the intellect gets in the way of perceiving the truth. Listening, I knew again my simple and immediate truth. I must get back east. I must see the woman who doesn't know me. Has never known me. I've told Luna.

I sit here reading Chloe's pages until Florida sunset colors the balcony doors. Finally, dusk, then dark out there. I bundle the scraps of paper and give them a strange burial in the container under my pristine sink, six floors above Galt Ocean Mile.

On the humid balcony, lean on the banister looking up for stars in this urban sky. No chance. In a place of too many lights you see only haze against the night.

Boston

1998

ঌ

February

For ten days a strange note from Chloe has waited on my desk. A plea, actually, asking me to see her in Boston. "I can't come there. I need to talk to you, Rae, explain some things. Confess some. And, have you read the book I sent earlier?"

No, I haven't been in the mood to read about *The Thirst for Wholeness*. Does she want to point out I've given up on ideas we used to share? I'll be more disappointed if she wants to announce she's given up all beliefs herself.

Months ago I sent her a book I found, *Loose Change*, by a reporter Sara Davidson who wrote about the Sixties. Was that a mistake? The opening page asked, "How could so many bright committed people have miscalculated so badly?" Did that cut deep for both herself and Garth? I thought she would enjoy seeing that honest account.

I wrote back I couldn't very well get away now, but what's the problem up there? Heard no answer from that. Ten days ago. Longer?

When Brandon says he's flying to Boston, I offer to go. Eager to.

"It's a quick trip," he says, pleased. "Means a couple of days of seeing snow and warming me up two nights."

On the plane, I mention I need to see a friend. No problem, I know the place and can take a cab.

Unsure for some reason, I have the cab wait for me to knock on the door of the carriage house. Locked. No answer. Have the driver take me back up to the ivy covered stone house with its elaborate brass door knocker. The maid who appears shakes her head. The brother looms in the doorway, a tall man, thinning blond hair, chin lifted to eye me coldly, to tell me his sister is in treatment. And where. "Drying out, if you will," Norman Payne says, glaring his impatience before closing the door in my stunned face.

Shock and dismay make a cold day grow bitter.

I tell the driver where to take me, yes, even if it's an hour from here. I ride, eyes closed. Did the brother mean alcohol? Prescription drugs? Was Chloe—my one believable example of inner tenacity and spiritual serenity—drying out? And in the very place she sat with her mother who died there? Unbelievable.

The cab leaves me at the sedate building set back on dead winter grass. Inside, I'm directed down a hall. Palpable sadness, age and defeat prickle my skin. I'm left at an open door of a sitting room.

A double window sheds colorless light on two chairs. A limp leaf plant sits on a sill. Someone rises out of a chair and stalks toward me, a heavy body swathed in a long textured robe, the solid amber face studying me coldly.

"Rae Kendall is it? You took your time. She's looked for you for two weeks. Now you bother to come."

I am not ready for this. It's Luna, I realize, challenging me as one lover to another. Heat suffuses me. Indignation, anger.

Chloe walks into the room and sinks into the chair by the window. Sees us in the doorway, "Rae, you found me. Luna, bring Rae in."

The room's ashen light drains the blue robe, the loose long hair, this pale wraith-like person, beautiful in an other-worldly way. What is she doing here, like this?

Dismayed, I move past Luna, to stand by Chloe. Manage to say, "Yes, I came, but why? I see you don't need me."

Anger at her and my own jealousy spills out. I can't stop. She's done what I've always warned about, using all her strength on retreats and teachers and Garth and her bleeding heart services beyond a reasonable call of duty. At her own cost. Now look, what had she done to herself? Resorted to alcohol, pills, what?

Her weary whisper stops me. "Rae . . . I wanted to talk with you, tell you . . . but I can't right now."

Dismayed, I bite out, she has Luna so no reason for me to stay. "When you feel like it write and tell me what happened. Whatever it is." I walk out shaken, sick at myself and the whole scene.

Riding back to the hotel through the cold dusky light, I hear all my words again and realize how they conflict—that business about over and beyond the call of duty and then saying "Chloe, you were my one shining example of a human I could believe in. . . ." As if I had stood to the side, expecting her to always prove something to me.

I hope Brandon is late and not waiting. But I don't care, can't feel anything but dismay for myself and what I might have ruined back there.

Three A.M. Questions

1998

March

Again. Awake in the middle of the night after fighting my way through dreams.

Can't keep this up. The days are too demanding. Nights run too late when Brandon's in town. Three Scotches before he orders dinner.

So, turn on the bedside light again, get out the new journal. You're not the kind I used to fill, but a designer's pretty little book, pristine pages meant for midnight thoughts or instant bad poetry. Are other women writing hopes and quandaries in one of these things in the middle of their nights? They needed an aunt Vyola to tell them how. Write it down, as honest as you know at the time and you may find yourself coming up with your own answers.

April 10

Journal:

Dreams again tonight. Being in a phone booth, dark outside, trying to reach someone, but the phone doesn't work. Who? Ryan? Bertie, for heaven's sake? Even my mother, so long gone and far away? Vyola, of course. Still missing her when I realize she's not back at the cottage. And now Chloe.

The way I walked out of there still shames me. What to do? I've tried to reach her. The sanitarium told me yes, she left a month ago. But the carriage house doesn't answer. She must be well enough to go off with that Luna and her group. She was her Chloe-self when she sent me that short note from Boston. A Chloe-way to say good-bye. Just a card quoting Tao Te Ching. "Whatever is flexible and flowing grows, whatever is rigid and blocked will die."

Keep having to put this out of mind. Can't handle traffic and selling and conversation going on around me while going over that stupid thing I did, walking out like that.

❧

May 3

Journal:

Still angry with my gynecologist today. He knows I'm healthy and busy, so why the interrogation at my simple request? I only asked for something to take the edge off, not just a sleeping pill.

"Edge off of what?" he insisted. Before prescribing an anti-depressant he prefers a patient to talk with the staff psychologist, to "know what we were dealing with."

Told him I'm not having a cliché mid-life crisis. Wasn't about to bore some patient faced therapist with my crazy dreams, the tick of impatience in my pulse all day.

Kept my cool okay. Told him I was doing quite well in my work, engaged to marry an important man later in the year. Told him this need was personal.

"All the more," he said. I countered: Doesn't stress go along with being conscious in the Nineties? Selling in this market? Dealing with the traffic out there? Told him I had a closing in thirty minutes.

Walked out with the prescription for Zoloft. Will it do any good?

ঌ৵

May 8
Journal:

Made another excuse not to go to Houston with Brandon for one of his short trips. Three days in a hotel suite should rest me, but it doesn't. Not when the evening means late dinners with his cohorts and their bored wives. Any sex after that is like a quick night cap for Brandon. I can't tell him that.

ঌ৵

June 2
Journal:

Woke up thinking how I miss my support group back there in the other world. Jenny sends perky cards and pictures of her grandchildren. Josey has taken off with another woman teacher in an RV to do the national parks. "This is it for me, Cuz," the first postcard said. I'm glad.

ঌ৵

June 8
Journal:

Awake at 2 a.m. More tossing, more dreams. Tonight the recurring one, racing down a fast-track highway, focusing hard on the yellow line, fighting the desire to whip the steering wheel. Not a death wish but a desire to fly off airborne to a moment of freedom. Then what? Crazy unsettling dangerous thought. At forty-eight who needs to land in yet another crossroad to find your way out?

❧

June 12

Journal:

Four a.m. question: What to do when you have what you thought you wanted . . . only you have to hide a hunger behind your public face? A need for something not yet found that defies a name because it's an intangible.

❧

June 20

Journal:

Awake tonight thinking of deadlines. September the new Tower Five will open. New push to sell. October Brandon is retiring. Have to plan a wedding at the club, dinner party to follow. First have to put my place and his Miami property on the market and have other possibilities lined up for our combined lives. Deadlines.

A desire comes up so clear in my mind, alive in my skin.

Before those deadlines, if only I could claim two months for myself.

To do what? Go off alone. In a quiet space I might think clearly, to look where I'm going. Get sensible. Honest, anyway. Time, also, to find Chloe.

Do I dare?

And risk everything I have going for me here?

❧

Discovery

1998

When you're ready to make the reckless plunge, the body must know before the mind agrees.

This hot June morning is off to its usual pace, traffic below humming. I dash around preparing to join it. Choose the new green linen from Saks because it looks sassy and confident. Stand in the perfect little kitchen for coffee and half a toasted bagel, the vitamin that promises Increased Performance and the Zoloft pill, not that it is doing any good. I toss down the pills with hope if not belief. Check the Daytimer for appointments coming up. Punch in the phone messages avoided last night.

Lily's honeyed voice comes on with its usual tinge of petulance. "Hi, Rae. It's me, going crazy stuck home tonight. It's my sixteen-year-old who's out having fun and not sex, I hope. You should have a teenager to know what I'm going through. Let's have lunch tomorrow. Please. Town and Country Mall, that salad place we like. You can't always be too busy."

Next, Brandon's baritone, positive and quick as usual, "Rae, love. I want you to fly to Houston with me tomorrow. No backing out this time. You can swing three days off. I should be in by six, at the club for dinner by seven. Pack your little bag, meet me there and we can leave from my place in the morning."

In a flash I decide no, won't go. Don't want to go. Will tell him tonight. Easy.

At the office for the morning staff meeting, Big Sam Burden prances like a motivator on stage, reporting progress on Tower Five, ready in September to show. Two months from now, one of my deadlines.

Into traffic again, to the next polished table for a closing. Have to pull my thoughts back to the proceedings at hand. My client, a paunchy legislator from the Midwest, round face florid with new sunburn, is buying a condo for his secretary. The trim woman smiles and keeps her mouth shut.

Lunch with Lily brings me back down to reality, South Florida mall reality. Waiting at a windowed table, I look out on this showplace of upscale lures, shoppers streaming by. With a chill, realize there is nothing here I want. Berate myself for the thought. To be devoid of desire is sick. Dark side of this morning's elation trying to surface.

Lily comes mincing down the busy corridor, skirt too short and long blonde hair swinging. Lily, a few years younger than myself, always trying to look like a twenty-year old model. Carrying a bag from Bloomingdale's. Drops down at the table, exuding tea rose scent and a coquette's smile. "Don't frown, Rae. It makes lines. These darling shoes were on sale."

"Fine." I'm not going to remind her again shopping is not the panacea for her credit card worries. "We all need our escapes. Different kinds."

Lily purrs up to the young man bringing the salads. We spear pink shrimp, the mall humming around us, Lily chattering on with an involved story. "So there you are," she concludes. "Now, what's new? You look so great in that linen, only you're still so restless, no fun anymore. Come on, take the afternoon off, go with me to check out this neat new boutique."

I have to hear myself say it: "Nothing here I want. Sounds smug, but that's not how I mean it."

"Really." Pouting, Lily pushes aside the untouched lettuce, pulls out her compact, reshapes her lips with coral. "You should have my real problems." I wait through the familiar litany, her mortgage, lawn bills, daughter's tuition at

Gardencrest. "You've got it made, Rae. You don't appreciate what you have."

Meaning Brandon, of course. And my place, but not my job.

"Guilty," I say.

"What in the world do you want?" Lily demands.

"To take off for a couple of months, away from here, alone."

"Really? When did that crazy idea come up?"

"It's been waiting. I've been ignoring it."

Lily blinks.

I peel out enough green bills for both lunches and tip.

Lily looks up. "I guess you're kidding but I'm telling you as a friend, Rae, you're not being very smart about Brandon Price, always turning down his short trips when he wants you to go along. A powerful man like that—well, you have to let him set the pace."

"How well I know." I say good-bye and walk out of there. Back to the car, the job, the traffic, the usual, feeling like a runner caught, trapped, jogging in place.

Where would I run, if I did? I know and squelch the image. Think instead how it would help right now to go home and dead-sleep before meeting Brandon tonight. No, I wouldn't stand up Emma Blumfeld, wanting to take a third look at the fifteenth floor resale.

The effusive little widow from New Jersey is waiting at the entrance of Pier 66. Emma hops in, a birdlike woman about seventy, sun-punished face, gold bracelets clinking on skinny wrinkled arms. Launches into her usual rush of compliments before switching to complaints about the last salesman.

"So I told myself, call that nice Rae Kendall again, the one who sounds like a Southern lady suggesting lunch, but has good sense just the same. Knows how to listen. I want to take another look at that condo with the godawful light. My, but you look cool and Irish today. And in this heat."

I murmur a gracious reply and swing back onto AIA.

We walk into the place, the light harsh as ever from glass doors bringing in midday glare of open sky and Atlantic below. Two white leather chairs sat on the expanse of nubby pale carpet, left by the divorcing former owners. I offer the usual, "Of course window treatment and furnishings will make the difference."

"Just let me look around," Emma insists.

Already four o'clock. I pace, trying to squelch what's building in me. Emma minces back, decisions working behind her once-gamin face. "Damn kitchen looks like an sterile lab with the test tubes taken away. Bet they never used it."

This woman should have bingo-minded, gossip-sharing neighbors, not impersonal strangers in these elevators, fellow cliff-dwellers, who would be trophy wives or solemn- eyed Arabs, or winter people from wherever. I tell her as much, more gently. Suggest we could look again at the townhouse on the canal with the lush landscaping.

She plops her little self in the white leather chair, gives me her best smile, thin stretched from too many face lifts. "No, I want this place for my own ornery reasons. What kind of check you want today? My son might come down before the closing to bluster but not to worry. It's my money, Herm Blumfeld would have wanted me to enjoy it. It won't be Herm Junior's and that wife of his until I die and I don't intend to do that anytime soon."

It feels good to laugh. "Emma, I'm sure, with your spirit. Wish I had as much."

I imagine Chloe saying, *That's the problem, Rae, your spirit is hungry for something real.*

I pull out the contract. Emma keeps talking with the enthusiastic relief of a buyer who has just made a decision. Her bridge friends, old widows like herself, will love coming here. She'll bring down her own stored stuff from New Jersey, as much as will fit. Still excited, she wants to know, "You married, Rae Kendall? Or, one of these career women too busy for a man?"

"No to both questions."

She beams, waiting for more. She'd love to hear about Brandon but I don't feel like telling it. Because she waits I say, "I've been married twice and foolishly in love once. Past history. The man in my life now travels out of Miami a great deal. Will until he retires." I focus on the contract.

"Well, you're young," Emma says "With that nice skin and bouncy brown hair, you look thirty-two though you probably aren't. Oh, listen to me. I hate being labeled by age, don't you? But wait till you're seventy and you'll know how young the forties are."

Emma digs in her purse for the checkbook. "You get around to realizing you need a partner as well as a lover. Better hope he works out as a friend, too. Whether he does or not, when you get older you need women friends. They can understand where you've been."

The bright room swims before my eyes. "Emma, that is so true, any age." Want to hug the woman's boney shoulders, forget my rule of keeping myself out of the conversation, to tell her about Vyola, about Chloe, how many years we'd been part of each other's lives, different as our lives were. Silent, I frown into my contract, aware of loss, and quiet panic to get finished here.

In the elevator, Emma wants to know, "You have children?"

We reach the lobby before I answer. "I did, once. I'm sorry. I mean I don't know where he is. In Hawaii, I've heard. I was a working mother who failed at the mother part."

"Oh, dear, I'm an old busybody, asking so much. Some things work out wrong no matter what you do. Now my son. . . ."

In the car, Emma Blumfeld talks and I drive, knowing with clarity what I intend to do and will stop fighting it.

At Oceanview Tower Properties, I march in, heart doing a fast beat. Receptionist Marleen looks up from the phone, nods, as she tells the caller, "Rae Kendall is not at her desk, but she's expected." She mouths the question to me, "Are you here?"

I shake my head. Marleen does her polite speech, takes the message, hangs up as I ask, "Is Big Sam in his office?"

"In there on the phone. What happened with your New Jersey widow today? That woman must be a pest."

I pat my briefcase. "Have the contract here. I need to talk to Sam, alone. Can you keep him off the phone for awhile? "

Marleen nods, studying me from her broad honest face. "Must be torrid out there. You're flushed. Say—that fiancé of yours called to remind you to meet him for dinner at seven. He sounds like a big deal, all right. Baritone, man-in-charge. I hear he's a silvered hunk."

"All that." I head for my broker-boss's office.

Big Sam Burton is on the phone cussing out a decorator doing the Oceanview Tower's model apartments. He waves me in, keeps on bellowing about urine yellow drapes. Behind his fuzzy, balding head, the wall holds the artist's idealized version of Tower Five soaring like a vain glorious windowed cube, sky and ocean as mere backdrop. I pace and wait.

Sam slams down the phone, leans back, grinning approval. "How's our ray of Southern charm? Who handles rich old babes like a niece working for the inheritance."

Usually, I counter his jokes with reminders I get rid of sight-seers with nothing to do but waste my time, also SOBs who turned lecher in the model bedrooms. This time I say quietly, "Sam, I need to get away from South Florida for a while. I'd like to leave now."

The grin fades from his ruddy face. "You in trouble, Kendall?"

"No trouble." None he'd care to hear. Sam sees women as bedable on his yacht or producers in his office. In my years here, I have been a producer. Now he will see me as incomprehensible woman, the kind he avoids.

"You crazy, Kendall? The new Tower's going to be ready to show."

"Not until September."

He rubs his fuzzy balding head. "What the devil's happened to you all of a sudden?"

"It's personal," I say.

Sam growls disgust. "Women. Do personal on your own time. You have closings coming up."

"Let Hollis do the closings. She needs them."

He studies me, curious now. "Thought you had it on with that big deal traveling engineer. Thought you wanted to keep on here when you married him. Has he dumped you? And you figure to run away and do your crying?"

"You know me better than that, Sam. No, I'm not dumped. Brandon doesn't know about this yet. You're the first. I'll be telling him tonight." The thought quickens my pulse.

"Hell, he oughta ditch you, springing that on him. You decided this today? Never took Rae Kendall for an erratic female."

"You know I'm not." I could tell him I need to do some thinking before I fit my life to Brandon's but it's none of his business. He wouldn't understand or care if I said I need a space of time to find a lost friend, a woman friend I walked out on months ago when she needed me. If I say I need to stop the world and get off long enough to hear myself think, he would glare and suggest a shrink.

Sam looks grim. "You want to stay with this firm?"

"Yes, I do." I've earned my place here. For awhile it felt like success. Maybe it will again.

Thirty minutes later, I walk out with my two months of freedom attached to an ultimatum—be back September one or loose out with Oceanview Towers and benefits. Will this deal hold? Don't know. It's the gamble I'm taking.

I clear my desk, focusing on details. Hand Marleen my list of appointments to give Hollis. She is curious. "Hey, this is sudden, isn't it? You going to take a fling to Spain, some place exotic? Even before you marry the fellow?"

"The opposite." The pen shakes as I write down my forwarding address. From the first moment I stopped fighting myself, I knew where I wanted to go.

Back in my own place, I try to call Brandon at the club. Have him paged. No answer. He expected me there at seven. Waiting, I do the necessary. Write bills in advance, a note for the manager downstairs. Pack a single suitcase with some basics. Find two pair of designer jeans folded, forgotten in a drawer. Cotton tees. Sandals.

Next task. At the alcove desk, get out the envelope I haven't touched since it came a year ago from Vyola's Montgomery lawyer. Read it once then, painfully and filed it out of sight. Now I'm eager to read it again, to imagine her husky but warm voice in those words.

April, 1997

My dear Rae

This news is not one for a phone call, therefore this note. The situation here isn't good, in fact it has become urgent. After the lung operation tomorrow, I won't feel like speaking or writing what is on my mind and heart.

It's this. I'm pleased for you, for your success in your palmy paradise. Yet in your hurried calls, I hear stress in your voice. So I must ask, how is your plan working as you put it, to leave the past behind a slammed door?

I can't tell you what to do but there is one offer I can make. I am leaving this note and a request with my lawyer, Wallace Johnson. He will send you the deed to this house, when I no longer need it. You may find times when you wish to get away from your busy life to be quiet. You know my belief. To stay in touch with what our hearts know and mind tries to tell us, calls for being quiet enough to hear and honest enough to listen.

With my love andbest wishes, Vyola

ꟷ

The old fashioned key falls out of the envelope. Cold first, now warm in my hand.

I wait for Brandon's phone out on the balcony, in the dark, lights moving below, rest of world going on as usual. Vyola, did you hear me, see me standing out here nights ago, talking to you and myself? I think you did. It helped anyway. Vyola, I'm going to the cottage.

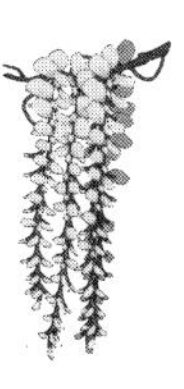

Lily

June 30, 1998

When the phone rings I brace myself to deliver a simple explanation. *While you're still traveling, Brandon. . . .*

It's Lily. "Rae, where are you? Brandon's at the bar talking but he's pissed off you're not here."

"I won't make it tonight Lily, please tell him to call me back from a quiet phone."

"Really . . . what's going on?"

"I decided to do it. Go away for awhile. So I have to talk to him. But not there over noise."

She gasps. "I don't understand you, Rae Kendall. Hey, I've got to run. He said if you aren't showing up he'll take an early flight."

"Go on. Tell him to call me. Tonight." I hang up.

Eleven now. Still no call. He's angry of course at the message delivered by Lily. Try his Houston hotel. Mr. Price hadn't arrived, but is expected, the desk clerk says.

Can't go to bed without talking to him.

Close the glass doors to stand in the hot night. Never did walk that beach somewhere out there in the dark behind this condo canyon. Wait, I hear it in the lull of late traffic. The sound of surf pulling back to surge forward again, moving with its unseen force. I know that feeling.

Back inside, waiting. One a.m. I call again. The hotel operator says yes, Mr. Price has just checked in, she'll ring the room.

I pull in a breath, waiting for Brandon's bluster and indignance. A petulant honey-sweet voice answers, "Room service? Where's our order?"

"No, Lily this is not room service."

Lily squeals in dismay hearing my voice.

I can guess that scene. Brandon always tired, impatient after a late flight, grabbing the phone to roar to me, "Goddammit, Rae, you haven't been exactly available lately, then leaving me the message you're taking off. Christ, what's going on with you?"

Had I expected any lover's apology? Ha. Brandon is being the male, seeing himself inconvenienced by both women, livid at Lily for picking up the phone.

I stay cool even with the heart beat. Tell him I need to be away for some weeks. Just a small lie there. I'll get back with him. Hang up.

I zip up the single suitcase.

The phone rings. Lily's distress gushes on the answering messager. "I know you're there, Rae, so pick up. You can't leave me feeling so horrible. I can explain. He has gone down to the bar."

I lift the receiver. "I can guess, Lily, so don't bother giving me your version. Or have you been subbing for me on these trips all along? I'm hanging up now, driving out of here in the morning. You're not the reason, actually. It's a decision—"

"He's angry at both of us," Lily wails

"Good-bye, Lily."

"Hey, wait. You really are leaving Fort Lauderdale?" Her voice perks up like a child who can stop crying now that she sees the ice cream cone. "Rae Kendall, you sly thing, you must have something going besides Brandon, that Steve somebody maybe, the hunk you sold—"

I listen with cold amusement. Why tell her that Brandon thinks she's a chattering bore, a foolish child- woman? Let her find out. "Wrong, dear friend who's been sleeping with my fiancé. I've told you. I've decided to get away for awhile, alone.

Personal reasons. Repeat that to Brandon in case he didn't get it."

"You're going off to hide? How awful."

"Not hide—it's more like finding what's missing." Chloe, and what else? Myself?

"Find what?" Lily insisted.

"Some decisions are too personal to explain."

"I figured you had secrets."

"Goodbye."

All women have secrets, Lily, they weave through our lives. And the time comes for some of us to stop and deal with them to know who we are.

I sit here, numb for moments before falling into bed for exhausted sleep. But no dreams.

Highways South

July 1, 1998

A four-hour sleep is enough when a road is waiting. A sugared second cup of hot instant helps. Decision must release a surge of adrenaline that feels like confidence, consequences to be dealt with later. Or ignored since they've already started. Last night's phone encounter tries to replay in my head, but Brandon, Lily, I'm doing a Scarlett. Will think about you later.

So close the mirrored door on silk suits, zip up the jeans and face who's looking back. Is this woman a runaway? No. What to call this thing I'm doing? A claim of time for a private experiment.

At the front door with my bag, the ringing phone stops me a minute. Am I glad or sorry the messager is turned off? Forget it. Lock this door. Ride down a thankfully empty elevator. Leave stamped mail and note in the lobby and head for the car.

Already traffic glitters in morning sun as I head north on I-95, turning up the radio clatter to drown out chatter in my head.

The dashboard bleats: "South Florida's in for a hot July opener . . . a new lead expected in the yacht party murder . . . two girls treated for heat exhaustion after the bikini shoot yesterday at the beach. . . ."

Past Boca Raton, I douse the noise. So, okay, I'll deal with last night. Brandon's angry roar, Lily's squeal of dismay.

I handled it coolly, didn't I? I know how to refuse to appear a dupe even when I find myself being one.

I drive, gripping the wheel. Lily was a surprise at first last night but for a moment. Haven't I always known the woman operates from a diamond-hard will under that wistful, well-kept surface? So face it, I allowed this to happen. Like the person who accidentally breaks a leg before the race his subconscious questioned.

Headlights flash behind me. Must have slowed speed without realizing it. The car whips past, a girl in the passenger seat glaring out the window. I wave back and focus on keeping a steady pace in stream of traffic moving north, so I can get to south Alabama.

From Jacksonville, thoughts race free of what I'm leaving behind. First plan: locate Chloe. Clear up this silence between us. Don't think of that awful, regrettable last visit. Maybe she's with that Luna and her group doing women's stories. Is she telling them what happened to her? She was going to tell me but I ran out. I hope she's hiding away somewhere to finish that book at last. *The Nurturing Feminist* will be the essence of Chloe McCullough, no matter what happened to her in the past year. Did I listen months ago when she was so quiet on the phone and I was so busy yakking about the palmy paradise?

Garth should know where she is. Means I have to locate him, hear his voice for the first time in years. He won't have to know what I'll be thinking, how I've hated him all these years. There's their daughter too, Emily, up east somewhere. And the brother she can't bear to be with, he would have to know where she is even if the man doesn't care.

Fast food marquees whip by. In a MacDonald's bathroom, washing my hands, I see a different self in the mirror. Pink faced, a few freckles without makeup. I've packed only lipstick, lotion, toothbrush and vitamins. Left behind the Zoloft.

Back on the highway now, sucking at the thick goo of a milkshake. Ahead, an endless ribbon streaking through summer woods, leaving behind small towns as names posted at rural exits.

Hours later, in a highway motel, a noisy air conditioner wakes me. Too bad. I lie here still weary but awake, debating.

I might have waited, dealt with Brandon. Handled those closings. This two month agreement by an angry boss, how good is it? No, stop the second guessing. Self punishment.

Beyond the wall, the muffled sounds have to be lovers next door. Outside in the parking lot night, bass guffaws and soprano laughs. All of them dealing with what they believe is living.

Are we on the same planet? Am I the only person between young and old, alone in a motel room tonight, rocked with questions?

What am I looking for?

Lying here I search for a sense of purpose—dare I say *joy*?—like a woman feeling her breast, afraid to find something hidden. In this case, it's the absence that's fearful.

Stop the debate. Middle of the night, alone in a generic motel, is not a wise time to question one's life. Instead pound the pillow into a new shape and give into sleep. Dream of highway lines streaming under.

A blue sky morning, a forgettable breakfast, but back on the road, the direction feels right. I punch an old tape into the dashboard and have to sing along. Frank Sinatra and Rae Kendall doing *My Way*. I'm leaving this highway, taking this exit. I want two-lane country roads.

An old farm house sits up there on its knoll under shade trees, looking proud, impervious. Does a family still live here I wonder. An old time extended family? As a child, I wanted to escape the family around me, those voluble, opinionated aunts, their solemn husbands, the women repeating their stories of others who peopled their lives. Most of my family gone now. Even the Alabama cousins are scattered, surfacing as names on Christmas cards that came with snapshots of children I've never seen. No contact really except with cousin Josey, in an RV van somewhere on an open highway.

Just ahead, a low wooden building promises Home Cooking. Next door an old time country station with a tin Nehi sign nailed to the side, two pumps in front. Waiting for me.

I fill the Mercedes' tank, walk over to Home Cooking, breathing in earthy summer air. At a plastic table, order turnip greens and candied yams. The too-sweet iced tea comes in a Mason jar, the greens, the frozen kind but cooked Southern. The drawling young girl who brought the cornbread does her hair like what she sees on TV. Before hitting the road again, I sit a-spell on a wooden table under pecan trees, eating boiled peanuts and drinking a bottled Coke.

This is being—what? Fully in the moment, Chloe used to say. Or like a runaway taking her time to wiggle toes in a creek.

In fading sunlight, I roll into Montgomery. The familiar stirs mellow memories, the old fountain still here, the Capitol still sitting at the top of Dexter Avenue. The new highways make me feel the stranger.

In beginning dark, it's time to find the cottage.

Headlights pick up the narrow street where old oaks make a tunnel of dark shade. Down toward the end there it waits. A faded yellow house with a peaked roof like some forest cottage in a child's fable. The moss-hung tree in front almost hides the driveway into the narrow front yard. Vines have crawled over the top of the door.

I pull in close. Turn off the ignition and wait. Listening to heartbeat, the key hot in my hand. In such silence, doubts rise like debris in murky water. Is this an utterly crazy notion, coming to this closed-up place, so filled with memories?

I get out, legs humming from hours of highway miles. At the weather-crusted door, the key turns but it takes pushing against inertia to plunge inside, into musty dimness of the front hall. Pensive silence here. Memories palpable as soft wings brush past.

Vyola, I'm here.

Motes slow dance in the dull gleam of the mirrored coat rack. Vyola's garden straw still hangs there. On the base, a metal box of matches and fat candle. Is this the one we held on a summer evening so long ago, listening to the thunder and crackle of lightning and talking about unseen power?

In the front room, behind drawn shades, the once- green couch, ashen gray now before a cold hearth. The air smells of faded smoke and damp passing seasons. Something scurries, and stills again.

With all shades drawn, the rooms are growing dark but I know my way. Across from the living room, Vyola's bedroom. I stand here looking. To touch the silver brush and mirror on the dresser is to touch solid memories. The little bathroom is laced with cobwebs, once white curtains, now gray and stiff. The old brass faucet yields cold water, thankfully, a welcome shock for hands and face.

I'm not ready to walk down the hall to my old room, or look into the kitchen where we always sat, calm aunt listening to whatever protests or confessions I was making at the time.

Weariness waves though every cell.

Back in Vyola's dark bedroom, I kick off shoes, peel out of tight jeans, to underpants and tee-shirt, and unhook the bra. Sink back onto blue cotton spread. Lie here, listening to faint creaking sounds. Fatigue is a magnet holding me against the solid bed. I let it draw me into welcome oblivion, as a lost child pulls up covers for comfort.

New Morning

The Cottage / July 3, 1998

Waking up in a musty room in underpants and top makes for a surreal moment or two. In the next breath, Vyola's old room is real enough. A gray sheen dulls the dresser and mirror like a sadness.

First thing to do here is force windows open.

Cobwebs lace the bathroom corners but a faint scent of lilac talcum lingers. Cold water shocks me truly awake. Pull on jeans, wander into the hall, bare feet remembering the old oak flooring.

Vyola, do you know I'm here?

I stand still, open for answers. That's what I'm here for, answers. I feel a benign, silent welcome. That's you, Vyola.

Pad down the hall, stop at the closed door of my old room before going in. This is really stepping into the past. Shades drawn behind faded chintz drapes leaves the brass bed, the oak dresser in shadow. The chair that rocked many a mile for a restless baby looks so empty. Have to back out, shut the door. I'm not ready for this rush of sweet and hurting memories. Didn't I know they'd be waiting here?

The old kitchen linoleum creaks underfoot. The maple table against the window holds a lone woven place mat. Outside the cloudy windowpane, the fence is covered with honeysuckle. The window repeats itself in the mirror over the sink on the opposite wall, both cloudy.

When was the last time I sat at this table? Three years ago maybe, when I breezed in and out, finding Vyola's dark hair streaked with silver. She was getting ready for another trip to England. It's the stopover six years ago, I'm remembering now. The time I left Atlanta behind after signing divorce papers. Came here to report I was about to reinvent myself and Vyola said don't leave your real self behind. Did I? Have I ever decided who the real self is supposed to be?

Looking around this old pine-walled kitchen now. The stove, an antique. The green refrigerator waits, propped open. In the big pantry at the end of the room, a few lone cans of soup sit on empty shelves. Behind the door, here's a note pinned on the 1997 calendar.

Welcome, Rae, on whatever day you see this. The place is yours for whatever it can mean to you. I have left you a gift in the attic-library. Vyola.

In the back hall, I look up from the foot of the narrow flight of stairs. The attic-library waits up there where I used to find her, sitting at the round table, dark head bent to some work, cigarette smoke curling from an ash tray. Whatever did she leave me? Pictures? I'll face the attic library later.

Breakfast is a pack of cheese crackers from my purse. Oh for a pack of instant coffee, but there's no hot water.

I have work to do.

In the hall closet, towels and faded leaf-sprigged sheets wait, neatly folded. A mouse leaps out, skittering over my bare feet, disappearing down the hall toward the back screen porch. Did I shriek? The still house must have absorbed it. Shivering, I track back to the front bedroom, slip into sandals before tackling stuck and locked windows.

New air moves in, warm but sweet. Alabama summer air, different from humid Florida heat.

In the darkened living room, the green leather chair by the reading lamp looks patient and timeless. The sad looking couch accepts a leaf-sprigged sheet as a fresh cover. The old

TV set is going to stay just as it is, tapestry covered. I'm not here for that kind of escape.

A filled ashtray sits on the hearth. I dump the gray dust into the fireplace behind the lacquered frame.

I have to stop, sink onto the couch to study what I love in this room, this painting over the mantel that has such a presence. The large oil painted by a famous French Canadian artist shows Vyola, at twenty, strong features beautiful with youth, long black braids coil around her head, poised against a dark background that hints of grand piano. The dark eyes and faint smile suggest a private joy.

How curious I was as a teenager visiting this house, wanting to know my inscrutable aunt's past. Didn't get many details. Only that Vyola had lost her mezzo-soprano voice before thirty, ending a beginning concert career. She'd lost the artist, too, for whatever reasons. He'd been an older man, but a lover. Maybe he died.

I would persist, asking how did she cope loosing all that, then marrying my Uncle Vance, the visiting Southerner who brought her home and in four years left her a widow. My Southern family treated her politely as an outsider. How I hated that.

I always tried to hear more of her story, why she stayed here, to teach English lit to girls at Huntington. Can close my eyes in this room and hear the answer she'd give about finding a new home and work and a Southern niece who makes up for the daughter she didn't have.

What an arrogantly innocent child I must have been back there, with my questions.

Outside, a car hums by and is gone. Quiet again.

I move on with my dust cloth. In the hall, pause at the cluster of pictures on the butler's desk. One of myself at twenty, taken in the back yard, holding a six months-old Ryan, his face against my sweatered chest. How can a memory hurt and warm at the same time?

In a leather frame, Vyola stands with a group of her students on tour on a rainy day in London. In another, five older women cluster in some living room, one of her private classes in myth, studying *Hero With a Thousand Faces*. She must have been teaching that with a focus on women before feminist became a label, its meanings debated.

On the weather beaten screened back porch, two old wicker chairs sit clumped at one end, at the other the tall wooden cabinet for her garden tools, door warped ajar now. Something rustles in the bottom. An orange-striped cat slips out of its hidey-hole, crouches a moment, regarding this intruder with amber eyes and a throaty growl. Inside the cabinet, three wiggling tiny kittens, eyes already open. It happens doesn't it, you unwed feline. No, I won't bother them. The mother cat slips under the torn screen and jumps into the yard.

I push open the squeaking screen door and go out. Stand under pale blue sky in this narrow, long rectangle of back yard. The old arbor is still here, covered with a tangle of wisteria vines. Here's where we sat summer evenings with tall glasses of lemonade and gingerbread.

The two oaks toward the back have grown so the lowest branches almost hide the alley fence. But here at the back of the house the yard is knee-high in weeds. I remember neat rows of lettuce, bunch beans, green onions and tomatoes along with marigolds.

The two-storied house to the left must be new. Don't remember the high board fence. Seems to be turning a proud back to this weedy yard. On the other side, the old Shaw place is still here, behind the wire fence, overgrown with honeysuckle and gnarled wisteria vines. They're so thick, I have a bulwark of privacy. Why does that please me so? Am I really here for a temporary escape? No, an experiment.

The old Shaw place, Lord, but it flushes up memories. One makes me smile. I must have been fifteen that summer I went through the gate to watch the tall red-headed college sophomore over there, tossing his basketball toward the hoop against the back of the house. I was the admiring teenager, watching that lean-bodied energy and upturned determined face. Even then, I guessed his throw was exuberant impatience to get out of Montgomery and to the world. Loren Shaw, yes, that was his name. Said he was going to the moon, like a brush-off to a kid admirer.

And Mrs. Shaw, whatever happened to you, dear soul. What a godsend you were back there, taking care of Ryan.

So many summers have gone by. What did I do with them? What did they do to me?

Now, a child's piping voice comes from the other side of the vines. Makes me shiver in the sun. More memories.

The cat follows me back into the kitchen. Okay, pumpkin colored mama cat, you can stay, but you're the only one allowed in this sanctuary. You won't ask questions I can't answer yet.

Hungry are you, cat? Me, too. Back to realities. Have to get the power and the old black phone connected. The car can stay parked by the front door. I want to walk this old neighborhood.

Pulling on one of Vyola's sun hats, I set out. Three, four blocks should do it. Destination, a phone booth and the corner store where an old man once bagged the beans and selected your tomatoes like gifts from his garden.

Achingly familiar here. I walk down oak lined sidewalks past old homes with porches and gardenia bushes in the yard. Already, Lauderdale seems to be on another planet.

Further on, trucks churn at one open lot where trees had been gouged out. A shiny plastic front convenience store is going in like an interloper in this neighborhood. The past is not always the best, but neither is the present that might replace it.

Beyond, the old man's corner has disappeared. Instead, across the heavy trafficked street, an island of asphalt fronts a shiny supermarket. At a booth outside, I fight with a lumpy phone book, call the power company, then go through more procedures to request telephone service. I don't want the outside world protruding on my hideaway but I have to reach out.

Inside the store, a plastic cup of hot coffee tastes wonderful. I push a basket along the miles of aisles with sudden quiet exuberance, the caffeine only part of it. *I'm a displaced person, posing as a regular shopper, here on a secret mission.* Have to shut out the strident female voice on the intercom to monitor my own gut message. This body is not salivating for, or willing to digest any contents in these pretty packages, nor any numbing libations on the liquor shelves, not any of these false panaceas for hidden hungers. Not even a quick fix of chocolate.

Instead, yellow squash, live green leaves, hard apples, bread and cheese with raisins to go in hot oatmeal if Vyola's stove still worked when the power came on.

The walk back seems longer, armload heavy. In front of the cottage, someone is waiting. A strong-bodied young woman, dark blonde hair tied back from a clear brow and serious face stands peering at the Mercedes' Florida tag. Looking up she explains, "I'm Georgiana Hale from next door. I was wondering who was here. This place has been closed for so long. I keep the front grass cut."

I adjust my packages and thank her. "Vyola was my aunt. I'm here for two months. To do some study."

With a polite smile and nod, Georgiana turns toward the Shaw house.

Back inside my sanctuary, front door closed to the world and neighbors, I dump my honest fortifications on the maple table.

Hi, my hungry feline friend, look what I brought. Shall I call you Pumpkin? It's candlelight supper for us tonight. Tomorrow, we shall have light. You're welcome to stay around and watch what happens.

The attic-library waits. Before twilight, I should go up, see what Vyola had left.

Pandora's Box

Throat tight, I climb the narrow steps. At the top, before facing the musty dim room, I force open the window and look down on the Shaw house back yard. Messy peach trees are gone but two old magnolias still make dark shade beyond a new brick patio at the back door. A child's tricycle there.

The young woman Georgiana who questioned my presence today comes out to stand, arms folded, pondering the sky. Or maybe her life?

Taking a breath, I turn now and look at the attic library. Just as remembered. Low bookshelves on each side under the slanted roof, windows at each end of the higher space where the leather chair is pulled up to the round table with its brass lamp. Vyola's old word processor sits there, she never got a computer. On top a note, addressed: Welcome Rae. Centered on the table, a familiar looking carton.

Oh, no.

Yes, it is—the box of personal stuff I left here to be dumped. Old saved letters, work notebooks, brochures from conferences, not looked at for ages, thrown into the box in Atlanta.

Now here it sits. I open the note and read:

ꟷ

My dear Rae:

I have saved these for you, against your orders to destroy them. I knew someday you would want to look back, as a traveler on a journey must do at times. The desire comes with maturity. You know I have quoted the wise who say: Life has to be lived forward, but is understood in retrospect. I found that necessary in my own life.

The only way to truly leave past disappointments behind is to understand them, then let them go. Slamming the mental door doesn't help. They will rattle in your consciousness. The contents here would surely help if you ever choose to look back. It's your choice.

Always, Vyola

ꟷ

I choose to run downstairs, to the back porch, grab a hoe, jump into the back yard to flail away at the weedy yard, crying good wracking sobs. Why? I keep on digging weeds and pushing out tears with equal fury.

Finally.

Sitting on the back steps now, in beginning dark, gulping new air. None of the Calhouns have been criers, myself included. That explosion just now was a surprise but I feel gratefully emptied. Maybe they were old, old tears. A breeze moves though the ragged arbor and honeysuckle-covered fence Now live, listening stillness. . . .

Vyola, I didn't come to relive the past but to get a clearer view of the present. That carton upstairs full of flotsam and jetsam amounts to a Pandora's box. I have two months here to find out how to go forward.

I hug my knees and rock looking at the mess I've made of weeds, the house dark growing dark behind me. No lights until tomorrow. I'll have to take that candle in the hall to find my way to the cold cereal and then to bed in clean, if musty sheets.

The Start

Fireworks echo from a distant street. Fourth of July means I'm waiting another day before the phone is connected. Are linemen out having an old Alabama picnic?

At least the power is on. Vyola's old stove works. The fridge hums away, trying to cool. Imbued with desire to do good to my sanctuary, I pull down dusty curtains before knowing if the old washing machine works.

A cat at my ankles. Okay Pumpkin, little mama, you'll get your Kibbles before I scramble an egg and look at the washer.

Glory. Water's coming in, the thing is starting to churn. I'll hang the curtains and the spread out in the sun. The weedy yard begs for my attention. And the little arbor is a mess with debris tangled with the wisteria vines. I have a great loving urge to clear it.

Evening. By the open kitchen window with a glass of tea and salad, what discoveries have I made? Besides the fact a can of tuna is a great thing to have for the secluded person without a filled pantry. More distant fireworks now. Takes me back to Alabama summer picnics in the park, kids in the swings, waiting for the call to food. The men pitching horseshoes. Women clustered around a long picnic table, with their sibilant patter, uncovering their prizes—plates of fried chicken, assorted bowls of potato salads. The sliced tomatoes would be from back yard gardens, the yellow cakes with chocolate icing made in their kitchen ovens. My mother and aunts among them, that Southern Baptist sisterhood who monitored my young life and handed down prescribed thoughts like family china.

How is it possible to love your past and resent it at the same time?

Tired now, but mellow. Should go to bed with a book. When did I ever have time to read except *USA Today* and *Time* and maybe *Vogue* at the hairdresser's. When have I thought of that little book I used to read and love? Called *Golden Precepts* about the path to the heart of the universe. Gave it to Chloe as a gift on a cold night in those Georgia woods called Freedom Farm. Wonder where they are now as women, those girls in their granny dresses.

The attic is sultry, the bookshelves dim. Here's Pandora's box, waiting. Open the top and look in. Layers of stuff here, old journals, letters and workbooks from the jobs that ruled my life at the time. Any snapshots and clippings would be in envelopes. Good, not ready to face them now. Oh my God, here's the little book Adam left with the good-bye note.

Yes, and here's the leather folder that was my first journal, waiting. My dear old faithful friend looks both familiar and strange as my own face would be in a dusty high school yearbook. Vyola handed this to me on a summer night, before the trip with my folks to San Francisco. Fateful trip.

Running fingers over the tooled surface, I remember Amy Rae Calhoun, just turned seventeen, in a broomstick skirt and peasant blouse, wearing Charley's school ring on a chain around her neck.

Memory can be so real once you allow it back. Alone here, these thirty years later, why not read what I wrote back there? Written in the back seat of my parents' Buick, riding into that first hippie "summer of love" in Golden Gate Park.

Morning. I wake to fresh curtains open to summer breeze.

Feed my mama cat. Have my coffee, waiting for the Vyola's black phone on the hall desk to be turned on. Finally, a

dial tone. Now to find the brother and Garth. Dialing information, I think of Chloe's murmured descriptions of her family. "I left and Norman stayed . . . a dead-souled man with only a bitter power-hungry drive to get his due."

Information comes up with a number for Norman Payne Investments, none for the Payne estate outside Boston. None for Chloe McCullough at the carriage house on that property. In Vyola's desk drawer, here's a neat stack of plain linen stationery and oh, groan, a crumpled empty pack of Pall Malls.

I don't risk leaving a phone message he could ignore. This has to be a letter to Norman Payne, marked personal.

Sir:

This request is brief and personally urgent.

I am a long time friend of your sister, Chloe McCullough. I know she occupied the smaller house on your property, but that phone seems disconnected.

It's important for me to locate Chloe. I would greatly appreciate any address or phone where I can reach her. Please reply to me here in Montgomery.

Sincerely, Rae Kendall.

Now to find Garth McCullough in either Washington or the Boston area. Garth, a Sixties' radical turned lawyer in a three-piece-suit with a new young wife. How ironic if his law firm represents the kind of establishment CEOs he warred against. Perhaps the reason for his heart attack at forty? I know about that from Chloe. She took him in, looked after him until he went back to his other life. At my angry response on the phone, she told me gently, as she's done often before, "Don't hate him, Rae. It's not good for your own spirit."

Finally, I have a number. When the crisp voice answers for Aylesworth, Macnair, Verbit and McCullough in Brookline, I ask for the mailing address and hang up. A letter can demand an answer and avoids questions.

❧

Dear Garth:

I am trying to get in touch with Chloe and am turning to you for help. As you might remember, we've been friends for a long time. Some months back, we had a misunderstanding. I haven't been able to find her since she returned to Boston. This is important to me. Please reply soonest to this address in Montgomery.

Sincerely, Rae Kendall

❧

I jog to the small contract post office near the supermarket with my two letters. Send them off priority. Now for patience to wait for answers. Patience while I continue to clear cobwebs in my private sanctum here. And go to bed with the old leather journal.

Last night I was a bride again on an airbase. Charley Kendall was real again, a man-sized blond boy with perfect teeth showing in his proud grin, silver wings on his jacket. Oh Charley, you're not forgotten. I just haven't had time to look back and remember.

Day Seven

Journal:

I brought you along to record this experience—this experiment of calming my urban momentum to hear something else. This isn't being Zen, Chloe, but willing to be open to my honest self. You would say, to my higher self, free of mind clutter.

No ahahs have come through. I've been busy about the place besides getting out the letters to the brother and Garth.

Cleaning away neglect has its righteous and therapeutic satisfaction but does staying busy negate what solitude might show?

No, because I'm going about what needs to be done, what I am doing here with loving care.

Looking at this sunny back yard. Cleared now. Weeds dragged back to the alley beyond the back gate. The red brown earth expects to be a garden. I answered back, it's too late in the summer to be a garden. Am I thinking it's too late for me? I've finally freed the arbor of trash from winter blows. Wisteria hangs there like a blessing, a memory of long ago summers.

Have pulled the wicker from the porch. Both need a can of white spray paint but the chair fits the body and Vyola's lounge will hold propped up feet and books I may bring out. Took my sandwich and tea out there for a midday break.

A jet drones over, a reminder other people are going places. My desk phone will be ringing back at the office, while I sit here in an Alabama back yard, in hot sun, with sweaty hands and broken acrylic nails.

Music would help. I've unplugged the radio as it only gave static and rock beat. Once I heard some strains of Wagner coming from the other side of the viney fence. The bearded one I've seen over there from the attic must have portable music. Don't think it's daughter Georgiana. She seems too preoccupied to sit in her shade and listen to Grieg. I'd love to hear some Grieg.

Watching Pumpkin allow three offsprings to knead at her willing belly, showing me there are times and circumstances calling for necessary acquiescence.

I've begun to talk back to the raked earth, to a cat, and to myself and to you, Vyola, though you stay silent. That figures. You want me to think for myself.

So—what do I know yet? What realizations at day seven?

Being alone, in this summer quiet, calls for patience. No surprise.

Also: solitude is a challenge to a body primed to move to an outside beat. So I must create my own routine. I'll walk these old neighborhood streets in the cooler night. Let a shower be a relaxing benediction. Eat with energy and pleasure, but not for escape. When images intrude, like Lily waiting for Brandon at the club, preening and pretty, working her conniving little self into his life for sure—well, put it away. Reacting to Lily is natural, but no reason to rush back to Brandon. That's not the answer I'm looking for.

Gardens

Mail has to come today. Waiting, I chop two carrots, an onion and two stalks of celery, set them to simmer with two cups of water and an easy-do package of soup mix. Sit back down with the leather journal. Reading . . . oh dear, that bus ride to Freedom Farm. Seems light years ago.

When the carrier strides up, his moist leathery face shows a big smile. He must think I'm a runaway female waiting for a lover who hasn't shown up. He finds me waiting at the door each noon.

Two letters. One from Marleen and Oceanview can wait while I rip open the formal looking envelope from Payne investments. My own letter, unopened, falls out with a folded note from a secretary, telling me Mr. Payne is at Mayo Clinic, not to be disturbed. Mrs. Payne is in Europe. My letter is being returned as it was marked personal.

Disappointment stirs the old impatience.

Garth will have to come through. I don't intend to wait. Dial his office braced to speak to him myself. A receptionist voice tells me Attorney McCullough is in court out of the city and will be going to Connecticut to see his daughter. Yes, she'll call his attention to my personal letter when he returns.

One of Chloe's theories: There are times you put out vibes, prayers, wishes with an urgency and it seems the universe is holding back on you, refusing to deliver. The silence must have its reasons before letting the answer break through.

Chloe, we have to talk about what happened to you.

Marlene's news: my last check has gone into my account, Hollis has handled a closing and sends regards, and Big Sam is still muttering about my leaving. The postscript is personal. "I should tell you I hear Brandon Price has been seen with that air-head friend of yours. Lily what's-her- name."

I deep breathe a minute, go back to the kitchen to take my soup to the table and look out on honeysuckle vines. The leather journal is open to trainee days at Sterling, Evan at the piano.

No, today I must stay in this present, focus on some hands-on task like cooking a Southern dinner my mother would have put out on a July evening. Is that being Zen, Chloe? Close as I can get.

This is better, walking these old sidewalks, past houses sleeping behind their porches so much like the kind I knew growing up in Birmingham. Jasmine bushes potent with sweet scents, they trigger images of gardenia corsages, funerals and dining room tables.

At the lot that has lost its trees for a convenience store, a truck churns out cement for the front paving. Two old kibitzers on the sidewalk look up to tell me they're not going to buy a bottle of milk or loaf of bread from this intruder.

Further on, the smell of freshly mowed lawn brings up a memory of my nine-year-old self in summer dark, lying on my back on pungent tickling grass, looking up to the canopy of a brilliant night sky, watching for a shooting star. How did such a kid, wanting the heavens to answer, become a doubter, a dutiful realist, focused on the job as the only and necessary reality? Story of my life in that question.

I slow by this next yard where a woman on her knees is working a lush border of summer annuals. She struggles to her feet, laughing at the effort, face radiant with exertion and pleasure. The image of my mother flashes bringing up poignant feelings.

I have to go up the walk, look at the riot of red poppies, yellow and orange nasturtiums, calla lilies and asters. Have to tell her that my mother used to have a garden of summer annuals like this. Suddenly, I'm remembering why those gardens stopped.

Beaming under her sunhat, she tells me, "Well now you must have the cuttings I'm pruning out. I'm so glad to see the teacher's little yellow house down the street with its lights on again."

Have to tell her I'm afraid I don't have time to do a garden. I have only a few weeks here.

In the supermarket, Georgiana Hale with her little boy stops to ask if I am settled. Toby, about five, looks up through his dark rimmed glasses, wanting to know about the mama cat. Did she have babies? So Pumpkin had been visiting through the vines. "Three babies, different colors," I tell him, "tumbling over each other now." I realize the child wants to come see. I hold back the invitation. I can't get involved with neighbors. Or a child who reminds me too much of Ryan.

Georgiana waits with a pleasant face so I say how I've watched Toby and the bearded one from my attic library window. How well they get along, the man reading to the child. I don't mention I've also seen the man stalking around the patio with his stick like someone debating with himself.

Georgiana's reply seems stiff. "My father. He's staying until his knee heals."

Resentment there? I could tell this young mother, you're fortunate having a child who wants to laugh and hug. You're lucky to have a caring male to add to the boy's life. But that's her business. I'm here to make sense of my own.

Her smile blooms back. "I see you're choosing to walk to the store, but I do have a small wire cart in the back of my car. Why don't you use it?"

Under slanting sun, I push my purchases home, including the turnip greens I'll have to wash, tomatoes and sweet potato plus a cornbread mix to bake and more necessities for my cat family.

Once home, there's a large wet bag of flower cuttings by the door.

ঌ৲

This afternoon I carefully plant gift cuttings in the cleared space as if I did have time to watch a summer garden grow. An act of faith, like this whole venture.

Looking at the woman's blooms memory burst clear from where it's been hidden so long.

A summer day on a quiet street much like these. Mother working in her garden, on the sunny side of the house. I am eleven, little sister Molly eight. We're crossing the narrow street in front of our house. From the corner of my eye, I see a white bakery truck swinging around the corner but I've already called out, Aw c'mon slowpoke.

A thud makes me turn to see something tossed and dropped to the street like a discarded rag doll in a red jumper dress. Molly's red jumper. Mother is running from the yard, falling on her knees, bending over little sister. People appear from the houses, from the truck, moving running forward. Remembering, I see it in slow motion.

That was the week I prayed so vehemently and didn't get the right answer. The forgotten garden died. So did Molly. At the funeral. We three Calhouns sat still as bruised people, nodding to others' futile platitudes. The room I shared with Molly become mine, all evidences of her gone. My parents moved about saying little, like guilty people going through the motions. I had to do the same.

Did they believe it was their duty to accept loss without release? We didn't talk about Molly only in beginning mumbles, quickly shut down. Were they too numb, too bottled in, to cry? So I couldn't let anyone see me cry. What happened back there? We never came to terms with failed prayers or imagined guilt.

My God, what a burden. Did I realize this back then? No.

Something else, too, comes up, hard to admit.

I resented my parents, for what they taught me by default. Does that make me the ultimate ungrateful daughter? There were no horror stories from my childhood, not from two parents who had to be the most responsible people on earth.

Mother, who believed wrapping you in worry was some kind of protection. Father, a solid presence, a dutiful hard-working, mostly silent man, awkward around a budding daughter, careful around a nervous wife. So he never showed or told me any clues how other men could be. And Mother, by example, you taught me to hide vulnerability behind a smile. The look of control, a smiling control, was the necessary shield to show the world, no matter how you felt inside.

So, I sit here aware of more hidden guilt. What am I going to do with this? It comes from looking back, doesn't it, Vyola? But I came to see ahead.

ACLU Attorney Speaks

Speaker drawing the most interest at the student assembly was Garth McCullough, 40, until recently an ACLU attorney and earlier a former activist with the New Left of the Sixties. Students showed little interest in the attorney's announced subject.

This junior college audience wanted to know about "hippie and counterculture" days.

The dynamic speaker seemed annoyed, but responded to questions from the floor.

"It was a cataclysmic time when fired minds believed in change," he told the students.

Asked did he miss that time or have regrets, McCullough said, "We had our personal casualties. But we woke people up to the social ills recognized today. The regret is real reform continues to be blocked by politicos whose vote go to big donors."

Intrusions

Garth McCullough's office yesterday said yes, he'd been in and left again. Surely he's seen my letter.

This morning I'm on my knees inspecting my planted cuttings, their little heads up. Each evening I pull out Vyola's ancient hose and wet them down.

Quiet here in the house. Getting use to hearing my own heart beat and ticking of the clock. Pandora's box speaks to be silently. I pour out clippings on the cleared table. Look again at the poem I wrote to Adam. A clipping Chloe sent about Garth. A brochure about a World Symposium in Pasadena . . . the sketch someone made of Chloe, sitting by the lake in Omega . . . a snapshot of Ryan on the beach when I had him down there the first time. The memories are so real I shiver.

By afternoon, I stuff it all back to go lie under the arbor concentrating on the occasional breeze. Pumpkin, you know how to relax, stretched in the sun, taking a deserved rest from kittens crawling around on the porch. I order myself to be still, embrace this quiet.

What quiet? A baritone voice booms out from the other side of the vines. The concerned grandpa over there shouts again, "Toby fellow, come down."

The vine-covered fence is shaking. On top, the boy is crouched, clutching the wire beneath the foliage, swaying on his precarious perch. I go over to call out, "He's more over here than—pull your foot free, Toby. So you can jump on this side."

He peers down, glasses askew, mouth open, uncertain, fence shaking under him. "Look at me, Toby. Let go and I'll catch you."

He struggles, falls, wide-eyed, arms out. I grab him in a swinging motion, steadying his solid weight for an instant against my chest. His explanation. "Wanted to see the kittens."

I call out, "He's okay, just some scratches. I'll bring him over." Don't want intrusions in my sanctuary here.

I let Toby watch the kittens on the porch for a minute before herding him through the house and over to his front door.

The bearded one I'd seen from the attic window is waiting in the open front door. A tall, angular presence, with a thatch of silver hair matching the beard, delft blue eyes more lively than expected. What's with the ridiculous beard? Is the man hiding behind that?

His greeting is courtly as a bow. "Very kind of you to retrieve Peter Pan." Toby mumbles his mama is going to be awful mad at both of them. Handing over the boy's glasses I look past the man into the foyer, knowing the beamed living room beyond.

"So we'd better clean you up right away, agree?" this granddad says. To me, "Won't you come in?"

Am I staring inside? "I'm remembering this house."

"Then do come in."

I follow him inside, into this old fashioned room that looks out to the patio and magnolias in the back. The couch is different but sitting where the big one was, where I'd find a sleeping Ryan.

Obeying his grandfather, Toby runs toward the kitchen then back as quick with the first aid kit.

"Yes, I'm remembering this room." Standing here, looking at oak pieces and carpet.

The man's silver head stays bent to his work, swabbing the child's scratched legs with alcohol, painting them with a line of iodine. Toby dances with the treatment, face bright, wanting me to know, "Grandpa knows everything about stars and mountains. He's writing a book about all the places he's been. Ouch! That burns. He knows—"

"Ah, but tell the lady what you know about the planets."

The child's big brown eyes go thoughtful, then with delight, "This earth has a solar system and that's the Sun, Mercury . . . Venus." Checks his grandfather's face to add: "And Mars. He knows about mountains too."

I mean to leave but a photograph on an open shelf stops me. Looking out of the frame, a round-faced little woman stands pleased between a dark-haired younger woman and the lanky young man. "Mrs. Shaw. She helped look after my son in this house until he was three or more."

"My mother." His long tanned fingers keep massaging the child's shoulders. "She visited us at Cornell. My wife, Helen, and myself."

Of course. I have to laugh. "Loren Shaw, the basketball player who was going to the moon."

He looks up, the blue gaze flashing recognition. "And you must be the girl in the bouncy skirts from next door."

"The same."

He's smiling behind that ridiculous beard. "It was destined, shall we say, that I discover this planet instead. Geological field work. And anthropology."

Toby pipes up. "Grandpa couldn't get in the Air Force 'cause he has dizzy ears."

"I found there were other mysteries to be plumbed in three billion-year-old rocks, when the earth was a hot, roiling mass beginning to sort into sentient matter. Also, fascination with the people who have inhabited its crusts."

"Your mother looked after my child when I needed that help so very much. My first job was downtown. Behind the desk of the Jefferson Davis Hotel. Gone now, I understand. So this house, her kindness, meant a great deal to me."

Loren Shaw gives the boy a pat on the bottom and sends him to put away the kit. He leans back in the wing chair. "She left the place to us. I'm afraid I never came back to it. Helen did. My wife lived here alone until Georgiana entered college. So my daughter thinks a great deal of this place."

He checks the boy is still out of hearing. "Georgiana lost her husband in Chicago, a policeman, killed on the street. She came back here, the only real home she's known."

I wait for whatever is working behind the man's face. Memory. A mellow recall.

"I was more often in the Kalahari desert in southern Africa, or a site as distant. Georgiana hasn't forgiven me for that. I don't protest, as I see it as a loyalty to her mother. I am temporarily her guest here."

He sticks out a stiff right leg. "The knee is demanding my patience. Nothing so interesting as a football injury. I have fallen on one boulder too many through the years. They had to reopen it. It's taking its time to heal."

I must go. Loren Shaw follows me to the door. Again, with courtly concern, "I hope we haven't disturbed your idyll over there."

"No idyll. I'm spending some time looking over old personal papers, journals. You might say I'm opening some old wounds, too. The idea is to heal them."

I realize the truth of that even as I say it. Is my face flushed? "Ask your daughter if Toby can have a kitten. I have three getting friskier every day."

I hurry back to my front door. It's early but I glance at the mailbox. A letter. Grab it up, get inside, and close the door on the rest of the world.

The creme linen envelope is not the mail I'm waiting for. Sinking onto the living room couch, I open the thing. Three smaller pieces spill out. First, a polite message from Brandon's secretary explaining she had obtained this address from Oceanview Tower Properties on request of Mr. Price. The second, an engraved invitation to a black tie dinner, honoring Brandon L. Price on his retirement, August 30. The last yields a note on his personal, embossed stationery, the message succinct and assured as the man who wrote it.

My Dear Rae:

Isn't it time you got yourself back here? The retirement deal is coming up and you are the woman who should be at my side. I'm ready and want you along. Forget this find-yourself crap, or whatever woman-thing you're doing and let's get on with it. Now or never.

Love, Brandon

He's inviting me back, ignoring that little matter of infidelity. And calling what I'm doing "that woman-thing."

A snapshot falls out, on the back a scrawled message: "We make a couple of winners, right?"

He means the two of us caught on a sunny day on the shaded club terrace, nothing but perfect green fairways for the backdrop. Brandon, tanned and silvered, just in from the game, having his first Scotch. At his side, Rae Kendall, broker, no trophy doll, I give him that credit, but slim and smooth enough to defy an age label. We could be a couple of models in a color spread ad, marketing whatever was being offered as the good life. The good consumer life.

To stay in that picture, I have only to write or leave a call. Poor Lily dispensed with, but probably standing by in the wings. Brandon, your invitation is an ultimatum, done with cavalier flair. No surprise. You're a man who calls all the shots. Inviting me along when you play hard as you've worked. And it's now or never to accept.

I sit here in this little house imagining the life. It means playing the charming hostess serving drinks on the yacht deck in Florida or the Bahamas. Golfing pals and cohorts clustered around you, Brandon, swapping conceits on how they ran the world better than the assholes doing it now. There'd be other women, yes, wives and recently added girlfriends, the young and older trying, maybe, to find common ground.

I could play the part as my public self. How many women have inner lives their lovers or husbands never know? Long as you look sharp and kept pace, some men wouldn't care to know. Like Brandon.

The image starts my pulse racing the old way. What should I tell you, Brandon? Now or never, right.

In the kitchen, I open an easy-do bran muffin mix and stir with quiet fury. Set the filled cups in the oven before it warms. Sit down at the table to look out at honeysuckle vines moving slowly in late sun. The browned muffins come out. Spread with butter, comfort food.

How to answer you, Brandon?

All these months in Fort Lauderdale, our relationship worked, didn't it? My independence was a convenience to you traveling as you did. As a wife, I'd be expected to follow. "Go along," like one of your board members with less voting stock and no opposing opinions.

For a man like Brandon, lack of a quick answer would say it all. He'd replace me with the same dispatch he'd replace a secretary who didn't show.

Someone at the door. I open it to a Fed-Ex delivery. I forget about Brandon, accepting the flat package from Garth McCullough,

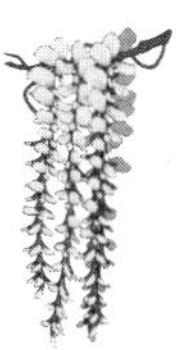

Garth

❧

In the living room I open the envelope. *Chloe, the universe has let my answer get through.* Under his office letterhead Garth has obviously typed his response himself, in haste.

❧

July 17, 1998

Dear Ray Kendall:

I received your request somewhat late. Sorry. I happened to be away, trying to see my daughter Emily. Our relationship has always been strained. At present it stands at total impasse. As you might know, being friends for so long with Chloe, Emily has grown up more a child of her aunt and uncle, the Paynes, than of our unusual and separated households. Emily was in Europe with Jean Payne four months ago when it happened. She is emotionally distraught over this, as a result, cannot forgive herself and has renewed her resentment toward me.

How can I tell you, but with the facts. You cannot know my regret, having to inform you of this.

Five months ago Chloe had a slight heart attack. I visited her at the house on her brother's estate. A week later she had a second attack. I sat with her two days in the hospital. When we talked, it was peaceful, ironic memories. Before she went, quite peacefully, I heard her say, "No more stops along the way." And more faintly, "This must be the place."

I find life delivers its sobering lessons like a belt in the gut to get our attention. Chloe's lessons were so subtle, so positive, her love so gentle, I took too much for granted. Didn't realize the strength underneath and the cost. As her friend, I am sure you know what I'm saying.

I went back to the carriage house to do as she had asked, gather up her manuscript "to put in Emily's hands, to do as she wished with it." Chloe hoped Emily would read it "to know who her mother was."

I put everything from the desk top into a fabric briefcase. I recall now she had been writing you a letter on my earlier visit. I saw the blue envelope. I don't know if you ever received it. If not, it might have been among the papers I gathered off her desk. I did manage to put the case in Emily's hands, even as she was in her car, ready to drive away from the Paynes and everyone else she knew in Boston.

Since Emily left, I have managed to locate where she is in Connecticut, but she remains inaccessible to both Paynes and to me. As you might surmise, I am dealing with a father's belated and harsh regrets about our relationship as well as the loss I have to sustain knowing Chloe is not in this world.

Knowing you two were friends for so long, I can understand how you must feel reading this. Accept my personal regrets for having to deliver such news.

Sincerely,
Garth McCullough

How long have I sat here like a hurting stone? The room is dark. Twilight outside. Must get up, move, breathe, walk shadowed sidewalks.

Chloe, can you hear me? I felt so close to glimpsing what I came here to find. Having our friendship back was part of it. Now that's ripped away and I have no right to cry at my own selfish loss.

What would you say to me now? I'm listening.

Walking and listening.

We all die sometime or another. Part of life. One sure truth.

Am I hearing you or do I know so well what you'd say?

Truth doesn't hurt. It's the resistance to the message that causes pain.

I hear that in my senses. Chloe, I believe you are alright. Always it's the ones left who hurt.

Back inside, I make myself read Garth's letter again. A hope flares. The letter Chloe wrote and was never mailed. It might be in that case with the manuscript. I have to reach Emily, I have to know what Chloe tried to tell me no matter what it is.

Emily

Eight a.m., the office in Brookline still doesn't answer. I try again minutes later. A receptionist tells me to hold. Garth's voice comes on. Formal, distant, but with the rich timbre I remember. When I tell him who's calling, he drops the formal tone. "Haven't you received my answer?"

"Yes." Silence hangs between us before I can speak again. "Garth, that letter you mentioned, the one in the blue envelope, it must in the papers you picked up from her desktop. Emily must have it." Have to pull in a breath to say, "I want that letter very much. I must ask Emily if she has it."

His heavy sigh tells me the subject is painful.

"Garth, I need her address, phone. I must call her."

Finally, "I can give you that much, but I doubt you can reach her. Emily is staying with some girlfriend up there who helps shield her. It took some time to even locate where she is."

"I'm sorry. I have to try. If you'll tell me. . ."

I write down address, phone number. Hang up from Garth, draw in a new breath and dial. It rings. I wait. A click and I'm disconnected.

More coffee, more waiting laced with praying. Dial again, someone answers. I sound breathy. "Emily McCullough, I need very much to speak with you."

A young voice answers. "You can stop calling for Emily. I'm trying to study and she will not come to the phone."

"Please. If you're her friend listen to me. Is she all right? Please."

A sigh on the other end of the line. "I try to get her out. She goes walking and comes in to curl up in there, back to me. I promised—"

"She needs to know what I could tell her. Her mother would never ever want this. I know because Chloe and I have been friends forever. No, don't go. Listen, does she still have the canvas brief case? Has she looked inside?" I wait, heart in my throat.

"A case is in there. Might as well be her mother's ghost. No, she hasn't touched it."

"Please tell Emily the contents are a gift to her. Valuable. There should be letters too, maybe blue envelopes, one to her and another addressed to me, but never mailed to Florida. I want that letter very much. If Emily would open that bag and look inside, she'd be doing something her mother wished. She should want to know that."

"I'll tell her, but can't promise anything."

"Let her know. . ."

"Call back if you like. I'll try to get her to answer."

"She could send the letter even if she's not ready to talk to me." I repeat the address, not knowing what's happening at the other end.

The line hums. I wait, visualizing one young woman opening a door calling to another. Wait some more, listening to my own heartbeat. Dial. Busy signal. Give up. Pulling a paper from the desk, I write a note that's a plea.

❧

Dear Emily,

I have known your mother so very long. So I know she would never want you to withdraw into any cocoon of hurt or self–blame. You never got to know the woman she was, but I do.

You have a great loving gift waiting in that canvas bag. The Nurturing Feminist *manuscript is valuable for more reasons than the fact it should be published. It will be the essence of Chloe's experience, her life. Inside you also should find a letter to you and another to me, likely addressed but never mailed to Florida. I cannot tell you how important it is to me to have that. And to your mother. Please look into that canvas bag of papers for a blue envelope addressed to Rae Kendall. Please, Emily, mail it to me here at this Montgomery address.*

Sincerely, urgently,
Rae Kendall

Georgiana

August 1

Journal:

I'm running out of July days according to the pocket calendar and I'm not thinking about the life and job expecting me back by September one. I'm waiting for a garden to bloom, as a proof of something. I'm waiting for Emily McCullough to mail me that letter.

The patience has a new feel. Not stoic, determined but willing. I pluck weeds from around my little plants early mornings and at twilight. I make soups the way Vyola did. From Pandora's box I read about flying for Excel and living in that blue house in Atlanta, as if I'm sitting high on a river watching how my life moved on to where it became clogged in the present that brought me here. I still can't see around the bend to what come next.

I move about and walk at night always listening, waiting. But patient. End of report August 1.

The sound of rusty front door bells pull me to the door. Mail from Emily? Georgiana from next door stands there, waiting with an eager-faced Toby, making his speech about a kitten. I invite them in.

The boy scoots out to the porch to hunker down where Pumpkin is grooming her kittens. In the kitchen, I fill two glasses with iced peppermint tea, behaving like a normal neighbor, not one in her own limbo. Georgiana leans against the old refrigerator, arms folded, talking about Toby wanting to name the kitten Cheshire, as in the Alice story.

I listen, looking back at her pleasant, pensive face. Recognize tension. She stops abruptly to ask, “Are you okay? Have I interrupted some work?”

“Not work. This has been a strange week. Had news that I’d lost a friend who’s been part of my life. I’m trying to reach her daughter now. The friend I lost would say I’m waiting for the universe to open with some answers.”

A wisful smile from Georgiana. “Don’t we all. I’m sorry about the friend. I should have called before coming over.”

“Oh, no, I need the company.” First time I’ve thought so, but today it’s true.

We settle down in the living room with our cold drinks. I explain how I’m surviving without air conditioning with this floor fan, lots of showers and night walks when it’s cooler. She sips her tea and looks around. “This is a sweet place. My mother would come over here to talk to your aunt. I remember a tall gracious woman, her dark hair with the silver streaks from the temples. I was in high school at the time, absorbed with my own life, but I know those visits helped my mother.”

“I can believe that.”

Toby runs in with the black kitten with white paws. I warn them this is Boots. He hasn’t taken to being held yet. I’ve tried. Boots leaps from Georgiana’s lap. Toby and kitten ran back to the porch. “He couldn’t wait to get one though we’ll have to leave it with my father for a week. I’m taking Toby with me to Chicago. We’re going to visit the man I’m thinking of marrying.”

The faint smile gives way to what’s obviously on her mind. I nod encouragement.

“Brent’s a police lieutenant, forty-two, never married, dedicated to his work. He was in the same district with my husband when Tobias was killed on duty.”

Toby again, another consultation. No, this gray and white cat wasn't going to be Chessy. He runs back to the porch.

"Brent hasn't seen Toby, not since he was born. We've been writing. Talking on the phone. I went up there a few days in April, alone. He's expecting me again, we have a lot to talk about, but this time I have to take Toby. Don't you agree? I can't decide anything until I go up." The direct gaze turns luminous with uncertainty.

"And see them together, decide what kind of a father Brent would be."

Georgiana puts her cold glass against her cheek a moment. "A child is shortchanged without a father. Ask me, I know. Brent is a true bachelor. No kids in his experience. But a good person. Do I sound like a dope, being so uncertain?"

"You sound honest." I don't hear any romance or anticipation in this situation. "If you didn't move up there and marry, what else would you like to do?"

Georgiana sits upright like a bright faced kid knowing the answer. "I'd start my school."

I invite her to tell me. She begins with enthusiasm. How she and a friend have talked, and worked out their ideal private school based on their experience in overcrowded public schools. "Beverly and I started this when we roomed together while getting our masters. It's a dream we share."

"A dream or a real plan?"

"Both. We still talk on the phone and email ideas. The plans includes small classes, of course, and a home atmosphere. Kindergarten through grades six. The early years are the vital for triggering a child's desire to learn. To lose that you've lost the best opportunity to wake in them the desire, the thirst for learning on their own. Trigger that desire early and you're instilling a gift that serves all of their lives." She pauses with a self mocking smile. "So here I am, a substitute teacher in crowded classes, teaching my own child at home."

"My aunt should be here. Vyola would tell you choices are the way around stone walls that appear impossible."

"I think you're telling me that now. But it's a big stone wall."

"Such as?"

"Start-up money, of course. I have a little insurance from Tobias. But that's invested for Toby, for his college. Ask my father? Oh, no."

"Does he know about this? I've seen how much he enjoys teaching Toby." I see her wince.

"I couldn't ask him for help. I haven't been the loving daughter these four months he's been here. It's the first time we've been together for any length of time. Besides, he has his own concerns."

She tells me about letters from Cornell he doesn't discuss with her. "I suspect he's miffed at not being given the position or program he expected after returning to campus this past spring with the bad leg. I happen to know academia politics are an anathema to him, so he's not one to fight the system. He loved the work he did and truly deserves recognition. He's back from his field work, doctors' orders."

Why do I care about this girl? Her sincerity, yes, and needing to say this aloud to another woman. She knows what she wants, but is about to go in the opposite direction. As I was with Brandon. What am I going to do about him now? Haven't wanted to think about it. All I do want is to hear from Emily.

"Couldn't your father help?"

"No, I could never ask him for money and I doubt he could come up with any. My father is a visionary as well as a scientist others quote, but when it comes to investments, he's an innocent by choice. Living so long with native people, the least of his interests would have been a stock portfolio or the gyrations of mutual funds. He probably only has university retirement coming."

We're quiet for minutes.

"All those years he wasn't in our lives he was happy out in the field. He's here, being stubborn, waiting them out, at Cornell I suppose. Pretending to write his book."

"Pretending?"

"He has tons of old records. Reads them out in the yard. When I happen to look into his room to say goodnight he'll be sitting at the computer but not typing. Just dreaming."

Toby marches in beaming, holding the orange kitten same color as Pumpkin. "This one is Chessie." His mother nods.

I bring out a small towel to transport Chessie home and a tin of kitten food and a bag of cat box gravel to get them started. At the door, Toby delivers his practiced thanks and Georgiana reaches out to hug me for an instant. "Thank you for listening. I hope something good will happen to you to balance the other." The gray-green eyes say she means it.

"You helped." I want to tell her, Georgiana, you don't want the man in Chicago, you want your school. It must be satisfying to know what you do want.

Loren

Beyond the viney fence, Loren Shaw is playing tapes again. Yesterday, Grieg, and something from Tchaikovsky. At this moment, exquisite sounds from a soprano throat float over to me. The woman's voice lifts and flows, conveying discovery mixed with pathos. I know, I know. Besides, I'm lonely.

I debate only a moment. Go to the fence to call out, "Hi, over there with the music."

The top of his silver head appears. "My neighbor speaks."

"Company is welcome." A pause. "Shall I meet you at the front door or will you try Toby's route?"

I surprise myself. "Won't need to. There's a gate here. Be there in a few minutes."

I run back to the porch like some kind of a fool, but what the heck. Grab Vyola's hedge clippers, come back to whack at the vines covering the old metal gate. Replace the clippers, pick up a squirming kitten, my calling card, my excuse, and I'm back at the gate, announcing myself, pushing it open enough to squeeze through. Loren Shaw is there to help, a lean, tanned Santa Claus in blue shirt and jeans. Still with that ridiculously curly beard.

"Daughter and Toby are away for now but stay," he says once I'm on his side of the vines. "They'll be back. Not going to Chicago until tomorrow. I offer a canvas chair and a cold lemon tea."

Was that a hint of a bow? The smile looks genuine. So this is the sun and shade yard I see from upstairs. Deck chairs wait inside the deep shade of the magnolias, back from the open patio. Already Loren Shaw is pouring me a drink from a frosted pitcher. The table also holds the radio-recorder, source of the soprano's voice.

"I'm interrupting your study," I protest. A second table by his chair holds a stack of books, and heavy black notebook, pen protruding from its pages.

"Not at all." Loren Shaw tucks a paper napkin around the tumbler and hands it to me, waves a hand toward the other chair. "On an Alabama summer day, a pause for iced lemon tea is a necessity, especially deserved for someone who has cut through a barrier between neighbors."

I take the tumbler and sink into the deck chair. No reason to bolt out of here as I did when I brought Toby over. The shade is great and I say so.

He nods, turning the soprano down to faintly audible. "As you see, we haven't clipped our side of the fence from its natural abandon. Georgiana lets it grow because the place over there looked so lonely. She imagines you want it to stay that way now."

"She must think I'm hiding away. Guess I am, but not from anyone else."

I watch him straighten the right leg out to match the other before leaning back to lift his own tumbler in a gesture of a toast. "Here's to Alabama back yards from the past."

It's a professor's voice, musing aloud to himself.

"And to this breeze," I add, lifting mine.

Magnolia leaves stir and still again with the soprano's faint notes. In the mutual quiet, I study the man's intent profile for a trace of the exuberant red-headed sophomore who leaped about this yard with his basketball. Lanky body, still straight shoulders, yes. What is he now? Fifty-six or so? Surely not old enough for a scientist and professor to spend a sabbatical in his daughter's back yard letting that crazy beard grow even with a knee to heal. So who else is hiding here?

"Sometimes," he says softly, as if aware of what I'm thinking, "one has to have his world shrink to take a look at himself. A hometown back yard will do."

I want to talk to this man. "My world was a crowded schedule in Fort Lauderdale with its lush foliage under glittering sun, impatient traffic heading for fairways and malls. I sold space as lifestyle and status, protected by electronic surveillance in the lobby."

A rumbling bass laugh. "Still studying? Has my music disturbed you?"

"Oh no. And this exquisite voice speaks to me."

"Kiri Te Kanawa. I have a fondness for sopranos. I found their female voices a comfort in many a lonely place on the earth." He glances over with a sly smile. "I've never admitted so before."

We're quiet again, looking out across sunny patio and back of the white frame house, a maple tree near the vines rising up against its second floor. I wonder if the basketball hoop is still up there. Looking at the back steps I can imagine Ryan, aged two, sitting there. Have to shake off the image. I ask Loren Shaw, "So, how is the knee coming along?"

He strokes the stiff leg. "The flesh is willing but the spirit is rebuking me for my impatience. And you, neighbor? You appear more relaxed than when you retrieved Toby." His shadowed eyes are blue as his shirt.

"Something else." A curious acceptance. "I just learned I've lost the friend I came here to locate. She died four months ago. It leaves me quiet inside, has me talking to my garden and myself."

"Self-scrutiny? Most people don't take the time."

"I find when you stop and look back—it's all here again, little moments, and major traumas."

He taps the heavy notebook beside him. "Yes. Your old enthusiams and questions and stubborn assumptions."

I laugh with him. It feels good. "I've been looking back at forgotten landscapes."

He repeats the word. “Landscapes.” In his musing professor’s voice he tells me about far off places that fired his interest for forty years. Mountains and deserts that held for him the mysteries of the earth.

“You must have had that drive always. I’m remembering the college boy who wanted the moon.”

“Ah, yes. Certain experiences in childhood can be the defining moment for a life. An old book of astronomy for me, it led the boy’s nose to seek out other mysteries. The curiosity, once fed, can become a drive in the man. Or woman.”

He turns quiet, looking up at magnolia leaves. “In retrospect, one has to wonder at the cost of such myopic intensity. The cost, professionally, and personally.”

“I would guess you don’t regret. . . .”

“True.” His long fingers comb the white beard. “I can ‘t regret the focus. When it’s given, you accept it, pursue it.”

His words stir a familiar wish, a belief Chloe and I shared. “I’ve always thought having such a motivation, knowing what you want to do in life would be like a gift. It would mean you had a purpose, a meaning to your life.”

Should I tell him about his daughter’s desire to open a school? Her detailed plans and purpose? Or would that be interfering in their lives?

Loren Shaw looks over at me. “And you, neighbor? You seem to have given the premise some thought.”

“Oh, afraid I’ve never found mine. I’m basically a dreamer who got stuck being a realist, of necessity. Had to focus on earning a living.” I want to tell him I know Carl Jung said life is wasted if we don’t embody some essential. And I’ve read psychotherapist James Hillman’s acorn theory that we come into this life coded with a purpose though we don’t always find it.

A new breeze moves, sweet with honeysuckle. He says, “I would venture you’ll find it. Most people need a few decades of experience before making that discovery. You’re young, Rae—it’s Kendall, isn’t it?”

"I could use some discoveries. That's what I came for. Haven't found what's missing yet, only what's lost. Well, thanks for the lemon tea and sympathy. Time for the mail and hopes."

He braces his knee before pulling up to his lanky height. "My dear neighbor, I believe you're looking for the Philosophers' Stone, not only mining old personal artifacts."

I laugh with him. It feels good. "You've been kind to listen. I have interrupted your work, I know. You're writing?"

"You are looking at yet another researcher's attempt to put down forty years of accrued theories and experience. I've had this in mind for ten years. First chance I've had to read all my notes. Fresh reading complicates my original intentions, but that is as it should be. Ideas worth expounding should be possessed with the vitality of truth. And the truth can expand under scrutiny."

So he is writing a book. And his daughter doesn't realize how important it is to him.

"On with our present missions," he says at the gate, holding it so I can push through. I close it behind me.

August

On my knees at my patch of garden. It's rooted, growing. Strange how digging close to the earth frees the mind to go racing on its own.

Emily McCullough, I'm talking to you. Look into your mother's canvas briefcase. She wants you to know who she was. Really know. And send my letter. I have to know what's there.

Brandon, should I have told you thanks, but no thanks because this woman, forty-eight, is still wondering who she is meant to be, wants to be, when she grows up.

No, to write anything at all demands a response to the remark about the woman thing and find-yourself-crap. I'd have to inform him the phrase is a glib label bandied about, a cliché for a timeless human need to know why you're here and who you're meant to be. No, intangibles can't be explained to anyone closed to them, even bright and quick engineers.

Is that why I couldn't love you, Brandon? I tried. Tried longer to fool myself. It didn't work.

I'm thinking of that snapshot, the two of us looking like a couple of models advertising the benign good life against a background of green fairways. I could tell Lily it takes more than the money, honey, for some of us. If we haven't dealt with past husbands, lovers, children, career battles—yes, and stupid affairs, secret depressions and private guilts.

I survived all of the above, didn't I, Vyola? But how do you clear out that closet? Haven't found that out yet. And my time's running out here.

Ryan, do you still hate me? What could I possibly do to ease that for both of us?

And Bertie? Something's left there unfinished between us.

Mother, so much left unsaid between us way back there.

Adam. I didn't expect a future. Just needed love at that time from a man like you. What to do with that frustration?

And Whitney, do I owe you any explanation?.

Admitting unfinished issues doesn't answer what to do with them.

Vyola, I know why you saved Pandora's box. Now, how to dump it from my life?

Confidences

Still nothing from Emily after my follow-up second careful note. So I go out and gather new blooms from my wildly spreading nasturtiums to take to Georgiana. At the fence I call out, "Is your daughter home?"

"Come over and I shall report."

I yank more vines free from the fence and go through, muddy-kneed jeans and all, carrying a fist full of color. "I wanted to tell your daughter these flowers prove something. It's not to late to have a garden. She'll understand."

He's still with the beard, half glasses perched on his nose. He finds a glass of water for my bouquet. "Georgiana and the boy are stopping by to see a friend. Sent me a postcard from Chicago but no comment otherwise." He waves me toward a chair. Toby's yellow kitten pops up on the patio table that's piled with books and morning paper.

I say, "You're working."

"Procrastination is allowed. Some of the best thoughts come in while letting go of the actual work."

I accept the iced coffee along with the shade and breeze. We talk of the newspaper headlines, a devastating earthquake somewhere in China. "All those people lost," I murmur. "I used to say God was unfair. I was a child and that's a child's simplistic response. Back then I really wanted confirmation otherwise. I was pushing my little nose into the Almighty's business."

"A scientist gets a glimpse." He leans back, telling me about earthquakes and plate tectonics—how a fluid mantle lies beneath this live earth and how the poles wander.

We're quiet again in this sun and shade.

"Georgiana and I have talked," I have to tell him.

"So you know she's caught in indecision, as I am."

"Loren, she doesn't want to marry the nice man in Chicago. Are you aware of her real desire? To open a private school for beginning grades. She has a plan all worked out."

He glances over. "She spoke of it once. I'm afraid my daughter doesn't care to confide fully in me. I believe she will be quite relieved when I leave. That will clear her mind about whether to marry this man or stay here."

Did he hear me? "You'd be interested in her plans. She should have told you."

He is silent so long I think I have intruded..

"We haven't shared much these months. But I understand Georgiana's attitude toward me. I have an old, well-documented male guilt. As you must have gathered, I chose my work over a being a husband and father. Acknowledging the regret doesn't repair the damage."

"I know." How well I know. Just as I was thinking over there.

"If it were possible," Loren Shaw says quietly, "I would write my wife, Helen, say what I couldn't say before. Unfortunately, it's ten years too late. She died from cancer with a new husband by her side."

An idea flashes in me like a warmth. It might not be new but I've never thought of it before. I want to hear myself say it, but he's confiding now about the real letters he finds difficult to write. "My farewell thanks to my daughter, for one. The university for another, the powers that be there await a reply I'm not ready to make."

I bounce up, energized. I don't care if he'll be amused. "Loren, that letter to your wife—why not write it? Get it out of your system. We can't change the past but we might change ourselves." Affect our own closure, I'm thinking. "The letter doesn't have to be mailed. As for Georgiana, you can still talk to her."

He shakes his head like the usual stubborn man about such suggestions but follows me to the gate like the gentleman and scholar he is.

Letters

❧

At the cleared maple table I start writing.

❧

Dear Ryan,

I wish devoutly this message could reach you. Regardless, I need to write it.

I wake so often before dawn, wondering where you are, if you've found your direction, and the place you need to be, a home for the heart. We never had a real home together, I know. In my mind I see your mop of curly hair, the strong brow, the man-sized shoulders you had at seventeen. I try to imagine your answering gaze, but it alludes me. All I know is that you're still somewhere in Hawaii, which island I never knew, and that you use a different name. You must know the remaining drug charge was long ago dismissed, yet you stay away.

You wrote to your Aunt Bertie once without giving us a clue to how we could answer back. I wish you'd write her again. She's diabetic now, not well. Louella takes care of her now. You never doubted Bertie's love. She deserves to hear from you.

As I write this I am in Montgomery where you were born. Alone in Vyola's little house, looking back, realizing the void I left in your life was more than the lack of an established home, or my regular presence.

You needed to know about your father and I could never talk of him. Forgive me, Ryan, forgive me.

Young mothers make mistakes when they feel alone and floundering. They may hide it, but they're vulnerable with self-doubt as to what happens next. It's too easy to grab at whatever seems the way out. For me it was jobs. Did it for both of us when I brought you to Atlanta.

Here, alone in this cottage, I've been reliving all of my choices made back there. These weeks have been a private self-imposed experiment to do that.

Some people say it's the journey that counts.

Here is what I want most to tell you: I'm glad you are in this world. I've always loved you, even your ability to express anger with such articulate fire. If that anger can become purpose, what a role you could play in whatever field you chose. What a man you could be. I hope you've already found that out.

With love from your Mother

ᘛ

To my own Mother,

On this summer evening, 1998, alone here in Montgomery, your face is an unfocused memory, yet the sense of you has become real. So is the need to speak to you.

Yes, it's Vyola's house, though she's been gone for more than a year. You might say I'm here cleaning out the attic, opening up moldy guilts and unresolved frustrations. The idea is to trash what shouldn't be held on to, retrieve what needs to be saved. The unpacking had to come first. That's why I must talk to you, all these years later.

I realize you became a faded picture in an album for me because your memory was buried with resentment. You left before we really knew one another beyond our roles as mother and daughter. Martha Calhoun, we never knew one another as one woman to another.

Here other glimpses of you have come back. The rapt look you had in church. The pleasure you had with a garden. Your dreaming, eager profile watching a movie about lovers. I sometimes caught you preening or staring into a mirror.

We were living the roles we had inherited. Your overseeing, selfless, fussy mother made me the falsely dutiful child, hiding her reactions. My silent father, too. Later, I must have tried the opposite way. And I failed my son.

The best choice must be somewhere in between, I've decided. Mother, you don't know how difficult it is these three decades later. Popular culture changes fast as commercials flash on our screens. What's new is sold with as much subtlety as a shouting sideshow barker. Parents have to compete. What you and my father tried to do is remembered now only for its errors, or the opposite, preached from political pulpits as lost perfection.

Here alone, I've allowed myself to look back and see us all. With love and good humor, I've been forgiving us all. Right now I can tell you a loving goodnight and good-bye.

Your older but wiser daughter,
Amy Rae

August 5, 1998

Dear Bertie

This is the letter I couldn't write before.

How long has it been since we were on the phone together? Not since you were kind enough to call and share your letter from Ryan. Being left out did hurt, but I was truly glad he let you know he'd found a life there in Hawaii.

If only he'd given a clue as to where we might find him.

No, I've never received the same from him, or you would have heard from me. I'm writing this now from my Aunt Vyola's little house in Montgomery. I've been here for weeks, a self-imposed retreat, to look at my life, before making any new choices.

Bertie, I'm writing to send you genuine thanks for the love and the home you gave Ryan. In all my visits there when Ryan was with you, I tried to admit my appreciation but it didn't come across very well. For reasons. We were both assuming we knew what was in one another's mind and heart. Were we both wrong?

Those visits in Birmingham were a bittersweet time for me, arriving as I was from a trainee's long hours or later from hotel rooms. It meant stepping back into the kind of home I knew as a child. You and your family and a few cousins of mine were the extended family I no longer had.

I was glad Ryan had that kind of grounded home rather than baby sitters even though it meant your resentment to me. Yes, I was grateful he was there while I was learning how to be in the world. Things were changing for women but not soon enough in the seventies and eighties for most of us, thrown out there to sink or swim in a male-dominated world. You didn't understand but that is past.

Another issue always between us: You were calling me a lost soul until I asked God for forgiveness. I want you to know I believe that now, though not as you preached to me. I believe that forgiveness is always there. But before we know that relief, we have to forgive ourselves. Not from being born in sin, as you say, but because we're fallible humans who collect little guilts and regrets along the way. I hope you well, Bertie, and hope you will hear someday from Ryan.

Sincerely, Rae

ꕥ

August 6, 1998

Dear Whitney,

I'm writing to you these years later because I am clearing off my personal ledgers of past choices. Don't frown, this is not a bitch from a former wife. I may even find something to thank you for.

I imagine your life goes on in the way you always manage it. Perhaps there is another woman in that house on Lullriver now. You are an attractive enough man. Women notice you and you like that. You let them come to you without exerting any charm to keep them there. If you have remarried, I hope the woman is clever enough to redo that tiresomely blue house, strong-minded enough to ignore your protests. Why didn't I?

First the belated thanks. Whitney, you did force me to learn about money, value of, record keeping of. A practical lesson I needed.

By writing this down, I realize something else. I don't need to mail this letter.

Rae

ꕥ

Dear Adam,

Wherever you are, I hope you will feel this message from a foolish woman who needed your love back there in Atlanta. I have allowed myself to remember those months.

It helps to know the kind of person your soul recognizes. If for only a time. I hope you are somewhere painting now, with kind thoughts of that uptight girl at the Yoga Centr. I can still think of you with love, so maybe you still feel the muse you spoke of in that letter.

Love, Rae

To Sheila,

Thank you for being the hard teacher, wiser than I realized. You were more important in my life than Evan. Looking back I see you were capable of forgiveness. I hope Evan grew up and went back to you, if you still wanted him.

Your student, still learning, Rae

Countdown

Waking to sun on the curtains, wet glistening honeysuckle beyond the open window. These old curtains should be changed. Absurd thought.

Marleen has warned me to call the office today. I want to lie here as if deadlines weren't looming.

Need to be finding someone to take a cat family.

Have to go out and see if my garden still has its heads up after last night's torrent of rain. Something new and crisp in the air, promise of September. Deadlines. Have to make that call to Florida.

But not yet.

At the kitchen table with a scrambled egg and coffee, I dip into Pandora's box and pull up a notebook to browse. Have to smile at who I was.

Today, I will let happen what is to happen. Won't even stand at the door for mail from Emily McCullough. Last note I told how I first saw her in Chloe's arms, as Emilybird. The universe might relent, let an answer come through. right, Chloe? I've relinquished demand.

I set out to stroll to the store. A woman is in the front yard of the big house next door putting up a realtor sign. We talk. She says the owners are selling because of the convenience store. They're angry, believe the neighborhood will turn commercal. They hope someone will buy their place for a noisy restaurant and bar.

Their reaction, their choice.

The shaded sidewalks are rain fresh. Once at the main street I have to wait as usual for traffic whipping by. Today it's an assault to the senses, endless cars driven by intent robot profiles. Is this what quiet can do to you? What a conditioned lot we must be, living with the bombardment of noise, the need for rush until it 's part of our own pulse.

Now the bright-lit, chilled supermarket. Conditioned again, I slow in front of blatant headlines from celebrity purveyors. This week again, they fed me famous faces finding love, loosing love, having a love child, getting too fat, becoming too thin, denying rumors of impending death, changing partners or sexual inclinations. False lures for real hungers, like cheap candy on the next rack.

Stroll home with cheese, apples, cereal, milk, and kitty food. Take my time like a satisfied dreamer refusing to look beyond today. But waiting . . . yes.

At the front door here's Georgiana, the dark blonde hair pulled back from her eager face. "I need to ask you something." She follows me to the kitchen, drops in Vyola's chair as I pour her tea and bring out ice. "Chicago?" I begin for her.

"Brent has his life up there. And his long hours. I didn't see us as a family. I thought I'd tell you." Something else is clearly on her mind. I sit opposite to listen.

"We came in yesterday to find Dad gone. I feel terrible, as if I've run him off. Did you talk with him at all in the past week? I hoped you could give me a clue to his attitude."

"Did he leave a message?"

"Yes, a note, thanking me for his four months stay. A polite note. I feel terrible. We hadn't talked about the past but he must have felt the resentment I've grown up with, you know, not knowing him."

"Old stuff interferes with the present, I know."

"All the time he was here, I'm afraid I must have acted like an impudent teenager, punishing him for that past. And yet, I am proud of the man and his work. I really am. Did I tell him? No. Invite him to talk about it? No."

Georgiana hugged her arms. "He didn't confront me about anything. You must have seen how he is. All that insular dignity."

"From what I saw, it wouldn't have been accusative silence."

"I suppose his work has been observing, recording, without intruding on the subject. But I must have hurt him. And now he's gone back to campus to be a part of a department not of his choosing. I do happen to know his dislike of campus politics."

I let her talk. She needs to.

"So he left thinking I didn't want him. Now he's sending me a gift from up there. Like a payment. That really makes me feel terrible. Paying me rent is, oh, ridiculous."

"I don't imagine Loren Shaw does anything that's ridiculous, or even unkind. The thanks have to be sincere."

"That's what makes me furious with myself. Toby enjoyed him being here. He'll miss him terribly. There was a man in my son's life, his own grandfather, and I ran him off. Yes, I did. I kept telling myself he needed the push to get back up there, claim his rights. He was biding his time here."

"Enjoying Toby, yes. And working on his book."

"Oh, his book. I figured all that writing, the time upstairs, was something to keep him occupied."

"Actually, Georgiana, the way he spoke of it to me, the book is of major importance to him, has been for years. He's been absorbed with it here. You two really should have talked about your plans. Your father wants to put down the culmination of a career, which should be a major task. Did he take that large notebook with him?"

She sits upright, gray eyes bright, studying me. "He told you that? I didn't know. Now I'm really feeling horrible. He took the laptop he used upstairs, but all the rest of it, five heavy notebooks he left packed into a corner of the bookcase."

"You can still write him, say he was welcome. Say you're proud of him. Tell him you've saving his research papers. He'd appreciate that and you'd feel better."

She gets up to leave, looking lost. "I'm sorry you're leaving, neighbor. I've needed someone who would listen to what I've kept inside. Bev is coming tomorrow to stay a month. Once we started back on our plans we couldn't stop. We're doing some serious planning. It's a wild hope but we're going to try for a loan or endowment."

"I'm happy for you. It's meant to be."

Still she waits. "Thanks for listening. It's still in our heads though. My, is this your notes you've been reading? A box full?"

"My Pandora's box. I'm about to the bottom. Found lots of memories and chagrin in there."

"Well finish. Remember the last thing that comes out of Pandora's box? Hope."

At the front stoop she surprises me with a sudden hug before stepping back. "Wish you weren't leaving. If it ever happened for us, Rae, you're just the kind of person we need in the office, to speak for us, and work with parents. Listen to me. It's still a dream. When do you go?"

"I don't know. I really don't know."

As she crosses to her house, the mailman is walking toward me with his congratulatory grin to hand me a letter. It's from Emily McCullough in Connecticut.

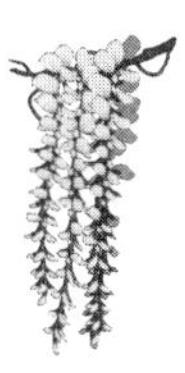

Chloe

Emily's large envelope yeilds a thick blue one addressed to me in Chloe's flowing script. I unseal it so carefully. Inside, two letters, folded separately, different dates. Gulping in a new breath, I read the first.

Boston / February 29, 1998

Dear Rae,

I'm here at the carriage house, wrapped in a blanket lying on a chaise lounge in the sun like a recuperating heroine in an old Bette Davis movie. Have been reading something that makes me think of you, of us.

It's Thomas Mann, writing to friend Hermann Hesse he hadn't seen in a long time. He says of that friendship, "our paths had taken separate courses through the land of the spirit. And yet we were always fellow pilgrims, always in each other's thoughts."

The reply from Hesse speaks for us both. "I wanted only to try to live in accord with the promptings which came from my true self. Why was that so very difficult?"

True, true, my friend. For both of us. Knowing our friendship, Garth once said we must be a "pair of dreamers, caught in the real world, trying to connect with the energy of the moon." I told him yes, "down the labyrinth of ways, chased by the Hound of Heaven."

Rae, we must talk. That meeting at the sanitarium was all miscues. You walked away too quickly. I realized why, once you were gone. At the time, I couldn't call you back. One's response is slow when the lungs are fighting for prana and the body has to relearn how to function without chemical help.

How long has it been? Weeks? A month? Clarity also suffers when you're pulling out of a medicated mire. Time is sand pouring through the fingers.

I wrote you a note. Luna mailed it for me. It wasn't meant as a reprimand, but perhaps you thought so since I've heard nothing from you. I'm writing now because I have been holding much to tell you.

First about Luna. She is a person who emerged from a wretched childhood to become an indomitable voice encouraging other women, not by writing books, but speaking to small groups at retreats across the country. She has been friend and catalyst to me these past five years. I realize her rudeness at the door stunned you. She can be abrupt. Yes, she's a lesbian, and yes, in my way I love her as I do anyone who has earned her wisdom. It's not a physical relationship, but a sharing of work and purpose.

Rae, haven't we've agreed many a time, laughing, but meaning it—an honest friendship between two women is a more dependable blessing than a lover?

Next, about your shock and disappointment seeing me in that dismal place.

You believed I floated above hurt and I tried to do that. Willed myself to do that. Should have remembered what a Sufi Master has said, "Who, with a living heart, can live in this world as it is and not suffer and not experience pain?"

Stress must have built, even as I thought I was accepting Garth's marriage, and the years of Emily's defection, seeing me as her hippie mother, hoping someday she'd understand me. Failing with her sent me back to my mother, to sit with her hours so many afternoons in that place, demanding myself to see contact in her eyes. I'd forgotten it doesn't work to demand. Some things aren't meant to be. It was too late of course. I should have let her go and not stayed like a sacrifice.

From that scene, I would rush back to work as therapist, dealing with angry teens, and pregnant girls and women telling their victim stories. Stubborn self-sacrifice is burning the candle at both ends but the light is not pretty. It's called burn-out. You begin to feel false.

I know, you've always warned me about giving too much of myself. It's true, the body can handle just so much.

*That book I wanted you to read—*Thirst for Wholeness*—explains what was happening to me. I wanted you to read it to find out what I couldn't tell you myself. The book is a wise and honest account of attachment, addiction, and the spiritual path. The author is a psychotherapist who has been there. I couldn't bring myself to tell you on the phone when you were so filled with your Florida life. I knew I'd be such a disappointment for you. All these years, even as you worried about me like a surrogate sister, you wanted to believe I was floating above it all, protected.*

Emotional fatigue can mount like a fog coming in, draining the color out of your days, the strength from your body. At Jean's insistence, and Emily's testy demand, I saw the psychotherapist they set up. A mistake. He was a clinical and chemical person, with no recognition of a spiritual emergency.

With his chemical help, Rae, I became lost because the spirit gets lost in a meaningless fog. For my mother it had been pretty alcohol drinks, then the bottle. She crawled into that dark cave and never came out. For me, there were little pellet and capsules that can be slipped into the mouth, to sleep, to forget, to keep moving with no regard for what they're doing to body and mind. Once you flounder in that dark pit, you listen only to your own devilish despair.

I wanted so to tell you about this, eye to eye, but then Luna was there, you ran out. Here it is.

I know you dislike the word surrender. I found it becomes a necessity. Not as you thought of it, not as you might have heard it preached, as a requirement from others to make some abject humbling announcement. Rae, it's an intimate, internal process.

Surrender is realizing you're in this hopeless dark pit and the only way out is up. First it calls for flushing down the false escapes. I had bad days and worse dreams for awhile about a pilot light inside, gone dark. I had to remember yes, it was once there.

At first I saw only the dull light of ordinary reality around me, the same old physical and work demands. This calls for accepting each new morning, knowing your body is still alive, functioning without false help. You hold on to that, refusing doubt. Then the light is there again, gentle but a sense of some strength within and beyond myself.

Call it God, Christ Spirit, Divine Intelligence, whatever one needs to call it. Haven't we always agreed, it's the naming that causes debate and wars?

I've seen why you don't trust it. You look at us fallible humans, vulnerable in our different ways, primed by egos, trained by circumstances. You can't wait until the stars answer or God taps you on the head as proof. Rae, it's in you. Just remember with the wisdom of your own heart to pump and your lungs to demand breath.

I'm here in the carriage house getting strength back and watching a new spring happening. Forgotten perennials are showing up. My cat is sleeping at my feet. I've been putting together the last version of my Nurturing Feminist *manuscript. I had hoped to hear from you but couldn't wait to share this experience. Not everyone would understand. You have to be there, as the cliché goes. And I was. I shall be wiser now for it, when I get back to my work.*

Write to me Rae. Call me. There is something more we need to talk about. Will close for now to rest,

Always your friend, Chloe.

So she was waiting for me to call and I didn't.

How cruel not to reply to a letter like that. But I didn't get it. Why wasn't it mailed?

I open the second letter.

Boston / March 10, 1998

Dear Rae.

My recouperation has a second chapter. Since writing you, I have been in a small hospital. It may not be my lungs that's the problem but my heart. I should tell you Garth is concerned enough he's coming to see me in the morning, determined to take me to some heart specialist.

But here I am back at my desk. I see my letter to you is still here. I am adding a message about something I had wished to tell you in person. Perhaps I shouldn't wait. I've given this long thought in these past months. Trust me.

Rae, I've always known Ryan is Garth's son.

It was clear to me far back, once I remembered your visit to Berkeley, knew you were not pregnant then, remembered I had to leave you there that night. Also, I knew Garth.

When you held back news of Ryan and kept pictures so close to your chest, I was sure. You thought I'd hate you for having Garth's son when I couldn't. I didn't hate. I was wounded, at first. I still loved the man so totally. Back then, I told myself that his sexual proclivity was male release of tension. His real passion was political, women were brief escapes and forgotten. He would have forgotten that night with you.

So why did I stay with him? My confession, I was holding on. You know the answer. I believed I had to save him for what he could do in the future. I had more foresight than an angry Garth did at the time. Actually he has since acknowledged that. Back there, I married him in that meadow at Freedom Farm because of Emily.

Now and again, I have lain with another warm body giving and taking some measure of comfort. Behind our public facade, behind our closed eyes, we are all so needy with our hungers. Most people think it's sex or success. There's this other hidden hunger to know you're not just this lone body playing some role. Or stuck in one.

I had to tell you these things.

Rae, have you thought that Ryan may need Garth?

Garth has been a driven man, self-absorbed, but time teaches and shapes. He has learned to deal with realities of a situation larger than his own intents. He's quite successful now, professionally, though a lonely man, married to a younger woman who is coolly ambitious and not about to have a child. He needs a son. I always knew that. It's true now he's older.

No, Garth doesn't know about Ryan. I have said nothing. I won't when he comes by, concerned about the heart scare I had last week. I know this man. I am giving you the secret I withheld all these years as you have from me. It's your choice, Rae. Do as your heart tells you,

As always, your friend Chloe

I'm holding the letter, my eyes closed, seeing, hearing her voice telling me all this when the phone rings. Try to block it out, but the sound is insistent. Get up to answer. It's Big Sam in Fort Lauderdale, angry. I was supposed to call him before now.

"Are you there, Kendall? Goddammit, I need to know when or if you want to keep your place here ."

I deep breathe until he slows down. "Sam, I'll be in your office September one."

Fort Lauderdale

September 8, 1998

Lily minces around my Oceanview living room like a chocoholic opening a box of Lady Godiva.

Her little bird voice has a tremor of need and uncertainty. "You know I adore this place, but I feel you don't approve of me having it."

"I'm selling and if Brandon wants to buy it for you, that's between you two." I go on cleaning out my desk.

Lily sinks into the deep couch, running her hands over the plush surface. "Keeping up my big place has been such a drag. Brandon can certainly afford this as an investment. It'll be a sweet place for me until Bitsy is in college and we can make other plans."

"Don't count on Brandon marrying you, Lily. I was only suggesting you want to be sure what you're accepting. You are an attractive bright woman. You could learn my job, go to work for Big Sam, sell your own house and make your own money. You could buy this place for yourself."

Lily studies her silver nails. "The job wasn't so great as to keep you here. Going back to Alabama of all things. Really, you're always a surprise, Rae. I can't imagine what you found down there. Look at your hair. Don't they have any decent salons? You've let it grow without a good cut."

"Alabama has hairdressers, too. And a Saks, I'm sure." I check to see if I've hurt her feelings. No, it went over her frosted blonde head.

"You're not taking any of this furniture, the china? It's all so perfect here."

"Only my clothes, personal files and myself."

She sounds wistful. "So you found whatever it was you were looking for."

I don't try to answer, too busy looking around at this place I'm selling, taking the money and running. Brandon's pride didn't let him bicker.

"Well so what is it? What's so mysterious?"

"Not mysterious. I found the right place to be."

"Rae, I don't understand you at all. Acting happy about leaving here for a little house."

"It's more than that."

Lily has kicked off her heels to try the deep carpet. She doesn't ask again what I've found back in Montgomery and I don't explain.

The Cottage

September 20, 1998

Walking through your little house talking to you, Vyola. Do you know what's happening here? Hear my heart, my thoughts, because I want you to know.

The workmen I hired before driving to Florida have packed up and gone for the day. I step over and around their work with goosebumps of pleasure.

The back porch is being extended out to become a windowed-in sunporch. When new wicker furniture goes out there, your old porch will be worth a color layout in *Southern Living*.

The wood floors down here are being refinished. Your old green couch and beds have gone out to Goodwill. Know you don't mind as coming in will be some beauties, couches covered in rich English chintz, jewel tones. Nothing's going to disturb your desk in the hall. The laundry room, all new.

And the kitchen, Vyola. New tile floor, appliances and cabinets to be refinished. Hope you don't mind that an antique dealer is taking away the stove. I'll never replace the maple table by the window.

I'm having a glorious time looking through a catalogue of bed dressings and curtains. I have to admit buying stuff can be satisfying when there's purpose behind it, like feathering your nest, making a home. Vyola, you knew too, as Chloe used to say, home means finding the right place for heart and body.

The attic is a mess but the fellows were careful to protect your bookshelves with plastic. The central air system has gone in the peaked ceiling. With wider windows and soon new tile flooring, your attic-library will be lighter, cooler, and the perfect place for my office because I have myself a new job. The thought brings a hum of pleasure along with the goosebumps.

Did you watch me? See me these past weeks reaching out to look in on the lives of the people next door? Georgiana, the young woman in the Shaw house, will open her private school by the first of the year. What she used to call her dream is going to happen. I might have had a something to do with it. And I shall be a part of what's to happen.

Before going to Florida to sell my condo, I negotiated with the selling out neighbors on the other side of me. That big house will be office and classrooms for this special school with atmosphere of home study.

Georgiana is buying the house thanks to a gift from her father, professor Loren Shaw. He has a contract with a publisher and is donating his advance to daughter's project.

Georgiana accepted the gift with guilty disappointment that her father is back at Cornell. I knew, and now she knows, he had sent in a proposal for the book and wanted to work on it quietly here, upstairs. Now she has to ship his heavy notebooks to Cornell, though she asked him to come back.

We even have a solution for space problems. The fences on both sides of the back yard will come down to open the back of the three properties for parking, paths, and playground. The magnolias will be saved and two of your old oaks and the arbor. I love that arbor of wisteria.

Chloe used to tell me answers sometimes wait on another level of mind, or time. Being here, I must have let that happen.

Chloe is on another plane of exisitence, too, Vyola. I've lost you both but not in my mind and heart. I want you to know, too, I've dropped my old private struggle about what to believe. Let's say I've stopped waiting on God to personally tap me on the head to prove to me I'm known.

I hope you both know I've found the right place to be. My heart knows and so does my body. I have a reason to wake in the morning with something I've always believed could be possible, but hesitated to use the word. Joy. Not the restless tick in the pulse but a private pulse of joy for what waits to be done that day.

My job with Neighbor Schools will be as spokesperson and office manager and especially, liaison with parents. All those jobs before taught me how. Prepared me for this. This job has meaning as it reaches into all the tomorrows because it deals with children. How about that for a woman who failed as a mother?

I should leave roses on the grave of that old guilt.

Wish you knew what else I've set in motion, Vyola.

The bedroom that used to be mine is being redone for a special reason. I want it to be inviting and calming, clear of all old memories except one—how you offered me a sanctuary when I was young and troubled and needed it.

I've invited Chloe's daughter Emily and I am praying she'll come. Have told her I am the friend who can tell her about the most special person who was her mother. That would be my belated gift to Chloe. When and if she comes, I hope I will be as wise as you were, Vyola, when you listened to my own confusions. I know not to push but offer and wait.

Something else: I have written to Garth McCullough.

No preambles. Just the truth. I said: *You have a son, Garth. Somewhere in Hawaii. Ryan Kendall, using some other name, what I don't know, but with your contacts you can find him. He doesn't know anything about you Garth, but his life has been cheated because he needs to know his father. He deserves to know.*

I wrote, *Find him if you will. When you do, tell Ryan I want only for him to be whole and proud and to know you. If someday he cares to walk into my door, I will be happy to see him. That will be his choice. What's important is that you find each other.*

Sending that letter gave me such a quiet satisfaction. Relief. Of all the unfinished issues in my life, that must have been the heaviest.

That message must have shocked the man. Set him into action. Some office secretary has called back with the message: "Mr. McCullough wants you to know he left yesterday for Honolulu. He'll be in touch."

Vyola, I'm poking around in the attic library now to pick a book. I have to read to simmer down and sleep.

The larger window is still unpainted but has a sill. I sit here looking down on the Shaw patio below and the fence that will go down soon.

Someone's moving down there in beginning twilight. A lanky figure. He just hurled a basketball toward the old hoop buried in the branches against the house.

I have a moment of *deja vu*. Have to laugh, recognizing the basketball player's lean face, no longer hiding behind a curly white beard. Tonight, the upstairs light in the Shaw house will go on again. A man will be writing his life and discoveries up there.

Looks like we're all at home, Vyola.

The End

About the Author

Marian Coe is an Alabama native, a former feature writer for the *St. Petersburg Times* in Florida, now a transplanted North Carolinian. She lives on Sugar Mountain in western NC with her artist husband Paul Zipperlin and winters in Largo, Florida.

Reviewers and readers praise her fiction for insights, strong sense-of-place and character-driven stories.

An endowed Marian Coe Creative writing scholarship serves students at Appalachian State University in Boone, NC.